"Fallen is
Mic

ƒALLEN

By midnight he still hadn't killed anyone.

Dr. Dakota Thomas isn't prepared for the gunshot victim who rolled through his emergency room doors. Michael Ricco looks like an average young Marine. His dog tags, however, tell a different story.

How could this fresh-faced Marine have a birth date of 1898? What was he doing wandering in the desert at night, alone and wounded? And why were thirteen people murdered to try to keep his secret?

In a world where genetic experimentation pushes the boundaries of how far someone would go to live just a little longer, the main question is…how many must die to keep one person alive?

FALLEN

By

Ann Simko

To Bethita!
What Can I say Girl, So many
years, so many many stories.
Here's only one—
Love ya & Missya!

Don

Lyrical Press, Inc.

New York

LYRICAL PRESS, INCORPORATED

Fallen
10 Digit ISBN: 1-61650-143-x
13 Digit ISBN: 978-1-61650-143-3
Copyright © 2009, Ann Simko
Edited by Pamela Tyner
Book design by Renee Rocco
Cover Art by Renee Rocco

Lyrical Press, Incorporated
337 Katan Avenue
Staten Island, New York 10308
http://www.lyricalpress.com

PUBLISHER'S NOTE:
This book is a work of fiction. The names, characters, places, and incidents are products of the writer's imagination or have been used fictitiously and are not to be construed as real. Any resemblance to persons, living or dead, actual events, locale or organizations is entirely coincidental.

The publisher does not have any control over and does not assume any responsibility for author or third-party Web sites or their content.

Published in the United States of America by Lyrical Press, Incorporated
First Lyrical Press, Inc print publication: April 2010

DEDICATION

To Dale who always believed in me.

ACKNOWLEDGEMENTS

Special thanks to Dale Rhodes who understands my writing better than I do. Also thanks to Corporal Robert Ridale, Army Ranger retired, for his help and expertise.

CHAPTER 1

Ricco ran. Fear pushed him forward. Fear of what hunted him in the dark, of what he knew would happen if they caught him again. Fear kept him on his feet long after his body had given up. He put one foot in front of the other, the word, move, repeating in his head like a mantra.

Sweat dripped down his face. His left arm hung useless and limp at his side. Blood oozed from the bullet wound in his shoulder, soaking his fatigues, pasting them, warm and sticky, to his side. His right hand clamped over the injury in an attempt to slow the bleeding, but he had already lost a great deal of blood. Every breath tore at his lungs like broken glass. Muscles cramped and begged for rest, but he ignored the demand. He hurt, not only from the bullet that had ripped through his flesh, but from the dozens of scrapes and cuts inflicted as he stumbled and fell through the Nevada desert night. One thought kept him moving—to get away, to escape or die in the attempt—move.

Ricco's military training controlled him. Even now, injured and confused, that training made survival second nature. Through blurred vision, he risked looking up at the star-filled sky, but finding the North Star amid the millions that gazed down upon him proved more daunting a task than he had hoped. He was relatively sure he still moved in the right direction. That would be any direction away from the base where they had kept him. Where they would kill him, eventually.

Sometimes in his dreams, he would remember sitting on the back porch with his father, gazing up at the stars. In reality, he couldn't remember the last time he saw the night sky, or felt the breeze on his face. He couldn't remember when his life had been his own. Memories were strange things. They warped and twisted over time, becoming what he wanted them to be, instead of what they were. Memories could not be trusted. Ricco had learned that long ago.

Mesmerized by the sight above him, he didn't see the small rock that tripped him, and went down hard, shredding the flesh of his hands and forearms on the sandstone and shale of the desert floor. The sand, cool and gritty against his sweaty face, felt soothing. Ricco needed to rest, just for a moment, to catch his breath. He rolled from his side onto his back to take weight off his injured shoulder, and closed his eyes.

The mantra played its one word symphony inside his head; he tried to ignore it and failed. It took everything he had to listen to the voice, then the Marine took over, and he obeyed. He rolled to one side and pushed himself to his knees, ignoring the pain the movement cost him. He stood on watery legs, blinked sweat out of eyes that were no longer trustworthy, and he moved.

The incline he had just struggled up, gave him a view of the small valley below. He stopped and stared as he tried to catch his breath. The boulders beneath his hands grounded him. The coarse, gritty texture of the rock he gripped kept him in the present. Ricco stayed on his feet, fighting the insistent demands of gravity.

He narrowed his eyes at the sight. The image confused him, until he realized it was not a part of his imagination. A small, orange glow penetrated the darkness and reminded him of swamp fires back home. It took a moment for the realization to make it through to his scrambled brain. He was looking at a fire. Out here that could mean only one thing—people—and people could bring him something he had refused to dream of for years—freedom.

He needed ten steps, that was all, and then he could stop fighting. Ricco pushed past the pain and fatigue, and moved forward, falling after the first two steps and crawling the last eight. Then he collapsed in the comforting glow of the campfire. His body began to shut down as blood loss, shock, and exhaustion overcame the adrenaline that had fueled him to this point, but he kept his eyes open long enough to see a man edge toward him, his every step more hesitant than the last.

Ricco could tell the man was scared from the way the he held himself. His quick, unguarded movements marked him as a civilian.

"Jesus, buddy, you okay?"

He couldn't answer, but he wanted to laugh. *Do I look okay to you, buddy?*

He closed his eyes and let fate claim him at last, pretending he had some choice in the matter. Death was the one thing Ricco did not fear. He welcomed it. There had been times he even begged for it. All that mattered now was that he had gotten out. He would take his last breath on his own terms, and maybe, just maybe, the man in the light would see to it he finally made it home. After all this time, his father might finally have a body to bury.

With his last conscious thought, he reached for the dog tags around his neck and gripped them tight. He hoped the man understood the silent message.

This is who I am. This is me. Take me home.

this hour, not that it mattered. His taste buds had died during his undergrad days. Too many all-nighters and bad dorm room coffee had destroyed his ability to determine between a decent cup of Starbucks and sludge.

A table near the window offered him the sole company of his reflection and a day-old newspaper. He picked the paper off the chair and smiled as he read the headline. *Local Firefighter Rescues Cat Caught in Drainpipe.*

Yeah, he would take home over New York any day.

The silence of the cafeteria gave Dakota time to sort through the list of things he needed to do over the upcoming weekend. The toilet was leaking, he needed to call the landlord about that. His fridge had nothing but ice cubes and baking soda inside it, guess he couldn't put grocery shopping off any longer. He also needed to find out if his brother was back in town.

He nearly spilled his coffee as his pager trilled, then laughed at his reaction and scanned the room for any witnesses to his jumpy nerves. He unclipped the small device from the waist of his powder-blue scrubs and read the four-digit extension and text message. The emergency room had a trauma coming in.

It was after midnight on a Friday, and as he rose from the table, he recalled his own youthful, misspent Fridays. With any luck, some drunk probably fell off the bed of his pickup and needed to be stitched up, or maybe a bar fight got a little out of hand—a broken bone, a smashed nose—nothing he couldn't handle. He took the stairs down to

CHAPTER 2

Midnight approached and he hadn't killed anyone yet. That was a good thing. Doctor Dakota Thomas checked the batteries in his pager, then the time on his watch. The pager had a full charge, and the watch informed him there were six hours left until his call ended. He hoped that with all of his in-house patients stable, and God willing, sleeping, he would make it through his first week back on staff without anyone dying.

A lot could happen in six hours, but considering this was Caliente, Nevada, and not New York City where he had done his residency, a quiet night was in the realm of possibilities. He remembered his first days as a resident intern, when all he wanted was a good, messy trauma. Now, after wading through more blood than he cared to recall, he prayed for uneventful nights.

Too wired to sleep, he wandered up to the small cafeteria on the third floor for a little carbo-loading and some unneeded caffeine. The cafeteria was long closed, and only vending machines were available at the ER at an easy pace. The text message stated the ambulance was a few minutes out, so he should make it to the trauma bay before they did.

He didn't. He exited the stairwell, turned the corner and hit the button to open the electronic doors to the back hallway of the ER, and heard sirens wailing and the screech of tires. That ambulance was in a hurry.

As he broke into an easy run down the long hallway, his pager trilled again. A second text message told him the trauma was a possible gunshot wound. Years of training took over, and he ran a mental checklist of tests he would need to order. Gunshot wounds were the norm for New York, but it concerned him that one had ended up in Caliente. Maybe it wouldn't be as bad as he feared. Maybe some farmer chasing coyotes off his property had shot himself in the foot.

One of the nurses he recognized from earlier that week fell in beside him as she ran out of the employee lounge. "Doris, what's up?"

"How should I know? EMS just pulled in with the guy."

She didn't sound happy over the interruption of her break, but Dakota had seen her handle the chaotic pace of the ER with an efficiency that humbled him. "Dispatch says he's gunshot. Have you got—" He was cut short by a loud commotion and shouting voices. They raced around the corner and found the town's only two paramedics struggling to hold their patient down while they wheeled his stretcher through the wide glass entranceway into the emergency room.

"Mister, you've got to lay still!" The paramedic leaned his weight into his struggling patient, and pushed his shoulders down onto the narrow stretcher. The boy cried out in pain, then went limp as Dakota rushed to his side.

"Hey, take it easy. We don't know what we're dealing with yet." Sliding fingers along his throat, Dakota felt for and found a pulse there. He lifted one of the boy's eyelids and flashed a small light, checking for changes in the pupil. "Good, let's get him into the trauma bay."

The frenzied medic helped wheel the stretcher around. "I'll tell you what you're dealing with, Doc—a freaking nut case, that's what!"

"What happened?"

"Beats me. We picked him up near Beaver Dam. A couple campers found him. He has a through-and-through in his left shoulder. We tried to control the bleeding and started some fluids on him, but he ripped the IVs out twice before he passed out. By that time, we were nearly here, so we didn't see the point in trying again. He's been out of it until now. Just opened his eyes and flipped out, man."

"Doesn't look like he woke up in a good mood." Dakota and the medic grabbed opposite ends of the sheet the boy lay on and slid him from the stretcher to the exam table.

Doris immediately went to work cutting away his shirt, but in a sudden movement that startled everyone, the boy sat up, shoved Doris into Dakota, and jumped off the table. When he saw the entranceway blocked by the two paramedics, he grabbed the scissors Doris had dropped and retreated into the far corner of the trauma bay.

Dakota kept Doris from hitting the floor and helped her back to her feet. "You okay?"

"Yeah, fine." She smoothed down her scrubs and gave Dakota a wry smile.

"Jesus! See, I told you, a freaking nut case," the medic said. "I got a twenty-two out in the ambulance. You want I should get it?"

"What? Hell no, we're fine. We can handle this." He looked to Doris and her nurse's aide. "Can't we?"

When Dakota got no reply from his staff, the medic shook his head and turned to leave. "Don't say I didn't offer." He motioned to his partner. "Let's go, Jess." They walked out of the room, leaving Dakota and his staff to handle the situation on their own.

"That's just great," he hollered after the two men. "Thanks a lot! You've been a big help!"

"Freaking nut case," the medic mumbled.

Dakota felt a little uneasy watching them leave. Traumas he could handle, armed, possibly psychotic, patients—not so much. He turned around and searched the room. The boy had wedged himself between the wall and a portable storage bin. One bare, bloody foot stuck out from his small hideaway.

He backed Doris and the other girl out of the room to regroup. "Okay, now what? I suppose calling security is out of the question."

Doris made a noise that sounded like *Phffft*. They both knew that "security" was Charlie, an overweight, geriatric, semi-dried-out alcoholic who slept through most of his shift. All one hundred and twenty pounds of Doris would be better protection.

"Well, someone's gotta' go in there. He's going to bleed to death if we just stand here looking stupid." Calling Charlie was beginning to sound like a good idea.

"Wow, Doctor, all those years of higher education has graced you with astute powers of observation." She took the stethoscope from around his neck and kept it. "No sense in giving him another weapon."

"Thanks for the concern. So, you're not going with me, huh?"

"Hmm…" Doris gave him a shove in the direction of the trauma bay doors.

"Wow, Doris, all those years as a nurse has graced you with the ability to instill great confidence in your fellow coworkers."

That got a smile out of her, but she took another step back anyway. "I promise I won't let him hurt you, Doctor D."

Dakota stepped through the open doors, and for the first time felt thankful for his thorough, if not gruesome, experiences at Mount Sinai.

Blood smeared the floor in great, sweeping swaths. His eyes followed the trail to the storage bin that had been pushed out of place. From behind it came the sound of rapid, labored breathing, followed by a few unintelligible words. It sounded to Dakota like praying or bargaining. He couldn't tell which.

He approached carefully, remembering his patient was armed.

With all the blood he saw, it would be surprising if the guy could put up much of a fight, but then, adrenaline is an amazing thing. "Hey, pal, I just want to talk to you, okay?" *That's right, Mr. Smooth, Mr. Non-threatening. Let's keep it cool.* Sometimes the approach worked, and sometimes it didn't. His words brought movement from behind the bin. He crouched down to his patient's level, sidestepped to the far wall, and saw a mess that used to resemble a human being.

A cut over the bridge of the young man's nose caused twin lines of crimson tears to roll down either side of his face and drip from his chin. His khaki t-shirt and desert-brown military fatigues were shiny and wet with fresh blood, most of it coming from his left shoulder. He had a gunshot wound all right, and it wasn't from shooting at coyotes. He stared at Dakota with vacant, dilated eyes set in an impossibly young face. Milky-white skin peeked out from beneath the blood that covered it.

Dakota gave his patient a quick once-over. Shock, he expected that, but the kid was still on his feet, so to speak. He also saw fear—lots of it. The fact the kid was scared didn't surprise him. What did surprise him was the level of terror he saw in those eyes. Dakota felt it coming off him in waves. He thought the guy couldn't be any more than eighteen, nineteen tops. He wondered if he would ever see twenty.

The boy blinked his eyes several times and seemed to focus, and then every muscle in his body tensed as though he just realized Dakota was there. His eyes darted around the room, and he made a frantic effort to push himself farther back against the wall. He took on the look of a trapped animal, and brought the scissors up to his chest in a quick, defensive manner. He held them there gripped in a bloody fist. Dakota had no delusions that the kid would use them if pushed too hard.

Careful to keep his movements as slow and non-threatening as possible, he sat on the floor, a few feet in front of the boy. "My name's Dakota. You look like you could use some help." He motioned to the boy's injured shoulder. "You're hurt." His gesture caused the boy to flinch, and he tightened his grip on the scissors. Dakota watched the hand carefully. "I'm not going to hurt you, pal. How about giving me the scissors?"

"You're not from the base?" The voice was high-pitched and on the verge of cracking from panic.

Dakota suddenly realized the fear wasn't focused on him, or even the hospital, but on something else entirely. He gave a quick headshake. "Nope. I'm not sure which base you mean, but you were found about thirty miles from here. Lucky for you, some campers came across you and called EMS. They brought you here. Do you remember anything about that? Who shot you?"

The boy's eyes automatically went to his shoulder, and then drifted back to Dakota. "Where am I?"

Dakota glanced over his shoulder at Doris and her aide, standing in the entrance to the trauma bay. "You're in Lincoln County Memorial Hospital."

A look of confusion swept across the boy's face. "Where...where is that?" His voice faded out on the last word.

Dakota felt pressured to get the kid on the exam table and start working on his injuries, but as long as he was talking, and he still held the scissors, he would take it slow. "This is Caliente, Nevada. You're pretty much in the middle of nowhere, my man."

"Nevada?" He leaned his head against the wall and closed his eyes. "Yeah, makes sense. Keep us away from people." His eyes blinked open again, and he looked past Dakota at the blood-smeared floor. He followed the bloody trail back to where he sat, dropped the scissors and stared at his hands as though realizing for the first time that they were gloved in blood.

Dakota slowly inched toward the boy and pulled the scissors out of reach. Now that he was more in control of the situation, he concentrated his attention on his patient once more. He knew the rest of his staff was just behind him, watching, and waiting to jump into action, but all he could see was the bloody young man trembling in front of him. Nothing else mattered.

Still staring at his hands, the boy whispered, "I won't go back." His chest heaved with a deep sigh as he slowly shook his head, his hands clenched into tight fists. He raised his eyes and glared at Dakota with fierce determination. "I won't."

The finality of his statement shocked Dakota. Whoever, or whatever, this kid was running from, he was prepared to die rather than return—but not on his shift. "Just take it easy, all right? The only place I want to take you is to x-ray, capisce?"

Fear swept across the young man's face again. "You're not safe. Nobody's safe. If they find out I'm here, they'll come for me. I have to get out of here!" He struggled to get to his feet, but didn't get far. With a groan, he slid back to the floor, leaving a smear of fresh blood on the previously white wall.

Dakota could see the fight leave his eyes, and hurried to his side. "You're not going anywhere in your condition, man. Come on, you're safe here. We have a hell of a security team." Doris chuckled in the background, and he frowned over his shoulder. "Not helping," he said, and turned back to the boy. "I won't let anyone hurt you. That's a promise." He felt for a pulse on the boy's wrist. The skin he touched had the icy-cold feel of someone in shock. "How 'bout letting me check you out, okay? I can help you." The kid's eyes dilated again, only this time, it wasn't from adrenaline. "Will you do that? Will you let me help you?"

The boy leaned against the wall and closed his eyes. "Yeah...okay. Doesn't matter, I'm dead anyway."

"Like hell you are. I don't remember giving you permission to die." He looped the boy's right arm around his neck, then grabbed his waist and helped him to his feet. "What's your name, kid?"

He made a small sound of pain before answering. "Ricco, Michael J., private first class, US Marines." He rattled off his sector code and a few other tags Dakota didn't recognize as they moved toward the exam table.

"Come on pal, just make it to the table and I'll do the rest, I promise." A few feet from the stretcher, the boy slipped in his blood and they both went down. Dakota turned to his staff outside the room. "Now might be a good time."

Doris pulled on a pair of latex gloves as she hurried into the room, carefully sidestepping the blood on the floor. She circled around Dakota, slid her arm along Ricco's injured side, and together they lifted him back to his feet. He hissed in pain and leaned his weight into her.

"I gotcha', honey. Just hitch your butt up here." Doris helped Ricco swing his legs up on the narrow table, where he finally collapsed.

Dakota grabbed another pair of scissors from the trauma tray and sliced what was left of Ricco's shirt off in one quick movement. He ripped open a package of gauze and pressed it over the still oozing wound on the boy's shoulder. Ricco scrunched his face up in pain, but offered no more objections.

"Get me two large bore IVs, normal saline, wide open."

"Already on it." Doris prepped Ricco's arm with one quick swipe of an alcohol pad, and tied a tourniquet above his elbow. Palpating the large vein in the crook of his arm, she took a needle and expertly slid it into the vessel. She released the tourniquet, hooked up her primed IV tubing, opened the roller clamp and secured the site with tape. Fluid ran into Ricco's body as fast as his depleted system could take it.

Dakota slid a bloody hand to his patient's neck. "Shit! I can't even feel a carotid on him."

"IVs are in, saline running wide open in both of them. Want me to call the blood bank?"

"No, I need you here." He turned to the nurse's aide standing in the corner. She appeared as pale as the boy did. "Blondie, what's your name?"

"Sandy," she whispered.

"Sandy, I need you to go to the blood bank and tell them we have a trauma, okay? Tell them I need all the O neg they can give me, and stat. Have you got that?"

She nodded, but just stood there, her eyes huge and focused on the blood covering the floor.

"Then, move it!"

Sandy snapped out of her stupor and took off at a run.

"Doris, get me a set of signs so I can see just how screwed this kid is."

"Let me get him on the monitor." She ripped open a package of sticky monitor leads and clipped the cables on before slapping them in place on Ricco's chest.

Dakota removed one hand from Ricco's shoulder and gently slapped the boy's face. "Hey, Michael, you still with me, man?" His eyes fluttered open, and he managed a slight nod. "You gotta' help me out here. See, if you die, my reputation is toast around here." Ricco gave him a half-hearted smile before closing his eyes once more.

Doris pressed a button and the monitor came to life, accompanied by the blare of low-limit alarms. "Shit."

"Yeah," Dakota agreed. "Michael, you aren't even meeting me halfway, man."

Ricco couldn't comment, as he had slipped into unconsciousness.

"Those numbers are ugly. Let's get him in trendelenburg." Dakota pushed a lever on the side of the table, and with Doris's help, tilted it so Ricco's head was down and his feet were elevated. "Start him on pressors...and where's Blondie with my blood?"

"Here!" Sandy ran into the room and dropped a box with a dozen units of blood at Dakota's feet.

"Great, but my hands are a little full." He looked at his bloody gloves keeping pressure on Ricco's shoulder, then back at the young girl.

Sandy lowered her head and mumbled an embarrassed apology. "Sorry."

"I'll take them, honey." Doris spiked another bag of saline as Sandy slid the box of blood over to her.

"Doris, let them fly as fast as he'll take them, then prep him for a central line." Dakota leaned into Ricco's shoulder, he grunted in pain, but his eyes stayed closed. "What's his core temp?"

Doris glanced at the monitor. "Thirty-five degrees celsius."

"Crap! You got any more good news for me?"

Doris simply smiled as she hung the first unit of blood, and then her eyes followed Sandy as she retreated into her corner. "How are you doing there, Sandy?"

The girl gave her a short nod, but the pale face that stared back at her, spoke the truth. She appeared as traumatized by her ordeal as Michael Ricco did by his.

Doris seemed to understand the signs and gave her a reprieve. "Good, I need you to run down to distribution and bring up a thermal unit, okay? Oh, and tell radiology we're almost ready for him on your way down."

Sandy gave another quick nod and left the room at a trot, obviously grateful for the chance to leave the gory sight in front of her.

Doris grinned and shook her head at Dakota. "I was never that young." She finished programming the IV pump. "Okay, pressors are running at five mcgs. You want to look for an exit wound?"

Dakota released the pressure on Ricco's shoulder and removed the saturated gauze. He took a fresh square and wiped it over the wound. Blood still oozed out the ragged hole, but at a much slower pace. Ricco's body was either doing what it was supposed to and clotting off the injury, or his pressure was so low it couldn't pump anymore blood. Hoping for the former, Dakota left the wound open to air. "Yeah, let's roll him."

Doris placed one hand on Ricco's shoulder and another at his hip, and together they rolled him on his side. She held him there while Dakota opened a bottle of sterile water and spilled it over Ricco's back. As the blood washed away, Dakota took a good look at the bullet hole. "Well, that's nice."

Doris's hands slipped on the blood covering Ricco's body, and she readjusted her grip. "Sorry. What you got?"

Dakota frowned as he examined the wound again. "Our exit wound is an entrance wound. Someone shot this kid in the back." Dakota shook his head. "What is a Marine private doing out at Beaver Dam in the middle of the night, and who the hell did he piss off?"

"I'm sure I don't want to know." Doris sounded indifferent, but Dakota could see the concern in how she held the boy, and in the way she told him it would be all right, even though she knew Ricco couldn't hear her. Doris wasn't fooling anyone, least of all, Dakota. "You want to roll him back?" she asked.

"Yeah, but gently, I think his shoulder joint is pretty messed up."

Together, they eased Ricco down until he lay flat on the table once more. The front shoulder wound had started bleeding again. Dakota sighed and pressed more gauze over it. "Okay, get me a stat H-and-H on him so I know how low his tank is."

"The blood going in is going to give you a false number," Doris reminded him.

"Yeah, well, I would rather treat a false number than watch him die while waiting for the real ones." He smiled an apology. "Sorry, I know, but it will have to do."

"No sweat. You want an electrolyte panel sent off with the H-and-H?"

Dakota snapped off blood-slicked gloves as he checked the

numbers flitting across the monitor screen. "Sure, then let's line him up. Titrate the pressors for something that's at least compatible with life, okay?"

"I can try." Doris grinned and reached for the ringing in-house phone. She listened for a moment, tucked the receiver under her chin and got Dakota's attention. "X-ray's ready for him, you want them to wait?"

Dakota glanced at the screen again and rubbed the back of his neck. "Yeah, I want him a little more stable, and I want that line in."

"You got it." Doris told x-ray to wait on their word, and hung up the phone as Sandy returned with the thermal unit. "Do you know how to set one of these up?" Doris asked her.

"Yeah, it's easy. Just take the plastic cover and insert the hose here." She pointed to the hole in the cover. "After that all you do is turn it on, and hot air blows up the blanket." She nodded. "It's called a Bear Hugger. Pretty lame, huh?"

"As long as it warms him up. Just cover his lower half. Doctor Thomas is going to place a central line in his chest," Doris told her.

Sandy nodded and began setting up the Bear Hugger.

Dakota retrieved a trauma procedure kit from the storage bin Ricco had hid behind and tore open the seal. "Can someone kill those alarms for me? They're giving me a headache." Sandy reached up and silenced the alarms as he fanned opened the sterile pack on a tray table. "Thanks, much better." He stepped to the sinks to scrub for the procedure. In the ensuing silence, he asked Sandy, "First week?"

She shrugged as she flipped the switch to turn on the thermal unit. "Second, actually. Does it show that much?"

"It gets easier, promise," he said.

She returned a shy smile. "God, I hope so."

Dakota finished scrubbing, dried his hands, and then turned his attention back to Doris. "I'd like to give him something for the pain, but I don't think his pressure can handle it. Just get me some local, and have anesthesia standing by in case we need them."

"Already done."

He pulled the procedure gown from the pack, slipped his arms through the sleeves, then turned his back to Doris so she could tie it for him while he put on a fresh pair of sterile gloves. "Where did you work before coming to Caliente?"

"L.A. This is nothing. How about you?"

"Mount Sinai, New York."

"Ewww, give me L.A. any day. The blood is the same, but the weather is way better."

Dakota laughed as he prepped Michael's chest with a green-tinted antiseptic. "Can't argue with that. What made you leave?"

"I got tired of fourteen-year-olds killing each other over a perverted sense of loyalty and the latest trend in footwear."

"I hear that." Dakota flushed the line and got it ready for

insertion.

Doris held out a bottle of saline for Dakota to prime his syringes. "What about you?"

"That's easy, this is home. I grew up here. Hey, look." He motioned to the monitors. "Nothing's alarming and his pressure's better. Way not to die on me, Private Ricco. Maybe I will give you a little pain med after all. Doris, please give the man fifty mcgs of Fentanyl, and Sandy, call x-ray and tell them they can have him as soon as I get this line in."

Dakota covered Ricco from head to toe with sterile blue paper drapes, leaving only the right side of his chest uncovered, as Doris pushed the narcotic into the IV line. Dakota probed along Ricco's chest, just under his clavicle, until he found what he was looking for, a shallow indentation indicating where the subclavian vein ran. Using his fingers as a guide, Dakota slid the needle in just under the clavicle and got an immediate blood return. He passed the introducer, and threaded the line through.

"Nicely done, Doctor. I think you've done one or two of these before."

Dakota smiled under his mask and capped off the line. "He made it easy—he's skinny. Slap a dressing on it, and let's get him to x-ray."

Doris picked the sharps off the sterile field, removed the drapes from Ricco's body, and cleaned and dressed the line. Ricco hadn't budged throughout the whole ordeal, and as Sandy helped x-ray usher him away, Dakota looked up and caught Doris staring at him. "What?"

"I think you just saved his life. Not bad for a country boy."

He smiled as he peeled out of the procedure gown and mask. "He's not out of this yet, and besides, I didn't do it alone. Nice work."

"Right back atcha'." She glanced around the room at the blood all over the floor and smeared down the wall. "He sure made a mess of my trauma bay, though."

Dakota chuckled as he tossed the gown and mask into the trash receptacle. Then he remembered something. "Hey, did you find any ID on him?"

"No wallet…" She reached around behind her where the tattered remains of Ricco clothing lay. "Just these." She handed him a set of dog tags.

He took the tags, turning them over in his hands. They appeared to be standard military ID tags—rectangular, aluminum discs embossed with his name, birth date, blood type, social security number, and bordered by a rubber frame to keep them from making noise—but something didn't look right.

"That's weird." He brushed both the dried and fresh blood off the tags with a gauze pad, held them up into the light and read them again.

Doris paused from cleaning the exam table. "What is it? You've got that look on your face."

He raised his eyebrows. "I've got a look?"

"Oh, yeah. Every time something doesn't add up, you get it.

You've got it now."

Dakota raised his brow. "I didn't know that." He glanced down at the dog tags again, then back to Doris. "It's probably nothing. Just a typo, I bet."

She waited for an explanation.

"The dog tags." He felt stupid bringing it to her attention, but she was right. It bugged him when inconsistencies couldn't be explained.

"What about them?"

"The birth date isn't right. It's got to be a clerical error. It's the only explanation for it."

"Hang on. Let me see." She washed her hands, then took the tags from Dakota. "What the hell? These say he was born in eighteen-ninety-eight."

"Like I said, it's a mistake."

Doris nodded, but her expression didn't agree. "I guess, maybe."

"Maybe?"

"Well, yeah, it has to be…but I don't know."

"Now you're the one with that look."

"This is weird. I was in the military for ten years. I mean, God knows they make mistakes, but not like this. These are usually the one thing they get right."

"Looks like they got it wrong this time."

"Obviously." She handed him the tags.

"Well, mistake or not…" He tossed the dog tags up in the air, caught them in a tight fist, and smiled at Doris. "At least these make him easy to find."

They busied themselves with the mess in the ER until x-ray returned with Ricco. Doris made sure all her IVs were still intact, while Dakota inspected the boy and checked the numbers on the monitor. "All right, his pressure's better. That's a good sign, for a change. Keep a close eye on him, call me with the lab results, and keep that pressure above ninety. I'll be at the desk if anything changes."

Doris paused from writing Michael Ricco's vital signs in his chart. "What are you going to do?"

"I'm going to find out who's missing a Marine private." He picked Ricco's dog tags off the desk and took a step, then stopped. "Wait, what about the gunshot wound? Who notifies the police, me?"

"Usually, yes, but EMS called them the minute they realized what they were dealing with. Cal should've been here by now."

Dakota raised his brow at the name. "Cal…as in Sheriff Calvin Tremont? Jesus, is he still alive?"

Doris smiled as she went back to recording Ricco's vitals. "Don't let him hear you say that."

"Well, it's too God damn late now!" A fifty-caliber voice echoed down the hallway, and Dakota turned to find a vision, that as a teenager sent ice coursing through his veins. In a moment, he went from competent trauma doctor to a fumbling mass of insecurity.

Cal Tremont stood six-feet-six and in his prime went well over two-fifty. Dakota guessed the scales probably groaned at three hundred pounds when he chose to step on them these days. Most of the muscle he remembered had rendered to fat, but the voice that approximated the sound of rumbling thunder still intimidated him. Even after all these years, Sheriff Tremont was a formidable sight. He strode into the ER, wearing a pair of Carhartt overalls over his pajama top, knee-high muck boots that smelled like the inside of a cow barn, and leaving a trail of manure in his wake.

"Doris, what the hell is so God damn important you have to drag my ass out of bed in the middle of the night?"

"Gunshot wound, Cal." Without looking up, she finished her charting and glanced at her watch. "And it's not the middle of the night. It's not even one o'clock."

"It's the middle of the night when your day starts at four in the morning." He ran a hand through gray, thinning hair and sighed. "All right, I'm awake. Let's get this over with. Who's the attending doc?"

Dakota stepped from around the desk and let out a breath. "That would be me." Dakota felt those eyes appraise him. He was an adult, he reminded himself, and not a sixteen-year-old high school student caught drinking beer after hours behind the football stadium.

"Dakota Thomas. By Jesus, they're not too particular who they let practice medicine anymore, are they?"

Then to Dakota's infinite surprise, he laughed and held a hand out to him. For a moment, shock overwhelmed him, but Cal took one meaty hand and swallowed Dakota's smaller one.

"Don't look so surprised to see me still breathing, boy. Come on, I'd like to get another hour or two of sleep before I gotta' get up again. What ya got?"

It took Dakota another few seconds to get back up to speed. "Uh, yeah. Marine private. Gunshot wound to his left shoulder."

"Is he dead?"

"No, not yet. Couple more hours and yeah, maybe, but I think we got to him in time."

"Damn, it's easier when they're dead. You got a name?"

"Private Michael J. Ricco, US Marines."

Sheriff Tremont took a pad of paper out of his overall's pocket and wrote down the information. "Okay, fine, you reported it. Who's his CO? Let him handle this."

Dakota shrugged. "I was just about to find out. Oh, and Sheriff, you might want to have a look out by Beaver Dam. A couple of campers found him there and called EMS."

"Yeah, Doc, I'll get right on that." He yawned. "Don't worry, I'll send my deputy out there in the morning. Doris, I'm going home. Try not to wake me up again tonight."

Dakota watched the sheriff walk away, adding to the trail of manure, and then shook his head in awe. "Man, has he mellowed."

"Kind of scary, huh? Now what?"

"Now, I find out who the hell Michael J. Ricco is. If we're lucky, the Military Police can handle it and we won't have to worry about Cal having a coronary."

"Works for me. I'll tell you one thing, though. If I remember anything about the Marines, you can bet your ass Private Ricco is in one hell of a lot of trouble."

As Dakota's eyes wandered over the boy's face once more, the fear he had seen in Michael's eyes came back to haunt him. He was scared to death and running from something, Dakota knew that, but the questions remained, what and why? He opened his hand and studied the dog tags again. Maybe they would provide him with the answers. He counted on it.

CHAPTER 3

Dakota stepped into the radiological reading room and sat down in front of three large, interconnected flat-panel screens. Gone were the days when x-ray films needed to be developed and processed. Now, those images were captured and manipulated digitally. He entered Michael Ricco's medical record number and watched as the images of the boy's shoulder came up on the screens. He had a vertical crack on the exterior portion of his left scapula, but the bullet's path had miraculously missed anything vital. One millimeter in either direction and it would have been a very different outcome. Michael Ricco was one hell of a lucky guy. He had massive soft tissue damage, and the cracked scapula was going to hurt like a bitch for a good week or two, but he would live.

He checked the desk monitors and scanned the boy's vital signs. After two hours of intensive resuscitation, Ricco was finally stable. The initial crisis had passed, and Dakota felt as if he could take a breath. He leaned back in the chair, closed his eyes, and rubbed a hand over his face. The adrenaline that fueled him earlier had long since vanished, leaving him wishing he'd slept when given the chance.

Doris peeked into the reading room. "Hey, sorry to bother you, but there's some captain from a military base in Carson City on the phone. Says you called him about our missing Marine."

"I've been expecting him. Can you put it through back here?"

"No problem."

"Thanks, Doris," Dakota said, and he turned back to the screens.

"Yeah sure, and hey…" She waited until he faced her again. "You did good."

Dakota smiled and gave her a nod, knowing that was the highest compliment he would ever get from Doris.

A moment later, the phone disturbed the relative quiet of the secluded reading room. He picked up the receiver, hoping for some answers. "Doctor Thomas."

"Doctor, this is Captain Anthony Talenco from the Marine division in Carson City. I understand you're trying to identify a possible AWOL private?"

"I'm not sure what he is, Captain. I have identification on him. I'm just trying to find out where he belongs." Dakota heard papers shuffling in the background.

"Well, now, that's where we have a problem. You told my clerk this boy's name is Ricco, Michael, J. PFC. Is that correct?"

"Yes, sir, it is."

"The Marines do not currently have a private, or anyone else for that matter, on active duty by that name. You might want to look at another branch of the military. I'm sorry, but I can't help you."

"But he was wearing dog tags that clearly state he is a Marine. Maybe if you look again…"

"Listen, Doctor Thomas, I did a thorough search. If he was one of ours, trust me, I'd know about it. As for the dog tags, hell, you can pick them up in any novelty shop. They look damn real too. As I said, I can't help you. You might try missing persons, or the army, for all the good that will do you." Without the courtesy of a goodbye, the line went dead.

Dakota stared at the x-rays in front of him. Now what? Who the hell are you, Michael Ricco, and why did someone try to kill you? He leaned back in the chair, laced his fingers behind his head, and stretched. Maybe Cal Tremont would have better luck figuring it out in the morning. Right now, all that mattered was that the boy was stable and resting comfortably in a bed on one of the few monitored floors in the hospital. He had done his job. It was three in the morning, and he was tired.

He left the dimly lit reading room and squinted his eyes in the bright lights of the main ER. "Doris, I'm going home to get some sleep. Try not to need me for the next three hours."

"No promises, but it looks quiet." Then she grinned and pointed her pen at him. "I do have your beeper number if anything happens, though."

"Don't I know it." Dakota smiled as he grabbed his bag from under the desk.

"Say, do we know who he is yet?"

Dakota shrugged. "Michael Ricco appears to be a mystery." He slung the bag over his shoulder and headed out of the ER. If Doris made a reply, he didn't hear it. His comment made him think of someone who was very good at mysteries. When he was more awake, he would call to see if his brother was back in town. Maybe Montana was up for a job.

* * * *

Tommy Lawson was not in a good mood. Sheriff Tremont promised him he could have this Saturday off. So why was he up at six in the morning driving out to Beaver Dam? Because Sheriff Tremont scared the hell out of him, that's why.

Tommy's father and the sheriff were good friends. Between the two of them, they decided the deputy job would be an opportunity for Tommy to make something out of his life. He had no objections to that; he just didn't want to be the sheriff's whipping boy. What he really wanted was to be a musician. That had about as much chance of happening as him standing up to his father.

Cal had given him the information from EMS on where they picked the kid up last night. All he had to do was look around, see if anything jumped out at him, and then report back to the office. Go in armed, Cal had told him. The kid in question had a gunshot wound. Cal also told him if his weapon was discharged, Tommy better be shooting his own foot, or Cal would do it for him.

"We're just going through the motions, boy," the sheriff told him. "Don't get all worked up. You're not going to see anything. Go there, come back, then you can have the rest of the day off."

"He better not be shittin' me." Tommy checked the coordinates on his map and decided he was as close as he was going to get to the directions the sheriff gave him, and if he wasn't, screw it.

He stepped out of the car, stretched, and yawned. No decent human being was awake at this hour. The desert was still cool under the early morning sun, but looking up at the cloudless blue sky, he knew it wouldn't stay that way. "Might as well get this over with."

It turned out he was right on with his directions. According to Cal, a couple of campers had found the kid and called EMS. About twenty yards from where he pulled over, he saw the distinctive tire tracks of the town's only ambulance in the soft dirt at the side of the road. He and Trevor, the medic who drove it, worked on the piece of crap enough for him to know what kind of tracks the overly wide tires made.

He followed the trail Trevor and Jess had made walking in and out the brush. Someone had been shot all right. Even Tommy could see the blood still on the ground. Big, fat drops of it, dried to a dull brown under the morning sun. Through the trees, he spotted the tent of the campers who called EMS, but he didn't stop. He would wake them later and flash the badge, ask some questions, and pretend he was important, but right now, the blood trail drew him on.

After an hour, and convinced he had lost the trail, he was about to double back and wake the campers, when he saw something. He walked to an area where it looked like the person must have fallen or stopped, because a large, dark-brown patch of sand stained the ground. Tommy had been so focused on looking for the same teardrop shaped splatters, he almost missed the bigger patch of blood drying in the desert heat. From that point on, the drops of blood got bigger and farther apart as if the kid had been running fast and bleeding heavily. This is so cool. He had no idea what he expected to find at the end of the trail, or what he would do when he got there; he only knew he had to keep going.

The bloody path led him down a steep hill into a hidden ravine. Sagebrush and yucca plants were uprooted and pushed aside, and the ground appeared torn up, as if someone had been digging there recently. Even to Tommy's untrained eye, it was clear a struggle had taken place on that spot.

"Awesome. This must be where it happened." He placed his hands on his hips and proudly surveyed the scene. "Maybe this deputy gig isn't so bad after all."

Then he noticed something unusual in the center of the disturbance. He edged closer and stared in open-mouthed disbelief. A large metal door lay half-buried in the sand of the desert floor.

"What the hell?" He crouched down to get a better look. The temperature had risen at least ten degrees in the last hour, but Tommy barely noticed. He reached out a tentative hand and grabbed the rusted metal ring that served as a handle. "I'm not hallucinating. Fucking-A! Cal can kiss my ass and give me the next month of Saturdays off for this." A big smile stretched across his face as he let go of the handle.

Tommy didn't feel any pain, and the smile stayed on his face as the darkness descended. Something was wrong, he just couldn't think clearly enough to understand what, and then he couldn't think at all.

CHAPTER 4

A slight vibration under his left hip brought Dakota out of a disturbing dream. He opened his eyes, confused and disoriented, reached for the source of the offending disturbance and found his pager still clipped to his pants. He vaguely recalled coming home and falling into bed. Apparently, he had done so fully dressed.

He rubbed sleep-blurred eyes and glanced at the clock on his nightstand. The bold red numbers staring back at him told him it was noon. He had been asleep for a little over eight hours. He sat up on the side of the bed, ran a hand over his disheveled hair, and focused on the pager display. The seven-digit extension wasn't familiar to him.

"What the hell?" The only people who should have access to his pager number were the hospital staff. Officially, his call ended at six that morning. If someone was paging him now, it could only mean his Marine had started going south, but the number wasn't a hospital extension. Apprehension turned to curiosity as he picked up the phone and made the call.

An overly cheery female voice answered. "Caliente Sheriff's Department, how may I help you?"

Dakota cleared his throat, his voice still thick with sleep. "Um, I'm not sure, you called me."

"Excuse me?"

"Ah, yeah, this is Dakota Thomas. Someone paged me to this number."

"Dakota Thomas?" the woman asked, and paused as it clicked. "Oh, Doctor Thomas! Yes, the sheriff wants to talk to you. Hang on a sec, I'll put you back to his office."

Dakota heard the connection go through and didn't have time to wonder why the sheriff wanted him. He pulled the receiver from his ear as Cal's gruff voice nearly blew out his eardrums.

"Thomas! Who the hell is this Marine of yours? I want his CO's name, and I want to know everything you know about the somabitch!"

That brought him from zero to sixty in under a second. "Whoa, wait a minute, Sheriff, back up. What's wrong?" Dakota stood, trying to make sense out of why Cal Tremont decided to be his personal, extremely unpleasant wake-up call.

The sheriff was breathing hard and heavy on the other end of the line. "I'll tell you what's wrong. I sent Tommy Lawson out to Beaver Dam this morning to cover my ass, and he never came back. That's what's wrong!"

"What's that got to do with my Marine? If you're talking about the same Tommy Lawson I used to know, he's probably in town or behind the graveyard with Earl Freemont drinking beer."

"Things have changed since you've been away, boy. Tommy's my deputy, and I admit he's not the sharpest tool in the shed, but there's no way in hell he'd take off without reporting back to me, 'cause I scare the shit out of him."

Dakota had to grin. "You do seem to have that effect on people."

"In case you didn't notice, I am not in a humorous mood. I want this Ricco's CO's name, and I mean now. Something ain't smelling right, and I need to know who the hell I'm dealing with."

His voice stabbed through Dakota's brain like an ice pick. He needed coffee, lots of it, and something decent to eat. "They couldn't help me, Sheriff. I spoke with their office in Carson City, and according to a Captain Talenco, there is no Michael J. Ricco on active duty with the Marines." He padded barefoot into the kitchen. "But I planned on following up on it later today."

"Well, it is later today, boy. I have a missing deputy and a serious case of 'I don't give a shit' about your excuses."

Dakota stopped in the middle of filling the coffee pot. "You know, Sheriff, I got home at three-thirty this morning. Ricco is my patient. He was stable when I left, and today is officially my day off. I hate to get all trekkie on you, but I'm a doctor not a cop. What the hell does your missing deputy have to do with me?" Dakota realized his mistake the second the words were out of his mouth. He squeezed his eyes shut, anticipating a major tirade, but Cal's voice got deadly quiet. He would have preferred the tirade.

"You called me, boy, remember? I sent Tommy out there, because of what you told me. As I see it, that makes this as much your problem as it does mine. Now, I'm going looking for my deputy, and you'd better hope to hell he is drinking beer behind the graveyard with Earl, because if I have to call the state cops in on this, I guarantee you'll live to regret it."

Cal slammed the receiver down. Dakota pulled the phone away from his ear, but the resulting echo was loud enough to make him wince.

"Jesus, did I say he'd mellowed?" He hit end, put the phone down on the counter and rubbed a hand over the stubble sprouting on his face. As he finished making the coffee, he tried to put the conversation out of his mind. Grabbing a chipped ceramic mug pilfered from some donut shop during his residency, he filled it to the brim with the strong black brew.

Leaning against the kitchen counter, he surveyed the naked walls of his clean, sterile apartment. He had rented it while still in New York and hadn't been back long enough to personalize it, he hadn't even had time to unpack yet. Well, he had the time, but not the motivation.

Despite his efforts, Dakota's mind kept circling back to the conversation with Cal Tremont. His hand went to the phone and he picked it up. He felt he should do something about Tommy Lawson or Michael Ricco, but for all his good intentions, he didn't have a clue as to what, or even who he could call.

Dakota slammed the phone back down on the counter in frustration. "Why is this my problem?" he asked the coffee pot. Mr. Coffee wisely kept his opinions to himself. "I did what I was supposed to do. I saved the kid's life, and I reported the gunshot wound to Cal. I don't owe anyone anything more." The words held as much conviction as a sieve did water. In hopes that a shower would chase thoughts of Michael Ricco and Tommy Lawson from his head, he decided to start there first.

Dakota turned the water on, stripped out of his wrinkled clothing, and stepped under the steaming spray. He tilted his head and let the hot water ease the tension in his neck and shoulders, then turned and braced his hands against the wall, letting the water cascade down his back. With closed eyes, he turned his face into the spray as unwanted images from his dream flitted across his brain. Images of Michael Ricco, running for his life across the desert, but then he realized it wasn't Ricco running wounded and bleeding, somehow he knew the face hidden in the shadows was his own. His feet moved with slow-motion madness and unnamed monsters chased him in the dark. He shook the disturbing pictures out of his head, turned the water off, and dried with the only towel he owned. Jeans, sneakers and a comfortable t-shirt instantly made Dakota feel more relaxed and almost at home.

He poured another cup of coffee, scrambled some eggs, managed not to burn the toast, and felt nearly human again as he sat down to eat his first meal in over twenty-four hours. It did wonders for chasing away thoughts of disturbing dreams and missing deputies.

Dakota had forty-eight hours all to himself. Cal's words wouldn't leave him alone. A smiled played across his face as he finally figured out exactly what to do about his mysterious Marine. There were a lot of things he needed to do, but only one he wanted to do. He stacked the dirty dishes in the sink, grabbed the phone from the counter once more, and punched in a local number. He was surprised when he didn't get an answering machine or voice-mail.

"Speak to me."

Dakota couldn't suppress the grin. "Woof."

"Dakota."

"Montana. Verbose as usual. When'd you get back?"

"Last night. Heard you were home."

"Home." Dakota considered the word. "Yeah, hey, what are you doing?"

"Now?"

"Yes, now. I want to talk to you about something."

Montana paused to consider the request. Dakota knew the routine. Nothing was ever easy with Montana, so he waited.

"I'll meet you at La Playa's in an hour. I want a pitcher of original margaritas and the fajita special."

Dakota heard the line disconnect, but this time he didn't mind. "Must be my day for people hanging up on me, but damn it's good to be home."

* * * *

The fajitas were ordered and the margaritas chilled. Dakota poured the green delight into a frosted, salt-rimmed glass and waited. Montana was late. Dakota didn't mind, he expected it. It only reassured him that Montana hadn't changed.

It had been five years since he last saw his brother. They kept in touch with emails and phone calls, but this was the first he would see Montana face-to-face in all that time. Dakota didn't think he had changed much, maybe a little thinner, but no gray hairs threaded through the black, and no new wrinkles. He wondered how the years had treated his brother.

Dakota checked his watch. He had been waiting for thirty minutes and knew Montana wouldn't show for at least another thirty, it was why he had them hold the fajitas when he ordered. It was all part of the game. Montana never did easy, he made you work for even his time. Normally his brother's lack of consideration annoyed the hell out of Dakota, and probably still would if he hadn't missed him so much. It wasn't a problem for Dakota; he knew Montana would show.

La Playa was his brother's one great weakness. Actually, Mexican food in any form, but La Playa in particular. It was, according to Montana, the only place north of the border that did it right. Dakota had a table facing the door, two days off, and was working on his second margarita. At the forty-minute mark he called the waitress over to the table and told her to have the fajitas put on.

An hour to the minute, Montana sauntered into the restaurant. The dazzling light of the Nevada afternoon momentarily framed him, and he looked exactly the same as Dakota remembered: tousled black hair that always seemed in need of a trim, faded jeans with frayed holes in the knees, and an untucked white oxford shirt with the sleeves rolled up against the afternoon heat. Montana never changed, he oozed confidence and always seemed comfortable in his own skin.

He took the Ray-Bans off in deference to the dimly lit restaurant, looked around until he spotted Dakota, gave him a slight nod, and headed for the table. Without saying a word, he sat down, drained the frosted margarita glass, and filled it once more. Only then did he center his attention on his brother. "Did you order the fajitas?"

Dakota laughed. "Good to see you too."

"I'm hungry." He stared at Dakota with an intense gaze no one else could have withstood, but Dakota had a lifetime of practice. He simply stared back.

Convinced he had won the staring contest, Montana finally spoke. "You look good."

Dakota tried not to smile. "You look the same."

The waitress, who placed a steaming plate of fajitas in front of Montana and reached for the empty margarita pitcher, interrupted the familiar game. "You want a refill?"

Montana looked directly at her and smiled. "Please."

The girl flushed from the bottom of her neck to the top of her head and nearly knocked over the glass pitcher. Dakota took pity on her and put it into her unsteady hands.

She mumbled, "Thanks," to Dakota, gave Montana a demure smile and left the table quickly.

"You love doing that, don't you?"

"Doing what?" Without looking up or waiting for an answer, Montana picked up his fork and attacked the fajitas.

Dakota wasn't sure if the innocence was feigned or not, but he knew better than to interrupt his brother until he was finished. He shook his head and took another sip of his margarita, then sat back and watched. Montana didn't even notice when the flustered waitress brought another pitcher to the table. Dakota filled both their glasses and waited until Montana scraped the last of the fajitas off the plate. Only then was he ready to listen.

He pushed away from the table and sipped his drink, his dark, black eyes on Dakota. "Okay...What?"

Dakota got right to the point. "Last night a nineteen-year-old Marine private by the name of Michael J. Ricco was brought into my emergency room with a gunshot wound to his left shoulder. He was running from something."

"Presumably from the person who shot him, yes?"

Dakota ignored the sarcasm and continued. "I called the Marine division in Carson City. They have no record of a Michael J. Ricco."

Montana shrugged, apparently not impressed. "Is the kid going to live?"

"Yeah, he's going to be fine."

"So, why is it your problem?"

Dakota reached into his hip pocket and closed his hand around the dog tags he had taken from Ricco. "Because things aren't adding up. Something just isn't right. I notified Cal to report the gunshot wound. He sent Tommy Lawson out to Beaver Dam where the kid was found. Then I get a page from him a few hours ago. Tommy hasn't reported back and apparently it's my fault."

"Tommy Lawson's an idiot."

"Yeah, I know, but there's more to it than that."

"What?" Montana leaned forward, resting his arms on the table. "What's got your shorts in such a bunch that you're buying me a meal at La Playa's?"

"I'm buying?"

Montana raised his brows.

"Okay, I'm buying."

"Look, Dakota, a Marine private gets shot. So what? Chances are there was either booze or a woman involved…maybe both. I don't get what the big mystery is. Carson City can't find him, this might be hard to believe, but the government makes mistakes. That's shocking, I know, but it happens. And Tommy Lawson? Please…the kid is a total fuck up. His father practically bought him the deputy job. Cal uses him as an errand boy, nothing more. You want to know who shot your

Marine? Why not ask him? Mystery solved. I'll send you my bill."

Dakota opened his hand to reveal the dog tags and dropped them on the table. "He was wearing these."

"Wow, now you've got my attention. Imagine, a Marine private with dog tags."

"Look at them." Dakota pushed the tags closer to Montana.

Montana picked the tags up and read them in silence. His face scrunched up in momentary confusion, and then his features relaxed once more. "It's a mistake."

"Maybe, and maybe I could buy it and let everything slide if it was just one thing, but it's everything together. A lone Marine private, shot in the middle of the desert, with no drinking buddies around and no alcohol in his blood work. Carson City not having any records of him. A missing deputy, even if it is Tommy Lawson, plus those." He pointed to the dog tags in Montana's hand. "Those tags claim the kid was born on April twenty-forth, eighteen-ninety-eight. According to those, Michael Ricco is one hundred-and-ten-years-old."

Montana put the dog tags back on the table. "You've been working too hard, little brother."

Dakota stared and held his tongue. It was his turn to do the stoic thing.

"What?" Montana asked. "What do you want me to do about it?"

"I want to hire you."

Montana laughed loud enough that the waitress and bartender

looked over at them. "You are freaking kidding me." He shook his head. "No. I just finished a case that took me three months of surveillance to get a handle on, and I only got home two hours before you called me. I'm tired. Forget it."

"I'll pay you."

"You can't afford me. Ask Cal to look into missing persons. Chances are you'll find your Michael Ricco there."

"I don't want Cal. He scares me. I want the best, and that's you."

"Ah, the flattery angle."

"Is it working?"

Montana sighed and picked up the dog tags again. "I'm a private investigator, not a miracle worker."

"I used a similar line on Cal just this morning." Dakota smiled. He knew he had Montana now. "What do you say? Will you help me?"

He kept his eyes on Dakota as he reached into his pocket and pulled out his cell, flipped it open, and pushed a preprogrammed number. "Yeah, it's me. I need some information faxed to my home office as soon as you get it. Subject, male. Ricco, Michael J., US Marines. Date of birth, four—twenty four—eighteen-ninety-eight." He paused and rolled his eyes. "Yeah, I know I said we weren't taking anymore cases for a while. It's not a case, just a little nepotism." He flipped the phone closed, then looked at Dakota. "Two days. You got me for two days and that's it. After that, you and your Marine private are on your own, got it?"

Dakota picked up Ricco's tags and tried to suppress a grin. "Two days. I got it."

Montana stood, took a few steps, and turned back and got his brother's attention. "By the way, Dakota…"

"Yeah?"

"Welcome home." He slipped on the Ray-Bans, and as he strolled out the door, daylight invaded the dim interior and seemed to swallow him whole.

Dakota smiled as every woman in the place watched Montana leave. Just once in his life, he'd like to know what it felt like to have that effect on women.

CHAPTER 5

Dakota paid the bill, added a generous tip, and then stepped outside and found Montana waiting for him inside a shiny, black Jeep Wrangler. The top was down, and his hair moved with the afternoon breeze. Behind the dark glasses and still exterior, anyone else might think he was asleep—but Dakota was not just anyone. He had grown up with Montana the boy, and had seen the many tumultuous moods of Montana Lee Thomas the man. He knew how to deal with his brother better than any other person alive. As he approached the Jeep, he decided that was the beauty of families: you knew what it took to make them bleed. The magic was in choosing not to.

He leaned in and checked out the spotless interior, then gave Montana a nod. "Nice. Is it new?"

Montana pointed to the odometer that read only five-hundred-and-seven miles. Dakota thought he detected the tiniest hint of a smile on his brother's face. "Get in. I should have some information back at my place by now."

Dakota shook his head. "Got my own ride." He pointed to the far end of the parking lot where, parked at an irritating angle and taking up two spaces was Dakota's baby, a bright red, sixty-six Mustang convertible.

Montana straightened in his seat, slid the Ray-Bans halfway down his nose with one finger, and peered over the rim. "That's just obnoxious."

"Yeah, beautiful, isn't she? Took me almost a year, but I rebuilt the engine myself. She doesn't run—she purrs." Dakota eyed the Mustang with pride, and grinned at Montana. "I'll follow you. You still at the same place?"

Montana pushed his glasses back in place, nodded, and turned the Jeep's engine over. "Park in front. I'll see you in ten."

* * * *

The day was warm, so Dakota put the top down and enjoyed a slow ride through the streets of his hometown. It was like entering a time warp. Caliente never changed. The main street still housed many of the same shops as when he was a kid, slightly updated and renovated, but it was still home. It gave him a comforting feeling, that lack of change. It made him feel that no matter what else happened in his life, he could always come home, and this place would always welcome him.

As Dakota entered Montana's apartment, he was struck, as always, by the distinct differences in the ways they chose to live their lives. While all Dakota required was a place to lay his head at day's end and something to fill his belly so he wouldn't starve, Montana was extremely detailed-oriented.

His apartment was as warm and hospitable as Dakota's was cold and antiseptic. It mattered to Montana what surrounded him. It always had. He was far more sensitive than he was comfortable with. Dakota knew his brother strived for the tough-guy image. The façade worked for almost everyone but Dakota. His living room was subdued in soothing shades of blue ranging from light, true blue to deep indigo. The couch was deep and made of butter-soft, burgundy leather. Sumptuous blankets were draped over the back. The furniture was a dark, glossy mahogany wood. Original watercolors and ink drawings covered the walls—many of them Montana's own, although he would admit that to no one.

Montana had graduated cum laude from Harvard law because their mother wanted it that way. Dakota had never seen Montana more miserable than when he was making a six-plus-figure salary as a corporate lawyer. After their mother had died five years ago, Montana quit and never looked back. The private investigator thing worked for him, Dakota decided. It fit in with his military background—the tough ex-Army Ranger-crime fighter. Hell, Dakota thought, all Montana needed was a cape.

Dakota made himself at home. He heard Montana down the hall in his study and launched himself over the back of the sofa, landing on his back in the soft leather just as Montana entered the room.

"I hate it when you do that."

Dakota laughed and propped his shoes on the arm of the sofa. "I know."

Montana shoved Dakota's shoes off the furniture and sat down next to him. Dakota sat up, his feet hovering over the spotless coffee table. He rolled his eyes at Montana's warning look, but let his feet fall to the floor with an exaggerated thud.

"Here." Montana handed him the papers that, as predicted, had been waiting for him.

Dakota glanced at the report, and then back to Montana. "What exactly am I looking at?"

"Your Marine captain was correct. There is no private by the name of Michael J. Ricco, either reported missing or listed on active duty. That, and there are no military bases located in this part of Nevada, let alone out by Beaver Dam. It's a state park, not a military facility." Montana stood and started back toward his office.

"Then what was he doing out there all alone in the middle of the night?" Dakota rolled off the couch and followed him.

"He wasn't alone. Someone shot him. And Michael Ricco didn't just fall out of the sky. He had to come from somewhere." He sat in the suede chair at the desk and typed a request into his computer.

Dakota took a seat in the overstuffed chair across from the desk, one leg dangling over the arm. "Does that mean you think I'm right, and this doesn't add up?"

Montana sighed and gave him the look. The one he used on him as a kid when he said something unbelievably stupid. "All it means is you have a misplaced person, nothing more. But…" He smiled. "That's something I can deal with. People get misplaced all the time. The only mystery is in the why."

"Ha! I got you." Dakota pointed a victorious finger at his brother. "You can't stand a mystery any more than I can, and you can't deny this is a mystery, can you?"

The printer saved Montana from commenting, as it spit out several sheets of paper. Dakota remained quiet while Montana read the information, which seemed to take him longer than it should have. When he was finished, he looked at Dakota. "Well, I found your Michael Ricco."

Dakota winged a brow up. "Yeah?"

Montana nodded. "Yeah. Only problem is, he's supposed to be dead."

"Excuse me?" He took the papers Montana handed him. "What's this?"

"Military roster. If your guy is, or ever was, in any branch of the military, he'd be listed there."

"And his name is listed?"

"Sort of."

"What does 'sort of' mean?"

"Since he wasn't listed as active, I asked for inactive personnel.

His name's on that list."

"Inactive? As in, retired or discharged? I thought you said he was supposed to be dead." It was obvious Montana wasn't telling him everything.

"Well, according to that, a nineteen-year-old private by the name of Michael J. Ricco was reported missing in action in July…of nineteen-seventeen. He was presumed dead, and his body was never recovered."

Dakota did a quick mental calculation. "If he was nineteen years old in nineteen-seventeen, that would mean he was born in eighteen-ninety-eight." He took the dog tags out of his pocket and tossed them across the desk.

Montana snagged the tags out of the air and read the birth date embossed in the metal once more. "Okay, Dakota. Now you've got my attention."

* * * *

Dakota called and got directions from Trevor, the medic who had picked up Michael Ricco the night before. He flipped his cellphone closed and climbed into the passenger seat of Montana's Jeep. Considering their destination, it was a better choice than the Mustang. In the twenty minutes it took them to get out of town and into the desert, they passed maybe a half-dozen other motorists. The road stretched out before them like a long, black serpent shimmering in the heat. Quiet for the moment, but always with the promise of danger if pushed too far.

They saw the bright yellow Thunderbird parked off to the side of the road a half-mile before they reached it. Montana pulled in front of it and parked the Jeep. "It's Tommy Lawson's."

They got out, walked back to Tommy's car, and Montana put his hand on the hood. "It's hot from the sun, but the engine's cool so it's been here for a while." He touched the white handkerchief tied to one of the side-view mirrors, and motioned to a second set of tire tracks behind the car. "Cal's been here and gone again."

"Where's Tommy, then? If Cal found him, why is his car still here? And if Cal didn't find him, refer back to question number one— where's Tommy?" Dakota glanced at his watch. It was almost five in the afternoon.

"Why don't we find out?" Montana started by the side of the road and found the tracks left by Trevor's ambulance. "At least we know we're in the right place." Then he followed the obvious trail into the desert. From there it got easier. "We got blood."

Dakota looked at the brown discolorations on the desert floor. If he used his imagination, he supposed it could be blood.

Not long into the trek Montana nudged Dakota and pointed. "There's a tent just through the trees. Might be the campers who called it in. Let's go check it out."

Dakota drained the last drop of water from a bottle he had taken with him and looked to where Montana pointed. "Good, maybe they have more water."

"You were supposed to ration that."

"I was thirsty now. It's not like we're stranded on a desert island, you know."

Montana only sighed as he took the lead along the narrow trail heading into the campsite. His cotton shirt clung to his back. It was nearly six in the evening and the temperature still hovered in the triple digits. Dakota followed close behind. At least the pinion trees the tent was staked under, offered some shade from the brutal sun.

Montana called out as they approached the campsite. "Hello, anyone here?" The only answer came from a pack of coyotes gathering for their evening hunt.

He put a hand out, stopping Dakota, who had just come into the clearing. Dakota watched with concern as Montana pulled out the gun he'd tucked into the waist of his jeans when they left the Jeep, and motioned for him to stay where he was.

"What is it?"

Montana ignored him and inched forward. The tent's zipper was open and flapped gently in the early evening breeze. He stepped to the side, flipped the tent flap up with one hand, and flicked the safety off the gun with the other as he entered the tent. Dakota followed a little behind him. As Montana lowered the gun, Dakota peered over his shoulder and let out a breath on seeing his brother's fears were unfounded. "See…nothing. They're probably out hiking."

"I don't think so." Montana pointed to a reddish-brown discoloration that speckled the inside of the tent wall. "That's blood."

"Montana, what the hell's going on?"

He ignored Dakota's question and exited the tent. He scanned the hard-packed ground around the campsite and pointed to a hastily concealed trail that led into the desert. "What do you say we find out?"

Big, fat drops of dried blood pulled him forward for at least a hundred yards, and then the drops became smaller and more difficult to find in the dense brush. Montana slowed his pace until he came to a complete stop.

"What?" Dakota asked.

Montana ignored the intrusion, backtracked a few feet and found the trail again. Forty minutes later, he still had his head down like a bloodhound on a scent. Dakota followed reluctantly. He was hot and still thirsty. All he could think of was every step they took needed to be repeated on the way back to the Jeep. "Come on, man. Shouldn't we let Cal handle this?"

"Cal's not here. We are."

"It's gotta' to be a hundred degrees, ever hear of heat stroke?"

Montana looked up from the ground and turned to face his brother. Brilliant sunlight reflected off his sunglasses, and sweat cut through the dust on his face to drip from his chin. "Tommy's footprints overlay the blood trail we've been following. He came this way."

"Great, then we know where he went. Let's go tell Cal."

"Dakota, there's only one set of footprints. He never went back."

"He might have gone another way."

"If you wanted to get back to the Jeep, how would you get there?"

Dakota looked over his shoulder at the trail they had made and understood what Montana was telling him. "I'd double back the same way I came."

Montana lifted a sweaty forearm and wiped an equally sweaty forehead as he nodded in agreement. "Yeah."

"You think Tommy's in trouble, don't you?"

Montana turned backed to the trail in front of him without answering. His silence told Dakota a lot. Mainly Montana was concerned, and *yeah*, thought Dakota, *Tommy's in trouble.*

"We must be getting close. They're trying to cover their tracks."

"They?"

Montana pointed to marks made in the soft desert dirt. "How many sets of footprints do you see now?"

Dakota squatted down and looked carefully at the marks. Shading his eyes with a hand, he squinted back at Montana. "More than one."

"A lot more."

Montana lost the blood trail again at the top of a hidden ravine, then found the path through the crushed vegetation. Dakota sat at the top of the ravine and watched him, having no desire to hike down the steep hillside, knowing he would only have to hike back up again on the way out.

Dakota looked at the unrelenting sun and wished for a little cloud cover at the very least. The sky mocked him by staying annoyingly clear. He figured they had about an hour and a half of daylight left. He regretted not listening to Montana and rationing his water. He wasn't just complaining now, he was seriously thirsty. A few Turkey Buzzards circled lazily high above him, their wings stretched wide and riding the thermals. *Not today, boys.*

As Montana searched the ravine below him, Dakota gazed across the vast expanse of desert all around him. He might be more concerned if he hadn't grown up here. When they were kids, the desert had been their playground. Dakota didn't fear this place, on the contrary, despite the circumstances and his thirst, he felt comfortable here. There were no structures, only the desert. Dried river beds that filled only once a year, if that, with rain trickling down from the mountains in flash floods. This was his Nevada, the true Nevada. Not the neon nightmare most people thought of, but this; the brutal heat and the life that existed despite the odds and then later the subtle softness of the desert at night, the cadence of a thousand living things that most people never had the privilege to see or hear. After all this time wandering, he knew he was home at last. He watched the buzzards one by one disappear over a bluff.

"Dakota, get down here!"

His response was less than enthusiastic. "Why? I'm comfortable right where I am."

"Because I need help opening this door."

Curiosity pulled him to his feet. "What door?"

Montana shielded his eyes from the sun and made no attempt to hide his sarcasm. "That would be the large metal door that is buried here in the desert floor. You know...the one that's at the end of the blood trail we've been following."

"Ah, of course. That door." He started down the ravine and grumbled under his breath, "Why did I call him? I could be in air conditioning somewhere with a cold drink."

He tried to pick his way cautiously down the loose soil of the steep ravine, but lost his footing two-thirds of the way down, fell head first, and slid the last ten feet on his forearms and hands. Wiping the dirt and blood on his jeans, he looked up to find Montana staring at him. He didn't expect any sympathy, and he certainly didn't receive any.

"Took you long enough." He gave Dakota a look of disdain for his less-than-graceful approach, and then gestured to a spot on the desert floor. "Look."

At first, Dakota couldn't figure out what he was looking at. Montana bent down and brushed aside sand, dirt, and dead branches, and a defined edge emerged. Dakota helped push aside the debris until all four sides became clear. Montana continued sweeping the metal plate clean, working toward the center, where he uncovered the recessed ring that served as a handle. The door had been painstakingly concealed and still Montana had found it. Dakota would have walked right past it.

"So, that would be a hidden door in the middle of the desert–would it not?"

Montana ignored him, stood to one side, and pulled on the ring. It opened with surprising ease. "This has been used recently." He took off his sunglasses and slipped them into his shirt pocket.

Dakota realized that he intended to enter the gaping, dark hole. "Hang on a second. We have one missing deputy and two presumably missing campers. Don't you think the reasonable thing to do, would be to call Cal and let him investigate this?"

Montana raised his head and spoke to Dakota with absolutely no emotion. "Yes, that would be reasonable." He reached under his pants leg, withdrew a small .32 caliber revolver, and handed it to Dakota. "Here. Just in case."

Dakota took the weapon and ran a filthy hand through his hair in exasperation. He was familiar with weapons; Montana wouldn't have it any other way. "What about you?"

Montana checked the rounds in his 9mm Berretta. "I'm good."

"Um…Montana? What if the bad guys are still home?"

Montana had started down the ladder leading into darkness. He stopped his descent and squinted up at his brother. "I wouldn't worry. They probably closed up shop and split after the kid took off."

"Probably?"

"Yeah, sure. Come on."

"You're so comforting," Dakota mumbled under his breath as he turned and tested his footing on the ladder.

Montana jumped the last four rungs and landed at the bottom of the shaft. He pulled a Mag-light from his pants pocket and flicked on the beam. Nothing but dust showed up.

Dakota followed him down, straining his eyes to see in the dim interior. They stood at the end of a long hallway. He felt the emptiness, the desolate loneliness of the place, and then the smell hit him. "Oh, Jesus." His hand went up to cover his nose.

Montana raised his brows. "Well, it would seem they left something behind. Come on." He took a step, and stopped suddenly. "Hold it." He focused the flashlight on a sensor in the ceiling. "Motion detector." He waved his arm under the sensor and nothing happened. "Electricity must be cut. That's a good sign."

Dakota's hand muffled a groan. "Thanks. I feel better already."

They continued down the passage, guided by the narrow beam of Montana's light and the horrific smell that grew stronger the farther they walked into the tunnel. The temperature, even though they were underground, was stifling. Sweat trickled down Dakota's back and beaded along his hairline. The only sounds were the scuffling of their shoes on the concrete beneath their feet and their heavy breathing.

Montana stopped suddenly in front of Dakota. They had reached the first of a long line of cells, and lying just inside the barred door was a body. It lay on its side with its back to them, limbs splayed out in disarray as if someone had casually tossed it inside.

Montana focused the light on the body and sighed. "I think we just found Tommy."

He tried the door, found it unlocked, and pulled it open on creaky hinges. As he stepped inside, he bent down and trained the beam on the head. "A single shot to the back of the head. Somebody wanted him dead." He turned the corpse over and illuminated the face. Glazed, lifeless eyes stared back at him. "Hello, Tommy." He searched the cell with his flashlight and found two more bodies thrown in the corner. After a brief examination, he looked up at Dakota. "One male, one female. Both killed the same way as Tommy. I'm thinking these are our missing campers."

Dakota shook his head in disgust. He looked down at Tommy and remembered growing up with the guy. Their lives went in distinctly different directions, and they could never have been called friends, but Tommy didn't deserve this—no one did. "Why would someone do this?"

Montana stepped into the hallway. "I don't know, but I have a feeling your private might have some answers."

They continued down the narrow hallway and found ten more cells. Each one contained a dead body dressed in military fatigues, and by Dakota's reckoning, none of them could be more than twenty years old. His mind struggled to grasp the senseless waste of life. So young! How the hell did they end up here?

"How long?" Montana asked him.

Dakota knew he meant how long had the bodies been there. Entombed underground as they were, decomposition had been slowed, but not halted. "Tommy and the campers, obviously just since this morning." He looked closer at one of the soldiers. "These guys...longer. A good day, maybe two." The skin had a sick, grayish pallor and the cheeks were sunken by the flaccidity of death. He tried not to look at the gray matter splattered across the boy's features. Fortunately, death had taken his individuality with it when it came; the face could be recognized merely as human.

Dakota followed his brother as he ventured past the dead men and found the remains of a command center. A control desk in the shape of a semi-circle occupied a spacious room at the end of the hallway. Bare wires protruded from the walls. The empty shells of computers lay scattered about the floor. All of the hard drives had been removed and the monitors destroyed. Nothing remotely helpful had been left, except the bodies.

Montana picked through the debris. "Well, they were thorough. I'll give them that."

They had been underground for nearly an hour with only the stench of death and decay for company. Dakota had trouble breathing as he turned in a small circle and surveyed the destruction surrounding him. When he came back to Montana, he pushed at the hair sticking to his face. "What the hell happened here? What was going on in this place?"

Montana stood and brushed the dirt from his hands. "The kid's the key. Whoever did this thinks he's important enough to kill thirteen people for."

Dakota suddenly realized it wasn't over. "They're going to try again, aren't they?"

Montana nodded. "Yeah, if they haven't already."

"What do we do?" That thought evolved into the conclusion that his staff was in danger. His chest felt constricted with the need to get out of there, to move, to breathe. His head was fuzzy, and he knew he was hyperventilating. He struggled to control his breathing. All he had done was ask one simple question. Who was Michael Ricco? Would he have tried to satisfy his curiosity if he'd known where the answers would lead him? As he got a handle on his feelings and his breathing, he knew he would have. An unanswered question was like an unopened door, you had to peek inside. For Dakota it wasn't a choice.

Montana stood next to him, placed a hand on his shoulder, and gave it a squeeze. Even in the dim light, Dakota could see the muscles of Montana's jaw working. His face might have conveyed nothing to the casual observer, but Dakota saw the tendons in his neck cord and the veins pop out as if he had just done a strenuous hour in the gym. Montana didn't answer his brother, just pushed past him and walked up the hallway to the still-opened door.

Dakota tried not to look at the dark humps, lying motionless in the cells he passed, but he couldn't help himself. Who were they? Who mourned them? They once lived up there in the light. They loved, they laughed, but they died alone and nameless down here in the dark. As Dakota followed Montana to the ladder and into the fresh air, he vowed he would change that. He would give those men their names back.

The stark beauty of the desert seemed surreal after what they had just witnessed. The sun was lower on the horizon and shadows had lengthened. The temperature had dropped down into the high double-digits, and the breeze felt cool in comparison to the bunker beneath them. The air smelled sweet, but it did little to wash the stench of death from their nostrils.

While Dakota sat on the ground trying to deal with what he had just seen, Montana pulled his cellphone from his pocket and attempted to get a signal. When he did, he punched a preprogrammed number. "Hey, I need a favor." He walked away from Dakota and spoke in a hushed tone, as though he didn't want him to hear what was being said. After several minutes, he put the phone in his pocket and strode back to where Dakota sat. "Okay."

"Okay, what?"

"I put a man on your Michael Ricco. He should be there in about twenty minutes."

"A man? What do you mean, like a guard?"

"Okay."

"Will you stop with the 'okays,' and just tell me what's going on, please?"

Montana leaned on a boulder next to where Dakota sat, and for the first time let his emotions show. He had yet to put the ever-present Ray-Bans back on and Dakota caught a glimpse of something pass over Montana's eyes. Dakota knew his brother thought that being strong meant never letting his feelings show, never losing his self-control. At that moment, he knew Montana was on the verge of doing both. Anger, grief, despair, and confusion all fought for a way out before Montana pulled the dark glasses out of his shirt pocket and forced them back into hiding. He looked away as though he were thinking. Dakota let him believe he had managed to hide the overwhelming emotions threatening to overpower him.

"All right, Dakota." Montana spoke to the horizon before turning back toward him. "You wanted my help, now you've got it. All of it. Here's the deal. Someone tried to kill your boy, and then they killed all these people to cover their tracks." He pointed to the open door. "We weren't meant to find that bunker or those bodies. Whoever was that desperate is not going to let Michael Ricco live to tell any tales. They are going to find him, and they are probably going to kill him." Montana caught his brother's eye and held it. "And anyone else who gets in their way."

It took Dakota a second to realize who he was talking about. "You mean me?" His mind tried to reject the thought. "But why?"

"Because you couldn't let it go. You asked questions."

Dakota looked at the sun sinking behind the buttes. The brilliant light of day had muted to blended orange and rose hues, painting the once neutral sandstone and giving it life in the fading of day. The beauty of the moment was not lost on him. He was alive to witness the sight, Tommy wasn't. "I got Tommy Lawson and those campers killed." Dakota turned back to Montana. "Didn't I?"

Montana shook his head. "Don't put that on yourself. You did right. And don't worry about Ricco. My man is armed, and he won't let anything happen to the kid or anyone else. Trust me on that."

Dakota took a deep breath and nodded. "Okay, so now what do we do?"

Montana pushed himself away from the boulder and gave his brother a hand up. "We go talk to Michael Ricco. I have a feeling he's got one hell of a story to tell us."

CHAPTER 6

The first thought that entered Michael Ricco's mind on opening his eyes was, Run! But his body didn't want to cooperate. Confusion, fear, desperation, and hopelessness crashed down on him, keeping rational thought at bay.

He should be dead. He wanted to be dead, but for reasons he had long ago stopped trying to figure out, he kept breathing. They took him again. He couldn't remember how, but the holes in his memory were not new. All he could think was they had found him, and he understood from long experience, there would be worse than hell to pay for what he had done.

His blurred vision cleared, and he looked around him. Something was not right. He didn't recognize this place. He had seen amazing changes and advances over his years of captivity, but nothing like this. He lay in a bed that was a technological wonder. The side rails were covered with illuminated symbols he had no hope of deciphering. The tubes and wires attached to him did look familiar, but the single thing that just didn't register was the fact that he wasn't restrained. As Ricco tested the boundaries of his mobility, he learned why. Pain, sudden and intense, nailed him to the bed without the need for restraints.

A small hiss escaped his lips despite his best efforts to conceal it, and the alarms above his bed started bonging. Feeling lightheaded, he closed his eyes and heard feet enter the room. Bracing himself for the worst, he opened his eyes and let confusion take hold.

A young woman stood over his bed with a stethoscope casually hung around her neck, her shiny brown hair pulled back into a sleek ponytail. She smiled at him and reached up behind the bed to silence the alarm. "You're okay," she told him. "You want something for the pain?"

He looked at her as if she were speaking a foreign language. Was she kidding? Something for pain? Maybe he was dead. Then he felt his heart flip in his chest. Nope, not dead.

He focused on the man who had entered the room to stand behind the nurse. He could have been carved out of solid, black marble. Dark, mirrored glasses hid his eyes, but Ricco knew they were looking at him. Reflexes had him sitting up, while pain forced him to lie back down. The monitor alarms started their klaxon once more.

"Take it easy, Michael." The nurse lowered the bedrail and took Ricco's hand in her own. "No one's going to hurt you." With her free hand she gently touched his cheek.

Ricco flinched at the contact. It was an involuntary response. The only time anyone touched him was to cause him pain.

She didn't seem to notice, or if she did he couldn't tell. She reached up and did something with the monitor, then gave his hand a little squeeze. "I'm going to get you something for pain." She turned to leave, but Ricco held her there.

"No." He shook his head, his voice barely above a whisper. He wasn't sure she heard him over the alarms that sounded again. "No pain meds."

The nurse wrapped her other hand around the one that gripped hers. "You're hurting. I can give you something to help. Come on, you don't have to play the tough guy with me."

He just shook his head and let her hand go. He didn't want to, it was so soft, and he had forgotten how soft girls could be. He had forgotten a lot of things he wanted to remember, and he remembered a lot of things he wanted to forget.

At that moment, the man who had been standing by, quiet and motionless, reached up and silenced the alarms, which brought an immediate and scathing reaction from the nurse. While Ricco had brought out a caring, almost motherly side to her, the man beside her seemed to illicit her wrath. "Hey… Your job is guarding him. My job is everything else." The tiny little thing was in no way intimidated by the walking mountain. She narrowed her eyes and pointed a demanding finger. "You don't touch anything in here. Got it?"

Ricco was in admiration of anyone standing up to that. He wasn't sure who he should be more concerned for, the nurse or the object of her annoyance.

The guard gave her a crooked grin and canted his shiny, bald dome in her direction. "Yes, ma'am."

She turned back to Ricco and switched on her smile once more. "You sure, honey? You really look like you could use something."

Ricco kept his eyes on the guard, but shook his head to the nurse. He was unsure about what to make of their strange relationship.

She sighed and gave his hand a reassuring pat. "Okay, but you're allowed to change your mind. If it gets to be too much, just push this button." She clipped a cord with a bright red button to his gown. "I'll be right down the hall if you need me." She gave him the thousand-watt grin again, then turned and frowned at the guard. "Hands off," she warned.

He held his hands out in feigned innocence as a broad, sparkling white smile spread across his face. He waited until she had walked out of the room and back to the nurses' station, and then turned his shaded eyes back to Ricco. "Don't think she likes me." His deep, rumbling laugh filled the small room.

Ricco couldn't take his eyes off the man. Even though well concealed, he could see the slight bulge of a weapon holstered under his left shoulder.

The man noticed Ricco's concern and his face softened, as much as rock allowed. "Relax, Michael. I'm here to protect you, not hurt you."

Michael. It had been so long since anyone had called him by his given name, and now, he'd heard it twice in the space of a few minutes. It had been Ricco or Private for as long as he could remember. The sound of his own name nearly brought tears to his eyes.

Despite the uncertainty of his situation, Ricco gathered up his courage and decided to ask a few questions of his own. After all, if the guard started getting physical he could always call the nurse back in.

He wrapped his hand around the call light, his thumb hovering over the red button. "This isn't the base?"

His guard shook his head. "Hospital."

So, it wasn't a dream—his run through the desert, the scattered fragments of memories, a dark-haired doctor with a kind face, the overwhelming panic. He had nearly convinced himself it was all a hallucination. He almost didn't believe it—he had made it out. He allowed one moment to relish in the victory before reality came crashing down and the panic he had felt on waking returned with a vengeance.

"They'll find me." Despite the pain, he almost made it out of the bed.

The monitor alarms sounded again as the man laid one hand on Ricco's shoulder, and with very little effort held him still. "They gotta' go through me first, boy. Not gonna happen, you hear?"

Ricco just stared at him. He wanted to believe this man was on his side, but years of captivity with nothing but lies and pain as constant companions had taught him a degree of cynicism that was beyond measure. It would take more than this man's word to have Ricco believing in him.

"Relax, Michael. You keep making the alarms go off like that and they're going to knock you out whether you want it or not."

He was breathing too fast, and sweat beaded on his face. Ricco willed himself to calm down. He took deep, steady breaths until the alarms quieted.

The guard released his shoulder and gave him a nod. "There you go."

Ricco still had trouble grasping the concept of an ally. Since his first question had been met without any harm coming to him, he pushed his luck and tried for a second. "Who are you?"

The broad smile returned. "A friend. Better get used to me, boy. For the next couple of days I'm sticking to you closer than your mama on the first day of school." He surprised Ricco by extending his hand. "I'm Ito St. James."

Ricco took the hand out of reflex, still not sure what to make of the man.

A movement outside the door caught Ito's attention. He turned his head, and Ricco strained to look past him. Two men stood at the nurses' station, their backs to the door. Both were about the same height, but one was much broader in the shoulders. The slighter-built of the two had shorter hair, and when he turned, Ricco recognized him as the doctor from last night, and his panic escalated. Doctors were a species he had learned to distrust long ago.

Ito sensed his uneasiness. "Nothing to fear, my man. They're the good guys." He raised his shades and gave Ricco a smile and a wink. "Don't go anywhere. I'll be back."

The three men met just outside his door, but were too far away for Ricco to hear their conversation. As if on cue, all three turned to face him, and then Ito took a position outside the door, while the doctor led the way to his bed followed by the other man. Up close, he could tell they were brothers. The most noticeable difference was in their eyes. The doctor had bright green eyes, while his brother had black.

The doctor spoke first. "Michael, do you remember me?"

Michael, again. He nodded.

"My name is Dakota Thomas. I took care of you in the emergency room. This is my brother, Montana."

Ricco nodded and tried to straighten himself in bed when a sudden spasm ripped through his back, to his shoulder, and he grunted with pain.

Before the alarms could sound, Dakota reached up and paused them, then turned back to Ricco. "My nurse tells me you won't take anything for the pain. Want to tell me why not?"

Ricco glanced from one face to the next, trying to figure out what they wanted from him. "I just want to stay alert." It was an honest admission. The only thing that scared him more than being sent back to the bunker was the thought of what they might do to him if they put him under.

"Look, Michael, no one here wants to hurt you, but there are a lot of questions we need answers to. Someone tried to kill you. Can you tell us why?"

Ricco's attention was drawn to the other brother. Everything about the man screamed military. They might not be from the base, but that didn't mean he wasn't in trouble. So far, all his questions had rewarded him with answers, so he went for broke and asked another. "You an MP?"

Montana stepped in front of his brother and thrust a closed fist in Ricco's face. Ricco, certain he had asked one question too many, flinched, turned his head to the side and closed his eyes, waiting for the strike. When nothing happened, he opened his eyes. Montana relaxed his hand and let the dog tags slide out. He dangled them in front of Ricco, patiently jiggling them, until Michael reached up with his good hand and took them. It was the first time he realized they were gone.

"Private Michael J. Ricco." Montana's voice was pure officer.

Ricco straightened as much as he could in the bed. "Yes, sir." The words were an automatic response.

"My name is Major Montana Lee Thomas, Ranger Delta Force, retired. Do you understand?"

Ricco swallowed involuntarily. "Yes, sir." He knew the Rangers were notorious for their badass attitudes, and retired or not, he had no desire to tangle with one, particularly one who outweighed him by at least seventy pounds and had attitude clinging to him like wet on water.

"I need answers from you, Private. You were shot. By whom?"

From the man's tone of voice, it was clear that keeping quiet was not an option.

"I can't say for sure, sir." It was an honest answer. He didn't even know he had been hit until he saw the blood dripping from his fingers.

"All right, then. Here's an easy one. Why were they trying to kill you?"

An easy one? Ricco could hardly wait until he got to the tough ones. His gaze went from one face to the other, trying to decide if he could trust these men. He couldn't rule out they were just playing him. He didn't know who they were, not really, or what they meant to do with him, or to him. Ricco took a breath and decided it didn't matter. They would either kill him, or help him. Either way would be a relief.

"I escaped. They were trying to get me back or prevent my leaving."

Montana stepped closer, his hands leaning on the bedrail, his eyes intense. "Michael, we found the bunker."

Ricco blinked and felt his heart trip faster in his chest. They already know! He tried to keep the fear that boiled in his belly from showing on his face. He almost choked trying to get the words out. "You found them?"

Montana pushed off the bed and turned his back on Ricco. He took two steps away before turning around once more to face him. "Yeah, we found them." Montana's hands clenched into fists as his eyes nailed Ricco to the bed. "Ten men in military garb, our town's deputy who went out looking for clues about you, and the two campers who saved your life by calling EMS…all of them dead, executed with a single gunshot to the back of the head. Thirteen people, Private Ricco, dead, presumably because of you." Montana moved forward, clutching the bedrail again, his knuckles whitening as he spoke. "And now you're going to tell me what the hell is going on before anyone else I know has a pair of crosshairs centered on the back of their head."

"They killed them?"

An unwanted slideshow flitted across his brain. He had been kept alone, isolation making him as much a prisoner as bars, but he had seen the other men like him, unwilling participants in an experiment in human endurance. The faces of the men he had survived and the ones he had left behind came to mind one at time. He never knew their names, they never knew his, but they shared something only they could ever understand. They were brothers, not of blood, but the bond they shared went far deeper. He'd heard their screams in the dark, the pleas for death. His own voice had been part of the chorus. A part of him envied that his brothers had finally found their peace. Ricco still searched for his.

His eyes never wavered from the major's, but his head felt like cotton. "All of them…they're all dead?"

"Talk to me, Private Ricco. I'm not known for my patience. You can start with those." He motioned to the dog tags.

Ricco opened his hand and stared at the tags. They too had changed over the years, but Ricco had always held on to them as a link to his past—to home. He blinked back a lifetime worth of tears as memories rushed the fragile gates that guarded his sanity.

"What year is it?" he whispered, wrapping his hand around the tags, clutching them like a lifeline to a past he had nearly forgotten.

"What?" Montana looked concerned by the question. "You don't know what year it is?" Ricco shook his head as Montana threw a questioning look at his brother.

"He doesn't have a head injury, if that's what you're wondering." Dakota turned to Ricco. "You don't know the date?"

Ricco shook his head again, and then wiped his eyes. "They had me there a long time. Always underground. No daylight. I never even knew what time of day it was, let alone what month. After a while, the years just blended together."

"Who? Who had you?"

Ricco looked away from the major's intense gaze and concentrated on the clock on the wall. If he centered all his attention on the sweep second hand circling the face, maybe he could get through this, maybe he could tell them. Living through the nightmare was one thing, talking about it was something else all together. If nothing else made sense to him, one thought was very clear—he would not go back.

"Military. Maybe, I'm not sure." One face, one name made it through the cacophony. The face of the man he would never forget. "I'm not sure of anything except for one thing. I am not going back. You won't take me back there, I'll die first. Do you understand that?" He sat up as he spoke, his voice quiet desperation. Then the pain had him backing down again.

Dakota pushed his brother aside as he stepped to the bed. "This is ridiculous. Let them get you something for the pain, man. No one's going to touch you in here. For Christ's sake, you've got a friggin' tree outside your room guarding your ass, plus my brother, who's just as scary as he looks. You want out of here, don't you?"

Ricco nodded, a little startled by the sudden rant.

"Great. Then let the nurse give you something for pain. You're not doing yourself any favors by playing the tough guy, okay?"

Ricco's tone turned to one of quiet desperation. "I can't stay here, you don't understand." His nurse came into the room with a syringe in her hand, and stood waiting for the go-ahead from Dakota. Ricco looked from the nurse, to the major, and finally back to Dakota. "It's not safe while I'm here—for anyone."

Montana spoke up. "What if we take you someplace else, someplace safe?"

"Do I have a choice?" He knew the answer before he asked the question. It had been a long time since he had any choices left to him.

Montana folded his arms over his chest. "No."

"Kind of what I thought." Ricco forced a smile. "Do you really think you can help me?"

"I won't know until I hear the rest of your story, but for now, I suggest you do as Dakota tells you, and trust me to keep you safe."

Trust me. The words sounded foreign, like a language he knew as a boy, but had forgotten long ago. Ricco was used to doing as he was told, but trust? He didn't think he could do that, not yet, maybe not ever. The smile faded from his face. "Will you promise me one thing?"

"Depends."

"If you can't help me, if it looks like he might take me back...I want you to kill me. Will you promise me that?"

Montana leaned down and looked Ricco square in the eye. "I can promise you one thing, Private...it won't come to that. Whoever this bastard is, you have my word he'll never touch you again. Now, shut up and let them help you."

"Yes, sir." Ricco decided he might have to like this man, despite his misgivings about Rangers and authority in general.

Dakota nodded to the nurse as she prepared to push the drug into Ricco's IV line. "Just lay back, honey. This is going make you a little sleepy."

"Wait," Ricco said. "You never told me the date. What year is it?"

The brothers exchanged looks, appeared to reach a silent decision, and Dakota turned to Ricco. "It's the year two-thousand-eight, Michael."

Ricco stared at him, not fully comprehending what he had been told. He saw the doctor give a nod to the nurse. This time, he didn't stop her. He watched her push the drug into the line, and as the narcotic dragged him under, he wondered how he would explain the rest of his story to Major Thomas, and what the major would think of him when he learned the truth.

CHAPTER 7

Dakota watched Ricco's eyes glaze over with the effects of the morphine. The boy fought to stay awake, but the narcotic was stronger and soon won the battle. He watched the monitors until Ricco's vital signs leveled out, then turned to the nurse. "Be generous with the pain meds. He's not going to ask for them."

"I figured as much." She left the bedside and sat at a computer outside the door to begin her charting. When Dakota followed and hovered she stopped typing and smiled up at him. "I'll call you if anything changes… Promise."

He glanced at the name tag clipped to her scrubs. "Okay, Ivey, I can take a hint."

She returned to her typing. "And I can do my job a lot better without you hanging over my shoulder."

Dakota gave her a smile and a nod of approval. "I like them sassy." He walked back to the nurses' station before giving Ivey a chance to reply.

He took Ricco's chart from a rack at the desk and wrote an order while intermittently watching Montana "Well, what do you think?"

"We need to get him out of here."

Dakota flagged the order and replaced the chart. "He's not in great shape. We won't be doing him any favors if we move him right now. Besides, I thought that was the whole idea of putting the moving wall outside his door." Dakota hooked a thumb in Ito's direction. Ito ignored the comment and continued to stare in the direction of Ricco's room.

In his frayed jeans, white tee, and opened long-sleeve denim shirt, Montana should have looked out of place, but he simply leaned back against the nurses' station, his arms folded across his chest, daring someone to make him move. "You have his pain under control. I say we move him now while we have the chance."

"I can't guard him if I can't secure him, and I can't secure him here." Ito didn't look at Dakota as he spoke, he had eyes only for Ricco's room.

"Why not?"

"Because, Doctor, this is a public building. All kinds of people coming and going, some of them work here, some of them don't. I can't secure what I can't control. Whoever is after this kid would have a field day if we keep him here."

"Yeah, reality check, guys. We are talking about Caliente." Dakota glanced at Montana, but his brother didn't acknowledge him.

"The same Caliente we grew up in."

Montana finally gave Dakota a little eye contact. "The same Caliente Michael Ricco ended up in, the same Caliente that is thirty miles away from a hidden underground bunker and thirteen murdered people. Small towns aren't immune to evil, they just hide it better."

"I read Stephen King too, but come on, you don't really think they would try something here, do you? With all these people around, and Mr. Personality guarding the door?"

"I would."

Dakota rolled his eyes. "Well, you would also break up a bar room brawl unarmed and outnumbered and call it a fun night. I am talking about people who would shoot an unarmed man in the back. That's cowardly. Besides, how would they even know he's here?"

"They followed the blood trail, same as us. They were shooting at him, wouldn't take a lot of deduction to realize he's wounded. They also know the authorities are involved because of Tommy. He was on the job. I assume he was carrying a badge, but it wasn't on his body. They also know every moment they wait they risk the chance of Ricco talking. They will want to…"

Dakota saw Montana stiffen, suddenly on full alert. Ito exploded from complete stillness to sudden action and pushed past him.

"What the hell?" Dakota turned in time to see one of the resident doctors in a white lab coat casually step past Ivey and enter Ricco's room.

Montana pulled his gun from beneath the loose denim shirt. "Stay here. Don't move."

Dakota felt like he was stuck in molasses, watching the scene play out before him in slow motion.

Ivey stood between Ito and Ricco, her hands on her hips. The look of annoyance on her face turning into one of fear as Ito took the shortest path between him and his objective and bore down on her. He pushed her out his way with a forearm and ran into Ricco's room. Ivey almost kept her balance, but tripped over the chair she had been sitting in and fell with a grunt onto the floor.

It was almost as if Dakota was watching a movie. Ito tackled the man in the white coat, just as he was reaching for Ricco's IV tubing. The man went down, the syringe flying from his grip. The combined weight of both men sent them flying across the room to crash into a storage bin. Medical supplies spilled out on top of them as the bin flipped. Ito wrestled with the man and fought to bring his weapon up.

The syringe forgotten, White-coat made a grab for the gun, but Ito was quicker and outweighed him by a good fifty pounds. That point suddenly became moot as Montana pulled back the slide of his gun and chambered a round. The snap of the weapon echoed throughout the unit.

Dakota waited for the sound of gunfire, but instead he heard Montana's quiet voice. "Hands."

There was no doubt that White-coat heard him too. He stopped his struggles and brought his hands up and out, away from his body. Ito trained his weapon on the supine man on the floor. They were both sweating and breathing heavily. Ricco, by contrast, was in a state of drug-induced bliss, wonderfully unaware his life had once again been in the balance.

Ito stood, never taking his eyes from the man. "Who the hell are you?"

White-coat laughed. "I'm a dead man." With one quick motion, he grabbed the syringe near his outstretched hand and pulled the cap from the needle.

Montana and Ito shouted in unison, "Freeze!" But the man only smiled and plunged the needle into his own neck.

Montana dove for the syringe, but too late; the plunger had already been depressed. He pulled the needle from the man's neck and tossed it on the floor. "Who sent you?" He handed his weapon to Ito, and lifted the man's head off the floor. "Come on, who sent you?" He slapped his face. "Tell me, you shit!"

Dakota remembered how to move and ran to his brother's side. He saw the man smile once more, but he never said a word. Then the eyes that laughed at them all, glazed over. As Montana held White-coat's head in his lap, the man's body convulsed. His back arched and stiffened. A wet gurgling sound came from deep in his chest as he slumped against Montana, dead eyes staring back.

Montana felt for a pulse at the man's neck. "Fuck!"

"Wait." Dakota turned to the shocked staff gathered at the door. "Get me some Epi!"

"Dakota…" Montana put a hand on his arm as Dakota knelt down next to White-coat and ripped his shirt open. He grabbed an Ambu-bag and started to pump air into the dead man's lungs, but Montana stopped him. "Dakota, he's dead."

"Where the hell's the Epi?" Dakota started CPR. The man beneath him twitched and flopped like a marionette whose wires had been cut. It was his last dance, the dance of the dead. Behind Dakota, his staff remained immobile. They already knew what he hadn't accepted.

"Dakota, he's dead," Montana said again.

Dakota ignored him as he grunted and sweated with the efforts of pumping stagnant blood through a lifeless heart.

Montana grabbed his brother's hands. "Stop it. He's gone."

Dakota tore his hands away. "No!" He glared at Montana, and then looked at the man on the floor. Pink froth had bubbled up and leaked from his mouth. His skin had taken on a bluish tint, and his eyes were dull and lifeless. Dakota knew Montana was right, and slumped back on his heels in defeat. "What the hell just happened?"

Montana motioned to Ito. "We need to get this kid out of here, now."

Ito nodded. "Give me a minute." He took out his cellphone and stepped to the window.

Ivey came to Dakota's side and gave him a hand up. "The

sheriff's on the way, someone should be here shortly."

Dakota nodded absently. Death was a frequent visitor in hospitals, but not like this.

Ivey stepped around the dead man on the floor. "I still have a patient to take care of."

Dakota just stared at her. She sounded all tough and in control, but Dakota saw her hands shake as she tried to reset the blood pressure cuff on the monitor. She pushed a wrong button, and a screen she didn't want came up. When she went to cancel it, she hit another wrong button. "Shit!" She jumped when Dakota came up behind her and gently pushed her hand down and reprogrammed the monitor.

"It's okay." He gave her a sideways glance. "I won't tell anyone, promise."

Ivey sniffed and wiped at her face before putting the professional mask back in place. "Thanks," she said quietly.

Montana came to Dakota's side. "We need to move, now." He looked to Ito. A single nod had Montana grabbing his brother's arm and turning him around. "Okay, unhook him." Montana motioned to the IV tubing and other equipment attached to Ricco.

"What?" At Montana's words, Dakota snapped out of the stupor he had been in. He jerked his arm free of his brother's grip and shook his head. "No, you can't just take him." He watched Ito move to Ricco's bedside and begin unhooking him from the monitor. "What do you think you're doing?"

Ivey regained her composure, reached across the bed and slapped Ito's hands away, and started hooking up what he had just unhooked. She glared at him as she worked. "I told you not to touch anything. I wasn't kidding." She pointed a finger at his face. "I might be little, but trust me, you do not want to mess with me."

Ito met her threat with a smile, calmly pushed her hands out of the way, and once again began unhooking Ricco. "My dear lady, if this were not a matter of great urgency, I assure you I would be unduly terrified, but believe me, we both want the same thing, to protect Private Ricco."

Ivey turned to Dakota and held her hands out as if to say, Well, don't just stand there, do something!

Dakota stepped next to Ivey. "Montana?" He wasn't sure whose side to take.

Montana ignored Dakota and handed Ito the keys to his Jeep. "I'm parked next to you. Bring it around back, but first, find this guy's partner. They never come alone. Find him and neutralize him. Try to keep it quiet, but go loud if you have to."

Dakota grabbed Montana's sleeve and whipped him around. "What the fuck are you doing?"

Montana gave him one seething glance, then continued giving orders to Ito. "Just do it. We'll meet you at the entrance in five."

Ito gave him a nod, winked at Ivey, and turned and jogged out of the unit.

Ivey's brow creased in confusion. "You can't really be thinking about letting them just take him?"

"Montana, Cal will be here any minute, I think—"

"Enough." Montana didn't need to raise his voice, the tone demanded instant attention and unquestioned obedience. "There is no time for this." He looked from doctor to nurse and back again before continuing. "Some very bad people sent this man in here to kill your patient. It's just lucky we were here to stop it, because if he knew about Ito, they wouldn't have tried the soft approach. Trust me when I tell you that the next time, and there will be a next time, they will not be so subtle."

"Cal can put guards on the door, or maybe the state troopers—"

"The next time, Dakota, they will come in and take out anyone who gets in their way. That includes Cal's guards, state troopers…" He glanced at Ivey. "Or any nurses who try to stop them. If he stays here, people are going to die. You saw that bunker and those bodies. These people are well organized, well financed, and obviously have no problems killing a cop." Montana pointed to the dead man on the floor. "He was willing to kill himself instead of being taken. Failure is not an option for them, and that makes them more dangerous than you want to think about." He turned his attention to Ivey. "None of you will be alive by morning if the kid stays."

Ivey paled a bit, but tried to keep up a tough front as she turned to Dakota. "He's kidding, right?"

Dakota shook his head. "I don't think he knows how to kid."

Ivey blinked several times, and then whirled around and started pulling monitor leads off Ricco's chest. Dakota leaped over dead White-coat and stopped her. "No. I'll finish this. Get me a wheelchair, his meds, something for pain, and some dressing supplies for later."

He shut the monitor off and capped Ricco's IV. Now, his hands were the ones shaking. "I'm going to lose my license over this, you know."

When Ricco was free from all the equipment, Montana put the side rail down, wrapped him in a blanket, and then gently picked the boy up in his arms. Dakota thought Ricco looked incredibly fragile in contrast. Montana waited for the wheelchair and locked eyes with his brother. "He could lose his life."

"I hate it when you're right."

"Yeah, I know."

Ivey rushed back into the room and positioned the wheelchair next to Montana. As he lowered Ricco into it, the boy's eyes fluttered but didn't open. Ivey took the bag of supplies hanging from the back of the chair and placed it in Ricco's lap. She bent down, placed Ricco's feet in the footrests, and tucked the blanket around his shoulders. She glanced up at Dakota. "Where are you taking him?"

He looked to Montana, who just raised his eyebrows. "I haven't a clue. It's probably best if you don't know." He blew out a breath. "Look, just keep everyone clear of this room and let Cal handle it."

"Handle it? He's going to have a coronary over it."

Montana's cellphone rang. He flipped it open, listened, nodded once and closed it. He didn't look happy. "We're leaving." He moved behind Ricco's chair and unlocked the wheels. When Dakota stayed where he was, Montana looked over his shoulder as he pushed Ricco out of the room. "Now, Dakota. Ito's in place and Cal's on the way."

"Shit!" Dakota realized Montana was leaving with his patient and jogged a few steps to catch up. He stopped, pulled a piece of paper from the desk, scribbled on it, and ran back to Ivey. "Here's my cellphone number. If Cal gives you any grief, let me know and I'll take care of it."

"If he gives me any grief?" Ivey asked. Dakota shrugged, and Ivey shook her head. "Take care of yourself, okay?"

Dakota gave her a wave and ran to catch up with Montana, who was waiting for him at the service elevator in the lobby. As they pushed Ricco inside and the doors closed, they could hear Cal screaming already as he got out of the public elevator around the corner. "Thomas! Get your ass out here, boy!"

Montana stared at the descending numbers. "And you wanted to stay."

"Momentary insanity."

Montana reached over and pushed a button, and the car jerked to a sudden stop. "You good with this?"

"No." Dakota looked at his brother. They had been back together for less than twenty-four hours, and they were where they always seemed to end up, in trouble.

Montana graced him with one of his half-cocked smiles and nodded. "Good," he said as if reading his mind. "Just wanted to make sure. Hey…"

Dakota saw the smile vanish and concern cross Montana's face. "What?"

"I won't let anything happen to the kid, or you for that matter. You know that." It wasn't a question, but a simple statement of fact.

Dakota sighed and gave him a nod in return. "Yeah, I do."

"You brought me into this. If you want out, just say so. You can still walk back up there and face Cal and the state troopers, but if you come with us, it's for the long haul. You can't decide you want out because things are getting uncomfortable."

Dakota looked from his brother to Michael Ricco.

"Dak, somebody wants him dead. If these people find out you're helping him, they will take you down without a moment's hesitation. Understand that, now."

Dakota swallowed the sudden lump in his throat and put his hand on the red stop button. He paused for a moment. How did it come to this? His entire future decided in one moment. He knew what he had to do, but he wondered how the hell he was going to pay off his student loans without a job. He pushed the button and sent the elevator on its way.

"You sure?" Montana asked.

"Hell, no! I'm not sure about any of this." Dakota ran a hand through his hair and blew out a breath.

The elevator doors opened, and Montana pushed Ricco out. Dakota paused, and made his decision, then followed him. He knew he couldn't leave Michael Ricco anymore than he could leave his brother.

CHAPTER 8

Dakota helped settle Ricco into the back of Montana's Jeep, then took the seat next to him. The boy opened his eyes, but he looked groggy and more than a little out of it.

"Exactly where are we going?" Dakota asked.

"Someplace safe."

"That's so comforting." Dakota buckled Ricco's seat belt. "I don't suppose you would care to be more specific?"

Montana turned to face him. "From time to time, it's necessary to keep a client out of sight for a day or two. Ito has a friend who helps me out. It's an unregistered address, a place where they can't find us— at least, not right away."

"He'll be safe there?"

Montana and Ito exchanged glances. "Yeah, for a little while, but the kid's got to talk to me, Dakota. I can't help him if I don't know what the hell is going on. Right now, all I know for sure is some heavyweight paramilitary group has been holding him against his will, and they want him back, or they want him dead. Neither of those options works for me." He waited for that to sink in before continuing. "When he wakes up, he'll tell me everything. I may not be gentle about getting the answers, and I need you to be okay with that."

Dakota knew his brother's gift for understatement, and a sudden image of when they were kids slammed into his head. Their mother had been at work, which gave a nine and ten year old Dakota and Montana plenty of time to get into trouble. Montana convinced him that the gently sloping roof of their single level adobe house wasn't that far off the ground, and if he took his skateboard down at just the right angle, it should be a cool ride. Dakota was doubtful, but didn't want to receive the look from his brother, so twenty minutes later he found himself climbing out his bedroom window and up the slope to where it peaked. It sure as hell looked plenty high to him. When the fall broke his leg, Montana refused to accept any blame, saying it was all Dakota's fault for not landing right. In Montana's world, anything was possible and "not gentle" could range from a slap in the face to some serious bloodletting.

"What exactly is 'not gentle'? I won't let you hurt him. I can't."

"Not my style. I won't touch him. He might not like what I'm asking him, but he's going to tell me what he knows. Do you understand?"

Ito made a sharp turn, and Ricco moaned as his body weight pressed his injured shoulder against the door. Montana eyed the boy, then turned away from Dakota without waiting for an answer.

Dakota spent the rest of the hour-long car ride lost in his thoughts and wondering exactly what Montana meant. He understood his brother better than anyone. At least, he used to. Montana had tried to run away from who he was for most of his life, trying to exorcise the demons of his past only to find that the demons were an inescapable part of what made him who he was.

Their father had never been a part of their lives and their mother had never seen fit to tell them about the man, even when Montana demanded the answers from her. Lilly Thomas was the one person who could stand up to Montana's anger. Montana reacted in typical fashion, for Montana. He cut their mother out of his life and searched for a father he never knew. What he found was that some truths are better left unknown, and some secrets are best never revealed.

Dakota watched Montana suffer for a truth that never existed, and he watched him make peace with that reality. It had not been an easy time in either of their lives. But it was that unspoken bond between them that gave Dakota the courage to trust his brother now, when every fiber of his being told him this was wrong.

Dakota turned his attention to the young man next to him and couldn't help but wonder what twisted turn of fate had brought Michael Ricco into their lives. He looked so peaceful and innocent with his head slumped on his chest and his eyes closed. His blond hair was cropped high and tight, and a dusting of freckles over the bridge of his nose fit in with the slight southern accent Dakota had detected in his speech. The innocence he conveyed in sleep was a stark contrast to the fear

Dakota had seen in his eyes last night in the ER. But in his sleep, he looked like a farm boy. That's how Dakota thought of him, a farm boy in one hell of a lot of trouble. He didn't think Ricco knew just how fortunate he was that Montana had decided to own him.

The Jeep turned onto a single-lane dirt road. Dakota had tried to keep track of where they were going, but the last few turns lost him completely. The rear view was nothing but a cloud of dust, and all he saw through the front windshield was empty desert. He was about to ask if they knew where they were going, when Ito drove the Jeep down off a slight rise in the rock-strewn path they were using as a road, and a house came into view.

It sat in a shallow ravine, hidden from sight by the natural rock formations that surrounded it. Dakota could not imagine what would possess someone to build a house this far away from anything. The headlights revealed faded, peeling paint that clung stubbornly to the exterior and gave evidence that no one had lived there in a long time. Yucca plants and sagebrush had taken over the path that led to the front porch, which had a noticeable lean to one side, and Dakota had serious doubts about whether it was sturdy enough to withstand their weight.

He groaned under his breath. "Great, the five star accommodations."

Ito drove up to the front of the house and turned off the engine, but left the headlights on for illumination. With the sudden stop, Ricco opened his eyes and blinked. He wiped his good hand over his face and squinted as if the dome light hurt him. His brow creased as he searched the faces around him.

Montana turned and met the boy's gaze. "Welcome home, Private Ricco." Then he stepped out of the Jeep and opened Ricco's door.

Ricco was still too out of it to respond coherently. He looked at Montana and blinked like an owl in the sunlight.

Ito closed the driver's door and stood just behind Montana, while Dakota helped Ricco out. For one moment, just before Montana touched him, Ricco turned his head to look at Dakota. Ricco's face paled, his eyes wide. It was the same look Dakota had seen on his face as he hid behind a storage bin in the ER clutching scissors as a weapon.

"Hey, Michael…" Dakota was about to tell Ricco that it was all right, he was safe, but he never got the chance. Ricco lunged for the gun holstered at Montana's shoulder and pulled the weapon free. Dakota witnessed an amazing thing—Montana taken by surprise.

Ricco stood barefoot in the dirt on wobbly legs, with his hospital gown flapping in the gentle evening breeze. His eyes shifted from one face to another. His hands shook as he stepped back, training the weapon first on Montana, then Ito, and finally settling it on the closest target—Dakota. "You won't take me back!" His eyes were wide, unfocused, and blinking rapidly. He brought one hand up to wipe them, and that was all the distraction Montana needed.

Montana threw himself at the boy, slamming into his injured shoulder. Ricco grunted, and the gun fell from his grip. Montana wrapped one arm around his neck and drove him to the ground. Ricco opened his mouth in a silent scream as he hit the dirt.

Ito quickly drew his weapon and stood over them with it aimed at Ricco's head. He sidestepped the boy and kicked Montana's gun out of Ricco's reach. "You good?"

Montana eased up when he saw Ricco's face pinched with pain and streaked with tears, but he growled his response. "Yeah, I'm good." He pushed off Ricco and stood up. "Where's my God damned gun?"

Dakota had learned long ago to avoid his brother when he had that look on his face. When Montana got pissed, people usually ended up getting hurt.

Ito pointed under the Jeep as Dakota decided Ricco was a safer bet and knelt down next to him. In the reflected moonlight, he could see blood seeping through the thin hospital gown. "Shit." He pulled the shoulder down on Ricco's gown and lifted the bandage. "Son-of-a-bitch!" The stitches had ripped apart. He twisted around and glared at his brother. "Hey! So much for not touching him!"

Montana was on his stomach in the dirt, stretching his arm under the Jeep to reach his gun. He grunted as he retrieved the weapon, and pushed himself to his knees. "Next time, I'll just let him shoot you."

He stood over Ricco, removed the magazine from his gun, and pulled the slide back to inspect the chamber. Not satisfied with what he saw, he put his lips to the chamber and blew the dirt and sand out of the barrel. He checked the action on the slide, then jammed the mag back into the grip.

Ito holstered his weapon and knelt next to Dakota. "It's the drugs, Doc. Kid woke up confused."

Dakota raised a sarcastic eyebrow. "Gee, you think?" He sat down in the dirt next to Ricco, put his head in his hands, and quickly scrubbed his fingers through his hair in frustration. Keeping Ricco safe was one thing; he had no problem with that. But guns being pointed in his direction, isolated houses in the middle of the desert, and mysterious bad guys, who for reasons he couldn't comprehend wanted him dead, was way more than he'd signed on for. "If this is what you guys do for a living, I would love to tag along on a fun night with you."

Montana ignored Dakota's sarcasm and knelt down next to Ricco. He had yet to holster his weapon, and held it against one thigh.

"So, what are you going to do now...shoot him?"

"Shut up." Montana leaned over and gently slapped Ricco's face. "Private, Ricco."

Ricco opened his eyes. He appeared lost and confused as his eyes traveled back and forth between the three men in front of him. "Where am I?"

Montana's entire demeanor changed as his tone softened. "You're somewhere safe, Michael."

Maybe it was hearing his name again, but Ricco focused on Montana. "I'm sorry, Major. For a minute... I thought you were..."

Montana grabbed Ricco by his good arm and helped him to his feet. "If I thought you meant it, you wouldn't be breathing right now."

Ricco swayed and fell into Montana. "I'm sorry," he said again, then his eyes rolled back and he lost consciousness.

Montana caught him before he hit the ground and scooped him up in his arms. He carried the boy up the rickety porch steps and waited for Ito to unlock the door.

"You're kidding." Dakota gave half a laugh. "Someone actually bothered to lock the door?"

Montana sighed. "I don't miss you as much anymore."

Dakota wisely kept his thoughts to himself as he followed Montana inside. He was expecting dust and spider webs, but when Ito flicked on the lights, Dakota stood speechless in the doorway. The inside of the dilapidated building was completely at odds with the exterior.

Red oak hardwood floors and cedar planking gave the room a warm, inviting feeling. The furniture was plush and comfortable looking. Navajo throw rugs were scattered about, and he recognized Montana's original artwork on the walls. The kitchen, seen through the open room, was fitted with modern brushed nickel appliances. Montana's touch was everywhere he looked.

Dakota turned in a small circle taking everything in. He found his voice at last and followed Montana into the room. "Damn."

Montana laid Ricco on the sofa in the surprisingly large room and glanced over at Dakota as he picked up a neatly folded blanket from one end of the couch and covered Ricco. "Just because we have to hide away from the rest of the world, doesn't mean we should be inconvenienced."

"Apparently." Dakota shook off his amazement and went to Ricco's side. He sighed as he peeled back the bloody hospital gown. "For not touching him, you sure did one hell of a job." He removed the blood-soaked dressing, and felt Ricco's sweaty face with the back of his hand. "All his sutures have split open, and he feels like he's running a fever, too."

"You're a doctor, fix him."

Ito handed Dakota the bag of supplies, his eyes following Montana as he started a walk-through of the house. Then he focused his attention back on Dakota. "What do you need, Doc?"

"Some iodine, a pack of four by fours, and five-oh silk with a curved needle."

Ito surprised Dakota by handing him exactly what he asked for. Seeing the question on Dakota's face, Ito smiled. "I was a medic in the army."

"Well, that's convenient. You can give me a hand. Did Ivey pack any fluids in there?" Ito pulled out a liter bag of normal saline. "Great. Hook him up and run it in wide open. You can use that floor lamp as an IV pole. Meanwhile, I'm going to try and put him back together again. We got any lidocaine?"

"That we do." Ito pulled out the numbing agent and a syringe, and handed them to Dakota.

They worked in silence for the next few minutes. Dakota pulled the lidocaine into a syringe and with a small needle, inserted some of the drug just under Ricco's skin all around where he plan to sew him back up, while Ito primed the bag of saline and connected it to the locked line in Ricco's arm. Dakota took a pre-packaged antiseptic sponge and cleaned the wound in Ricco's shoulder. He thought it looked a hell of a lot better than it should have this soon after the injury. There was very little bruising, and that alone was enough to make him raise his eyebrows, but the wound itself, was weeks ahead in terms of healing than in should be. Dakota filed Ricco's amazing healing abilities under "one more weird thing about the kid". As he pulled the first stitch through the open wound, he realized his brother had yet to return.

"What's Montana doing?"

Ito smiled as he adjusted the flow of fluid from the IV into Ricco's veins. "Not to worry, Doc. He's just securing the house."

Ricco moaned occasionally, and moved now and then as they worked on him, but he remained unconscious the whole time. When they finished with the stitches and had fresh dressings in place, Dakota stripped Ricco of the soiled hospital gown and left him naked under the soft blanket. "I don't suppose you have any clothes here that would fit him?"

"I'm sure we have something here that would suit the private's tastes. Let me know when you need them." Ito sank into the over-stuffed chair opposite the couch and stretched his legs out in front of him.

Dakota sat on the floor with his back against the couch. He crooked his arms around his knees and studied Ito. "So, where do you fit into all this?"

Ito eyed him for a moment, and seemed to be weighing his response. "I fit...wherever Montana wants me to fit."

Dakota gave him an understanding nod. "You were part of his team, one of his Rangers, weren't you?"

Ito returned the nod, but offered no more explanation as he laid his head against the back of the chair and closed his eyes. Dakota knew better than to push. He had learned long ago that the brotherhood of Rangers was a sacred one—no outsiders allowed. Having exhausted that avenue of questioning, Dakota changed the topic. "Tell me something." He waited for Ito's attention before continuing. "Back at the hospital, how did you know that guy wasn't a doctor?"

Ito grinned. "The shoes."

Dakota scrunched his face up in confusion. "His shoes?"

"Doctors spend a lot of time on their feet. Most of them wear sneakers." He pointed at Dakota's Nikes. "The ones who don't are clinic doctors. They wear fancy dress shoes. You might see those in a hospital every once in a while, but I never saw a civilian doctor wearing combat boots."

Dakota raised his eyebrows. "Damn." He couldn't have told Ito what color the guy's hair was, let alone what kind of shoes he had been wearing. Dakota took a moment and considered the man in front of him. "Mind if I ask you a personal question?"

Ito shrugged and made a noncommittal sound that Dakota took as an affirmative.

"What kind of a name is Ito, anyway? You don't exactly look Japanese."

Ito laughed. "No, but my mama did. I take after my father." He glanced over Dakota's shoulder to Ricco. "Kid gonna be okay?"

Dakota yawned and stretched his legs out in front of him. "Depends on what you mean by okay, but yeah, physically he'll be fine. In fact, I'm amazed he's doing as well as he is. Did you notice how little bruising there was around the wound? I mean, look at it. He should be black, purple, and all kinds of colors. He's as white as a baby's ass, and by now his shoulder should be swollen and just plain ugly. This kid looks like he's three weeks post injury instead of twenty-four hours."

Ito gave him a small nod. "He's a strange one." He had abandoned the ever-present sunglasses, and without them, Dakota noticed his eyes were the only soft thing about the man. They gave him the appearance of a huge teddy bear. Dakota thought he understood why Ito wore the glasses.

"Let me ask you a question, Doc, since we're getting all chummy."

Dakota lifted his shoulders. "Sure."

"In all the time I've spent with Montana, there is one question I've never asked him. Why Montana, and why Dakota? Your mama have some special affinity to those fine States?"

Dakota laughed quietly. It wasn't the first time he'd been asked the question.

"Our mother was, among other things, a unique individual. The short version is, we were named for the states she conceived us in."

Ito laughed, a small rumble in the quiet. "Uh-huh. And the long version?"

"The long version..." Dakota stretched his arms above his head and yawned. "Would take considerably more time, and would require Montana's permission in the telling."

Ito nodded in understanding as Montana walked back into the room. "All clear," he told Ito, and then turned to his brother. "Is the kid okay?"

"Yeah, just sleeping. He's wiped."

"Good, I can wake him?"

Dakota creased his brow. "Well, you could, but why would you want to?"

"He has answers—I have questions."

Dakota sighed. Montana had warned him in the car. He turned, put a hand on Ricco's uninjured arm, and gently shook him. "Michael?" When there was no response, he repeated the name a little louder. "Michael?" Ricco's eyes fluttered open.

Montana pulled a chair from the kitchen and came to the side of the couch to be on eye level with him. "We need to talk, Private Ricco."

Ricco blinked once more, and Dakota watched as his eyes came into focus. He tried to pull himself to a sitting position, but couldn't quite make it. Montana put an arm under his shoulder and helped him. Ricco nodded his thanks, and wiped sweat from his upper lip with the back of one hand.

"You with me, Ricco?"

Another blink and a nod. "Yes, sir."

"Good, because we're running out of time here, Private. Someone tried to kill you a little over two hours ago. Are you aware of that?"

Ricco swallowed hard, his voice little more than a whisper. "No, sir."

"Someone, pretending to be a doctor, walked into your hospital room and tried to finish what they started in the desert. This time it wasn't a deputy or two good Samaritans who almost got caught in the crossfire, it was my brother. The same guy who saved your life, by the way."

Ricco closed his eyes and leaned his head back on the couch as if what he was hearing was too much for him.

Montana gave him no sympathy. "Look at me when I speak to you, Private!"

The man's eyes snapped open, and he licked dry lips. "Yes, sir.

Sorry, sir"

"Then you start talking, boy, and don't stop until I have some answers. The son-of-a-bitch who tried to off you, killed himself before I could get jack from him. I still have no clue as to who wants you dead or why. That leaves just you, Private, as my only source of information. You are the key to all of this, Ricco, and I am not a happy man about that. I'm supposed to be on vacation, instead I'm in the middle of the freaking desert with nothing remotely female around, and I'm blaming this all on you." Montana leaned forward, putting his face in Ricco's. "Who the hell are you?"

He flinched at the tone of Montana's voice. "Ricco, Michael J., private, US Marines." The answer was an automated response. Ricco's voice rose in direct proportion to his nervousness.

"Bullshit! Michael Ricco died almost ninety years ago, so stop screwing with me and start talking."

Ricco automatically reached for the dog tags that were no longer around his neck. Before he could panic, Dakota withdrew the tags from his back pocket and gave them to the boy. Ricco reached out and grabbed the tags, his hand wrapping around them, the thumb absently rubbing the raised characters.

Montana gave him no time to think. "Who are you running from, Private? Who wants you dead so badly they are willing to kill other people, even themselves, to get to you?"

Ricco's eyes focused somewhere out in front of him as he spoke.

"I can't say exactly, sir. They're mostly military, but no specific branch. I've seen all types of insignia."

"Why? Why were you running?"

"I wanted to go home."

"So, you're AWOL."

That got a reaction, but not the one Montana expected. "No!" Ricco turned angry eyes to Montana. "Hell, no!" It was the first time he had failed to address Montana as sir. He gripped the dog tags in his hand until his knuckles whitened. When he spoke again, his voice was quiet but filled with the pain of things Dakota thought he would just as soon forget. "I just wanted to go home. All I ever wanted was to go home." The words didn't seem to be addressed to anyone in particular, rather just a thought that had found voice. He caught himself, and his face flushed as he hung his head. "Sorry, sir. I didn't mean no disrespect." Ricco sighed. "I'm no coward, sir, but if I tell you the truth, you aren't going to believe me."

Montana leaned back in his chair and folded his arms over his chest. "Try me."

Ricco turned his eyes toward Dakota. "I don't know where to start."

Dakota smiled at him. "The beginning usually works for me." He glanced at Montana for the go-ahead, before turning his attention back to Ricco. "So, where is home, Michael?" He hoped to get Ricco more relaxed and away from the hard stuff.

Ricco's face softened, and a small smile formed on his lips. "Corbin County, Virginia, sir."

Dakota nodded. "I thought I heard a southern accent."

The smile grew. "Yes, sir. My daddy had a dairy farm and grew some taters and corn. One hundred and ten acres of the prettiest land you'd ever hope to see." Ricco's blue eyes sparkled with a faraway look. "My brother Mattie, and my little sister Sarah, used to help bring the cows in at night."

"Dakota…" Montana's voice betrayed his impatience.

Dakota held up a hand, asking his brother for a little indulgence. "It must have been hard for you to leave your family and your farm."

Ricco shook his head. "No, sir. I wanted to serve my country."

"How old were you when you joined the Marines?"

"Eighteen. I would've joined sooner, but Daddy wouldn't sign the papers." The smile grew warmer. "Mamma wouldn't let him." Then, like flipping a switch, the smile and all the warmth it had brought to his face vanished. His turned back to Montana. "I remember it was July, sir. We were in France, outside of Calais, but I wasn't even in battle." He shook his head. "That's the one thing I can't get over. We were on leave when it happened."

That got Montana's attention, and he sat up in his chair. "What happened, Private?"

Ricco's face screwed up in concentration as he tried to recall the memory. "It was the girl, sir. It had to be."

"What girl? What are you talking about?"

"It's all pretty hazy, sir, but there was this girl. My buddies kept kidding me 'cause I wouldn't, well, you know. I have a girl back home, Emma. But this girl, she wouldn't take no for an answer, so I said I would give her one dance." Ricco shrugged. "We went for a walk, and she gave me something to drink. The next thing I remember is The General."

"The General?"

"Yeah…" Michael's face clouded over. "The General. I won't never forget—"

Montana held a hand out to stop him. "Hold it. Back up for a minute." He gestured to the dog tags Ricco still clutched. "How long ago are we talking about here, Private? You sure as hell don't look like you're a hundred-and-ten-years old."

"That one surprised me a bit too, sir." He ran his good hand through his short hair. "The last date I remember clearly is July tenth, nineteen-seventeen. I had just turned nineteen that spring." Ricco looked at Montana as if to dare him, maybe beg him, to tell him he was wrong. "I knew they had me a long time, sir. I just didn't know how long."

"But, Jesus…since nineteen-seventeen?" Montana slid to the edge of his chair, his arms resting on his knees, his eyes intent on Ricco. "You'd better not be bullshitting me, Private, because I swear to you—"

"It's not bullshit, sir. I'm telling the truth. You wanted to know why I was running? I woke up in a cell with no explanation of why I was there other than I was serving my country. When I complained that it wasn't my division, they beat me. I watched them kill other guys like me, and was told it was done in the name of science." Ricco stopped when he was met by a blank stare from Montana. He turned to Dakota in frustration. "I knew you wouldn't believe me."

Dakota had no idea whether to believe him or not, but he worried about his patient's condition. The questioning had begun to take its toll. Ricco's face was shiny with sweat, and his breathing ragged and uneven. The boy's obvious emotional turmoil was playing hell with his physical condition.

"Yeah, yeah, all right." Montana eased up on him and sat back. "Let's just forget that for now. Tell me who had you. Who exactly are 'they'?"

Ricco took a deep breath and let it out slowly. He wiped his face with his forearm, the fatigue evident in his sagging features. "Like I said before, sir, I don't know for sure who they are. The guy who leads it changes from time to time, but he always goes by the same name— The General. This last one has been in power for, I don't know, maybe the last twenty years or so." He laid his head against the back of the couch and closed his eyes, then remembered Montana's displeasure the last time he relaxed he snapped backed to attention.

Dakota got up and checked Ricco's pulse, and felt his forehead. "Can't this wait until morning? The kid's exhausted, and his fever's getting worse."

"No, it can't. Private Ricco?"

Ricco swiped at his eyes, struggling to focus. "Yes, sir."

"Even if I believe what you say, what I don't get is, why? You've been held a prisoner for ninety years. For what? What were they doing to you all that time?"

Ricco slowly shook his head. "They never would tell me what they were doing, sir. Some sort of medical experiments is all I know. They would inject me with all kinds of stuff—watch what it did to me—take notes. Later on, especially the last thirty years or so, they would wire me up to fancy machines that somehow kept track of my reactions."

"Why you? What makes you so special?"

"I'm not really sure about that either, sir. But this last General, he told me that in the beginning, when they first took me, they somehow managed to turn off the gene that causes aging. I don't think they knew what they did either, because they kept trying to repeat the results on other guys, but they always died. I'm the only survivor."

"Holy hell." Montana sat back and looked up at Ito, who just shook his head. It was obvious that Ricco's words had affected him as well.

"Michael?" Dakota pointed to the tags still clutched in his hand. "Is your birth date really April the twenty-fourth, eighteen-ninety-eight?"

Ricco locked innocent blue-green eyes on Dakota and gave him a single nod. "Yes, sir, it is." He paused before asking, "Is it really the year two-thousand-eight?"

Dakota couldn't comprehend what this must feel like to Ricco, what it must have taken to even ask the question. "Yeah, Michael. It really is."

"My family…" Ricco turned to Montana. "They're all gone, aren't they?"

Montana leaned in close and placed a hand on Ricco's arm. There were no words to soften the information. "Most likely they are, yeah."

Ricco looked like he was trying to hold it together and gave a quick nod. "I figured as much."

"I'm sorry," Montana said.

Ricco kept his thoughts to himself, unwilling or unable to say more.

Dakota broke the silence. "Okay, this might sound obvious, but I'm confused. This General, he had you all this time, and did medical experiments on you and others like you, right?"

"Yes, sir."

"Why?"

Ricco's face bunched in confusion. "Why?"

"Well, warped as it might have been, there had to be a reason, right?"

Ricco thought for a moment. "Sometimes, after they did things to me, The General would come and sit with me in my cell. He would tell me how proud he was of me and the others. He would tell me about all the lives we were saving with the research they were doing." Ricco shrugged. "I didn't care, all I knew was it hurt. It always hurt." He turned his right arm over to reveal an old scar that ran the length of his forearm. "They broke it on purpose while I was awake. Compound fracture…you know, with the bones sticking out of the skin? They broke it, and then they put me back in my cell and just watched me. I never felt pain like that before. They would come and take notes and wait for me to die from the infection." An odd look crept across Ricco's features as the memories invaded. "But I just kept right on breathing. Finally, after I decided they weren't going to do anything to help me, I pushed the bones back in myself. I should have died, but I didn't." He showed them the slight unnatural bend to his arm. "It never healed completely right. They broke it twice more like that. They told me I'm a quick healer." He gave Dakota a twisted grin. "Lucky me."

Dakota and Montana exchanged glances. Ito's only reaction was to shift his weight in the chair.

"How did you get out, Michael?" Montana's use of Ricco's first name was the only indication to Dakota of how the boy's story affected him.

Ricco smiled and shook his head. "Just dumb luck. They usually sedate me before bringing me to the medical facility. When they don't, I know it's going to be bad."

"Why's that?"

Ricco met his eyes. "That's when they want to study my pain responses. They didn't sedate me that last time, but I had stopped fighting them long ago so they weren't very careful. They hadn't restrained me yet when the power went out."

"And you ran," Montana concluded.

"Hell yeah, I ran...sir. Honestly, I was hoping they would kill me. I sure never expected to get out of there alive. I never expected to get free, but I did and innocent people have died because of me."

"Don't put that on yourself, that wasn't your fault."

"They wouldn't be dead if I hadn't escaped. Don't know whose fault it would be but mine."

"Try the ones who pulled the trigger."

It was clear from the look on his face that Ricco wasn't buying any of it.

Montana put a hand on Ricco's arm and looked the boy square in the eye. "Michael, you aren't alone anymore, and you aren't going back. That's the first thing you have to understand."

Ricco looked at the three men in front of him. It was clear he wanted to trust them, it was equally clear he remained skeptical about giving that trust. "And what's the second, sir?"

"The second, Private Ricco, is that if you ever draw a weapon on me again, there will be no second chances, understand?"

Ricco lowered his eyes, the corners of his mouth turning up into a small, embarrassed smile. "Yes, sir. I understand."

Chapter 9

The man was known only as The General. His life was spent in the shadows, away from the glaring light and prying eyes of those who would judge him. His world was dominated by secrecy and the suffering of others. Suffering brought about by his word, his hand, his vision. That was how he perceived himself—a visionary, a humanitarian. He existed for only one purpose: to protect and maintain the Program.

The General sat at a desk in the bunker they had hastily re-comissioned and reviewed the handwritten entries of his predecessors, lightly brushing his fingertips across the antiquated signatures as if they were religious icons. He smiled as he considered that analogy. The Program was very much like a religion.

The line of his predecessors went back more than ninety years. No one knew their true names, sometimes he almost forgot his own. Each General selected his replacement years before retirement, meticulously grooming and training them to take their place when the time came.

From that point on, they were known only as—the General. Theirs was a position of power, anonymity, and great responsibility.

The work they did was accomplished in secrecy because it would never be understood, but those who would condemn them had no moral or ethical dilemmas when it came to reaping the results the Program provided. Now everything they had accomplished, all the years of research and hard work, was in jeopardy.

The General clenched and unclenched his fists as he paced the small room and struggled to control the rage that simmered just beneath the surface. The fate of humanity was in his hands, he knew what he and his 'brothers' had accomplished was vital to the survival of the species.

"Human beings are such pathetically flawed creatures. They demand perfection, but are they willing to go to the lengths necessary to achieve it?" His words echoed off the naked walls as he verbalized his contempt. "No, of course not, they are squeamish when it comes to the real work. No one wants to get their hands dirty." The General shook his head, walking manic circles around his desk. "They play with words such as morals and ethics, decency and humanity, but are the first to demand a cure for whatever ails them!"

The General stopped his circling, and when he felt some measure of control, he smiled. He reflected on the Program's many achievements: the cure for polio, the varicella vaccine, the discovery of HIV, the discovery of the first antibiotics and all the new classes needed almost daily to combat more virulent forms of viruses and bacteria, new surgical techniques and orthopedic procedures to repair injuries that used to demand amputation, organ transplants, pain control, and even the recent cadaver face transplants to benefit severe burn victims.

The public bought the lies, that all the miraculous medical breakthroughs over the last several decades had been the result of research on lab animals and experiments with Petri dishes. Diligence and hard work had saved countless lives all right, but 'they' didn't have a clue.

"If not for people like me, men would still be huddled in caves hiding from the thunder!" Realizing he was yelling, he took a calming breath and straightened his uniform. He knew it didn't matter that the credit was never given to the Program. It was enough to know they were the true heroes—most days it was enough. The important thing was that medical advancements had been made decades sooner because of his work, because of the Program

"Surely the lives of a few dozen men are worth all that."

His attention wandered to the ancient metal desk and Ricco's file once more. Private Michael John Ricco. That is where it had truly all started. Ricco was their prized possession. The Program's greatest achievements had come about as a direct result of the experiments performed on the boy.

Private Ricco was unique. The records were unclear as to exactly what had happened, and his predecessors never understood what they did themselves, but Ricco's aging process had all but stopped. He did age, but at an extremely slow rate. How long he would live or how he would age was anyone's guess. More research needed to be done.

It was Ricco's immune system that fascinated the General. Either because of what they had done to him or despite it, his immune system had kicked into overdrive. He took everything they threw at him and always recovered. Over the years, they had tried to kill him any number of ways, just to see what his limitations were. His ability to heal himself was astounding.

The General opened the file and flipped to an old black and white photograph. There were more recent color photos, but this one was his personal favorite. It was the first photo taken of Ricco shortly after his acquirement. In it, Ricco looked directly into the camera. Even through all the years of degradement and handling, he could still see the fight in Ricco's eyes, the anger and indignation on his face. He touched the photograph with fondness, recalling the many years he had spent with the boy. In an odd way, he supposed he felt like a father to Ricco. Only now, Ricco was gone. He could not have been more disappointed in the boy.

Ricco's escape had put everything they had worked over nine decades for at risk. Unless they got the boy back and took care of the collateral damage, the Program would have to be scrubbed. One bunker had been abandoned already. There had been no time to dispose of the bodies properly, though he was confident they would never be discovered...but the situation was far from being contained.

The General stared at Ricco's image, and the rage boiled over.

"This project has been put in jeopardy, all because of you!" The General swept the file off the desk in one violent move. The ninety-year-old document scattered as it hit the floor, priceless information fluttering to rest on the cement.

"You have put everything at risk!" The General ground his heel into the image of Ricco's face, damaging the photograph beyond repair. His fists clenched tightly, the well manicured nails biting into the flesh of his palms, as a knock on the door interrupted his tirade.

He fought the rage back down, he needed to maintain calm in order to promote calm. He bent down and retrieved the ruined file. Fitting the pages together, he placed them between the covers of the folder and once again positioned it in the exact center of his desk. He closed his eyes and fought for control. Control was strength. Strength was what separated him, and those who preceded him, from those they served. When he thought he had gained enough control, he sat and placed his hand on closed the file.

He sat up straighter. It wouldn't do for his subordinates to see weakness in him. "Enter."

An older man walked through the door. His short buzzed hair was nearly white, and his face was lined and deeply tanned. He looked like he was in his early fifties, but was probably closer to sixty. He was in better shape than men half his age, but the General thought he looked nervous.

"Sir, we lost Brinks." Captain's bars graced the shoulders of the man's fatigues. The rank was only for show, but these men needed some symbol of their former lives. They needed to feel important and necessary. The captain stood with his feet squared, his hands behind his back, and his gaze not settled on anything in particular.

"Define lost." Under the desk, the General dug deeper into the bloody furrows he had created in his palm. The pain calmed him in the face of more disappointing news.

"Brinks is dead, sir. The attempt at reacquiring Private Ricco has failed."

"How is that possible, Captain? He is wounded and being kept by civilians. What happened?" The General's voice was calm, belaying the emotions he strived to control. Failure was not an option. His people knew that well.

"He had unexpected help, sir. Military from the way they operated. We weren't expecting them, sir." The captain swallowed hard.

"Do we know where they are? Is he still retrievable?"

The captain shifted uncomfortably. "We are working on that, sir."

The General gripped his closed fist with his free hand and increased the pressure. The blood flowing from the wounds gave him strength. "Excuse me?"

The captain licked his lips. "We lost them, sir, but we have a good idea of where they might have been headed."

The General blinked once, and his brow creased with displeasure. "Then I expect you to do your job, Captain, and bring Private Ricco home. Is that understood?"

"Yes, sir." The captain gave a smart salute and waited to be dismissed.

"Captain…" The General stood without returning the salute, his bloody hand behind his back. "You do know what happens if you can't bring him back."

"If Private Ricco is unobtainable, then he will be eliminated, sir." The captain stared straight ahead, holding the salute.

"And your team?"

The salute faltered just a little. "My team, sir?"

"You will not be taken captive by their civilian authority, Captain. Do you understand? The future of this program depends on your success."

"I understand, sir. If my team cannot return, then we will become collateral damage as well as Private Ricco, sir."

The General returned the salute, letting his blood drip from his hand onto his face and nodded. "Very good, Captain. As long as we understand each other. I want no one else to be obtained by their civilian authority, and I want to give whoever Ricco talks to something else to worry about besides looking into his story. Am I making myself clear on that matter, Captain?"

The captain stared for a moment. The General held his silence and waited for the captain to answer. "Very clear, sir."

"You are dismissed, Captain." The General waved him away and waited until he closed the door behind him.

He wondered how it had come to this. Private Ricco was to be re-obtained or killed. There were no other options. It was unfortunate, Ricco was truly unique, but the continuation of the Program was what mattered. They may never duplicate what had made Ricco the way he was, but it was the research that mattered. There were always more Riccos out there waiting to be found. Miracles happened everyday.

* * * *

The muted chiming of his cellphone woke Dakota from a deep sleep. He automatically reached down to the waistband of his pants and silenced it before it woke anyone. He winced as he sat up to answer the call. His back complained loudly, and he realized falling asleep in the chair across from where Ricco still slept on the couch, had been a mistake.

Blinking sleep out of his eyes, Dakota focused on the small screen and recognized a hospital extension. Not wanting to disturb anyone else's sleep, he walked outside trying to work some of the stiffness out of his back along the way. A slap of cold desert night air greeted him as he stepped onto the porch, and he found himself engulfed in complete darkness—no streetlights, no traffic, only stars.

He flipped open his phone and placed it next to his ear. "Yeah."

"Hey, Dakota, it's Ivey. Can you talk?"

"Ivey? Yeah, what is it? What's wrong?" Dakota's mind jumped from one assumption to the next as to why she would be calling him at this hour. He glanced at the illuminated dial of his watch to see exactly what time it was. Three in the morning, shit!

"Look, I don't have long. I'm at work and only have ten minutes left on my break. This is the first alone time I've had all night, and I need to warn you."

"Wait a minute, slow down. You may be awake, but I'm just getting there, okay?"

"No! Listen to me. Cal is having a bird here. They found Tommy Lawson's body and two other people they think were camping out by Beaver Dam, along with ten military personnel, all of them dead…murdered."

"I know. Montana and I found them, too."

"You know? What do you mean you know? Never mind, I don't want you to answer that. Dakota, I'm not sure about all the details, but according to hospital gossip, which can be extremely reliable, Cal and the Nevada State Police were out there all night, and the only evidence they found were fingerprints…" She paused. "Only two sets of fingerprints."

Dakota was awake now as the information sank in. "Let me guess, they belong to Montana and me?"

"They think you and your brother killed those people and took Ricco to kill him too, so he couldn't give you up. There's a state-wide man hunt out for both of you."

"What? That's ridiculous. Why the hell would I kill Ricco after I spent all of last night trying to keep him alive? You don't believe them, do you?"

"Would I be calling you if I did? Look, wherever you are, just stay there, okay?"

Montana had warned him it could get ugly, but Dakota had no idea what that meant until then. It was one thing for him to put his career, maybe even his life on the line; that was his decision. But endangering the welfare of his staff was another matter altogether. "What about you? What about the rest of the staff who was there when we took him?"

"I won't lie. It hasn't been fun, but we'll survive. No one knows where you went, and no one believes what they're saying about you."

"Exactly what are they saying?" Dakota looked out into the quiet of the night. An uncomfortable silence answered him. He heard Ivey sigh.

When she continued, it was clear something more than worry had prompted the call. Undeniable fear laced her words as she answered him. "It's not good, really not good. The police are calling you a vicious killer. They're telling everyone you're armed and dangerous, and unstable. Dakota, they have orders to kill you on sight, both you and your brother."

Jesus! Dakota pulled the phone away from his ear for a moment as the weight of her words fell on him. Shaking his head, he put the phone back. "No way I'm letting that happen, Ivey. I was nowhere near

Tommy or those campers when they bought it, and I can prove it."

"I don't think they want to hear it. Look, whatever you're thinking, don't do it. Stay where you are, and stay safe. Shit, one of those weird government guys is here. I have to go."

"Ivey, wait. What—" The connection went dead.

Dakota stood on the rickety porch with a cool breeze washing over him, bringing him the scent of sage and yucca. All he wanted to do was help Michael Ricco. Instead, he and Montana were now Caliente's most wanted. What the hell, a murderer?

This wasn't right. Dakota couldn't let Montana get hurt or his reputation damaged because of him. He needed to talk to Cal Tremont. The sheriff had to know he wasn't a part of this. Cal had called him to tell him about Tommy being missing. He had to know the timeline just didn't add up.

Keeping Ricco safe was a priority, and that meant Montana had to stay with the kid. It was Dakota's job to keep Montana out of this. If that meant Dakota taking the heat until this was all straightened out, then so be it.

Dakota dialed information and asked for the number to Cal Tremont's home.

"What?" a sleep-filled voice asked. "Who is it?"

Cal didn't sound quite as intimidating at three in the morning.

"You know Montana and I didn't kill Tommy Lawson."

Silence filled the line as Dakota let Cal figure it out.

"Where are you, boy? Do you have any idea the trouble you're in?"

"Cal, you know I didn't kill Tommy or those other people," Dakota said again.

Cal breathed a deep sigh. "Do you think I'm stupid? Hell yes, I know that, but why didn't you tell me you found Tommy? And why'd you run off with Private Ricco? And how the hell did an ex-special-ops man end up dead in your hospital? Dakota, you're in a deep pile of shit, and Montana just had to join you, didn't he?"

Dakota was relieved to hear Cal didn't believe him to be a murderer, but there was still a lot of explaining to do. "Cal, I don't know any more about what's going on than you do. All I know is that whoever killed Tommy and those people in the bunker, also sent that special-ops guy to kill Ricco. We stopped him, and then the son-of-a-bitch killed himself. It all happened so fast, there was nothing we could do. I'm sorry we didn't contact you right away, but I'm not used to people trying to kill my patients while I watch. This whole thing is way out of my area of expertise. Under the circumstances, Montana thought it safer to get Ricco out of there." It was Dakota's turn to take a deep breath. "At the time, I was inclined to believe him."

"Something's not right here," Cal mumbled. "This is not how things work. I never saw the state troopers they sent out to investigate this. They aren't from the local barracks. Special procedures, my ass. Something stinks here, boy, and I don't like it. All I have is a dead deputy and no answers. You tell me how I'm supposed to explain this to the Lawsons? We need to talk, and you need to come in, and Montana too. Hiding isn't going to help anything, it's just going to make you look guiltier than you do now. The evidence isn't conclusive. Come in and talk to me, boy. You know I won't let them take you anywhere on trumped-up charges. What's going on, Dakota? Where the hell are you?"

Dakota looked out across the desert. The night stared back at him, refusing to part with her secrets. Somehow, he needed to fix this. "I'll come to you, but Montana stays out of this."

"It's not my choice anymore, boy. I'll do what I can to help you, but the Feebs have control now, and my word don't mean dick. I'm just a hick country sheriff."

"Bullshit, Cal. I was sleeping when Tommy Lawson was killed, and Montana didn't even know Michael Ricco existed."

"Listen to me, Dakota. I know you didn't kill anyone, but these dickheads don't want to look at evidence. They want you, and I want to know why."

They want you. Cold crept through Dakota with those words. He wondered just how far and how deep this General's reach was. "I'll explain everything to you. Can you meet me at your office in few hours?"

"I'll be there."

"No FBI?"

"Just me," Cal told him. "I owe you that much."

"Thanks. I have a hell of a story to tell you." He pushed the end button on the phone before Cal could change his mind.

He walked to the Jeep covered with early morning dew, and saw the keys still in the ignition. Guess Montana wasn't too concerned about anyone stealing it out here. Well, anyone but him, at least.

He had a vague idea of how to get back to town. He knew if he kept going in the general direction they had come from, he would eventually find the main road. God, he hoped so. He got into the Jeep and turned the engine over, hoping no one in the house would wake at the sound. Then he realized even if they did, there was very little they could do about it. Dakota was taking the only transportation.

Man, Montana was going to be pissed at him.

CHAPTER 10

A half-hour outside of town, the Jeep started hitching and sputtering, and despite Dakota's efforts to keep it running, the vehicle stalled. He eased onto the shoulder and tried to get just a little more life out of the over-heated engine, but all he got was a low hum and a click when he turned the key.

He hit the steering wheel in frustration and swore at himself. "Stupid, stupid, stupid!"

The Jeep sat on the soft shoulder of a deserted, two-lane black top. In his haste to get back to town and speak to Cal, he had left without any thought of provisions. He had the clothes on his back and his phone. The car thermometer indicated it was ninety-six degrees outside, and he had no water, with the prospect of at least a half a day's walk through the parched land ahead of him.

"I am freaking brilliant." The early-morning heat seared him as he stepped out of the Jeep. The difference between the air-conditioned vehicle and the outside temperature left him momentarily breathless.

Dakota looked as far as he could see in either direction, and saw nothing but empty road shimmering in the heat.

It wasn't even six in the morning, he was a wanted felon, and he was stranded in the middle of the desert without any water. He slammed the door and pocketed the keys as he started walking. "Brilliant!" Shaking his head, he concentrated on just putting one foot in front of the other.

After twenty minutes, and soaked through with sweat, he almost wished for Cal's cruiser to come and pick him up. Jail sounded pretty good to him just then. He hadn't had anything to drink since the day before and was seriously dehydrated by the time he saw the vehicle far ahead in the distance. At first, he thought it might be a hallucination, a trick of his heat-seared brain. He watched in fascination as the car drew closer. It took nearly a quarter of an hour for the driver to see him, the flat terrain making distances deceiving.

When it was clear that the driver not only saw him, but was slowing down, Dakota simply stood on the shoulder and waited. He didn't realize something was wrong until the tan sedan stopped next to him. He wiped the sweat out of his eyes with a forearm, watching with detached giddiness as three armed men dressed in military khakis exited the vehicle and approached him. An image of Ricco running through the desert flashed through his mind, as did his dream. This is why Ricco ran. He took a step back and the men split up. Two flanked him, and one stayed in front of him.

"Doctor Thomas?" asked the lead man.

Dakota blinked in response and lifted a hand to shield his eyes from the sun's unrelenting glare. "Who wants to know?"

The man smiled and gave a nod to his companions, who started to close in on him. Dakota licked parched lips and looked from side to side, desperately seeking an avenue of escape. There was only the road before him and the desert behind him.

The man in front of him laughed. "Where are you going to go? Come on, Doctor Thomas, we only want to talk to you."

"You want Ricco." Dakota saw no sense in denying who they were or what they wanted. He knew these men had killed for less, and would kill again with very little provocation. It was in the way they moved, a self-assured cockiness that only comes with never listening to the word 'no.'

"Well, that too," the man agreed. "Get in the car, Doctor."

Dakota shook his head and tried to back away. If he got in the car, he was dead. He knew that. "How'd you find me?" It was a useless question. He knew that too, but he was trying to buy some time to figure a way out of the impossible situation.

"You can thank your friend Ivey for that."

Dakota's eyes widened at the mention of the nurse's name. "You didn't hurt her?"

"Relax, I can make quite a convincing state trooper when I want to. I actually used to be one in another life." Dark, reflective lenses shielded the man's eyes, but the smile faded with his words. He seemed to shake off the thoughts and grinned at Dakota once more. "I questioned her and confiscated her cellphone. When I traced the last number she called, this is where it led me. I couldn't get a definite fix on the exact location, but that doesn't matter anymore. Now, imagine our surprise to find you coming out to meet us."

The two men flanking Dakota moved in. Each one grabbed him by an arm as the man drew his weapon on Dakota. "Get in the car, Doctor Thomas."

Dakota considered his options. One thing was clear; they would have to kill him to get him into that car. He prayed he wasn't wrong about that.

Dakota shook his head, feeling more confident than he had a right to. "You won't kill me."

"You're absolutely right, Doctor Thomas. I have no intention of killing you… yet. I have someone I think would be very interested in meeting you." He gave a nod to the men who held him.

Quicker than Dakota thought possible, one of them pushed him to the ground and held him there with a hand to his throat and a knee on his chest. The other one grabbed his free arm and pushed his shirtsleeve up, exposing the vein in the crook of his arm. He knelt on Dakota's upper arm, using his weight as a tourniquet, then pulled a syringe from his pocket and discarded the cap.

"What the hell?" Dakota watched the man purge a clear liquid from the needle. The sharp steel glimmered in the heat and sun.

The man smiled down at him. "This was meant for Private Ricco, but I don't think he would mind sharing it with you."

Dakota felt a sharp sting in his arm, and almost immediately, a warm fuzziness enveloped him. His eyes lost focus and felt weighed down as the chemicals flooding his system took him under. He blinked once, twice, and then gave in to the inevitable, going slack beneath the men who held him.

The man kneeling on Dakota's chest released the pressure and stood. He looked up and down the road to be sure there were no witnesses. Satisfied there were none, he bent down and pulled the unconscious Dakota over his shoulders.

The man in charge motioned to the vehicle. "Get him in the car."

"What about Ricco?"

"The doctor's the next best thing. Before, we only had a guess as to where Ricco was being held. Now, we have a hostage."

The soldier carried Dakota to the car and waited for someone to open the door. "The General's not going to like this." He rolled Dakota off his shoulders and into the back seat of the sedan, and then crawled in next to him.

"I know, but he'd like it even less if we came back empty-handed."

The soldier who had injected Dakota took shotgun and turned back to look at the unconscious man slumped on the seat. "He has a point."

The driver waited until they were all in and secured. "We good?"

"Go," the point man told him.

"Where? To get Ricco or back to the base?"

"To the base." He silently hoped the decision he just made was the right one. The General was not known for his forgiving nature.

* * * *

Dakota opened his eyes and immediately squeezed them shut again in protest to the glaring fluorescent lights shining in his face. His head ached, and his tongue felt thick and useless in his mouth. He tried moving to ease the pain in his back, but he couldn't. Opening his eyes to tiny slits until they adjusted to the bright lights, he looked down the length of his body and found leather restraints around his wrists and chest. He couldn't move his legs and assumed his ankles were restrained in the same way.

Panic began to cut through the drugs, and Dakota pulled against the leather, testing its resilience. He quickly concluded he wasn't going anywhere. Adrenaline zinged through his system, only this time the cause was fear, not excitement.

"He's awake, sir."

Dakota heard a voice somewhere near his head. He tried to turn to identify the speaker, but was denied by the restraints.

A man stepped into his field of vision and blocked the light momentarily. It also placed the man's face in the shadows. "Ah, Doctor

Thomas, so nice of you to join us."

He reached up and swung the light out of the way, giving Dakota his first good look at the man's face. He was older, maybe in his late sixties, with a deeply tanned, almost kind-looking face. His eyes were blue-gray, and he smiled at Dakota.

"Who the hell are you?" Dakota's voice sounded rusty even to his own ears.

The man turned to retrieve a glass filled with what Dakota hoped was water, and held it to his lips. He sucked the glass dry without putting a dent in his thirst. "More."

"Perhaps later." The man cocked his head, his eyes slowly moving over Dakota, who felt for a moment as he imagined an ant might, trapped beneath the scorching rays of a magnifying glass. "You have caused me a great deal of trouble, Doctor Thomas, and now I am left with a problem. Just what do I do with you?"

A sudden realization hit Dakota. He knew with awful clarity who he was speaking to. Fear chilled him as it coursed through his veins, and his heart rate doubled in an instant. He tried to swallow, but he had no spit left.

The man continued his disturbing observation and smiled. "You know who I am, don't you?"

Dakota nodded. "You're The General."

The man laughed softly. "Private Ricco has proven to be most inconvenient to all of us."

Dakota's anger at the man's callous attitude caused his fear to recede for the moment. "Is that what you call murdering thirteen people...an inconvenience?" He saw, for the first time, a tray table behind The General; on it laid an assortment of surgical instruments.

The General followed his gaze and gave him a reassuring, almost fatherly smile. Reaching out, he picked up a scalpel and ran the razor-like edge carefully over the pad of his thumb. The pressure wasn't hard enough to draw blood, but the intent was clear. He sighed and shook his head. "You were never a soldier, so I wouldn't expect you to understand things like duty and honor."

"You don't have to be a soldier to understand duty or honor. What you did to Ricco and those others has nothing to do with either."

The fatherly face faltered just a little. "They were giving of themselves on a level you could never comprehend."

"They never gave you anything—you took it from them without permission. They had no say in what you did to them, no free will."

The General put the scalpel back down on the tray and turned to face Dakota. "Free will does not exist. It is merely a fabrication we partake in to give purpose to the things we do. Everyone needs a cause, Doctor, and this is mine. In a way, it is very much yours as well."

Dakota gave him a questioning look. "What do you mean?"

"The medical field has made amazing progress over the last century, wouldn't you agree?" When Dakota just stared at him in response, he continued. "I have heard it called miraculous, the advances that have been made. It's no miracle, just hard work and sacrifice."

Dakota felt his blood run cold as what The General was telling him slowly sunk in. "What are you saying?" He knew Ricco had told him they did medical experiments. He only half-believed him, until now.

"Doctor, really, do you think we would be where we are without the research my team has done? The new classes of antibiotics that are constantly needed to fight more virulent forms of bacteria, new surgical procedures to save limbs, to repair hearts. Better, more efficient ways to battle pain. We would still be in the dark ages if lab animals were all we used." The General sighed at Dakota's horrified expression. "You are a physician. I had hoped you would understand."

"Understand what? Torture? What you're doing here is wrong, no one asked for it. No one would want it done—not like this, not at the expense of innocent lives!" Dakota closed his eyes, and Ricco's face came to mind. Opening them again, he looked directly at the man standing over him. "You're insane."

The General laughed and looked beyond Dakota to an unseen audience behind him. "You see?" he asked his team. "You see why we work in secret? The work we do would not be understood. They would vilify what we strive to do in the name of decency, when what we do is for the good of all mankind."

There were vague murmurings of agreement from behind Dakota.

"Tell me, Doctor Thomas, don't you agree that the sacrifice of a few lives is worth the saving of thousands, perhaps hundreds of thousands? The good of the many being worth more than the good of the one?"

"No life is insignificant." Dakota pulled against his restraints as anger surged through him.

"You are reciting doctrines force fed to you and every other living soul for eons. Haven't you ever thought to question them?" The General sighed and shook his head once again, reminding Dakota of a disappointed parent. "It was too much to hope that you would understand the importance of our work here." He lifted his hands in acceptance. "But we do have work to do."

He reached into his jacket pocket and withdrew a cellphone. Dakota recognized it as his. The General turned it over, examining the device in detail. "Amazing how small they have become." He flipped up the cover and turned the phone on. "You know, I have the exact same model. I'm especially fond of the camera feature."

Dakota swiveled his head as he heard someone new come beside him. He recognized the team leader of the small group that had taken him on the road. The General spoke again, and Dakota turned his head toward the voice.

"Your brother's name is Montana Lee Thomas. He is a former Army Ranger, currently self-employed as a private investigator. He has my man. I want Private Ricco returned to me."

"Ricco doesn't belong to you." Dakota's anger, for the moment, was winning out over the fear curling in his gut.

"On the contrary, Doctor. He would have been dead decades ago if it were not for this program and my predecessors. I helped make him. I most certainly own him." He waved away any rebuttal Dakota might have, and scrolled down the numbers listed in the phone's memory. "Only one Montana listed—imagine that."

The General gave a nod, and the soldier beside him unbuckled the restraint on Dakota's left wrist. Any hopes of freedom were quickly dashed as the man held him more efficiently than the leather restraints. His eyes went from the soldier gripping his arm to the General holding his phone. Fear edged out over the anger as The General punched in Montana's number.

Apparently, the wait for an answer was not a long one. "You know who this is?" Dakota watched as the man smiled, and could only imagine Montana's reaction on the other end of the line. The General continued. "I won't waste your time. You have someone I want, and conversely, I believe I have someone you want. Perhaps we can come to an understanding, yes?" The General listened for a moment, and then placed the phone next to Dakota's ear.

"Montana?"

"Dakota, you all right?" His brother's voice was quiet, but Dakota could hear anger and overwhelming concern in the words.

"Whatever he wants, don't give it to him." Dakota glared at the General's smiling face.

The man withdrew the phone and placed it back to his own ear. "Mr. Thomas, you have a rather important choice to make, Private Ricco for your brother. If you choose not to commit to this trade, I want you to remember something."

The soldier lifted Dakota's arm, as the General held the phone out next to him. "I'm sorry, Doc," the soldier said quietly.

Dakota looked at him, confused. The man gripped Dakota's arm at the wrist and just below his elbow, and using his knee as a fulcrum, snapped both bones as if they were twigs.

Dakota screamed. The pain became his entire existence, and when he thought it had come to its peak, he found out just how wrong he was. The man gripped the shattered limb and savagely pushed until the sharp, broken ends of the bone penetrated skin. Hot blood, his blood, splattered his face and chest.

Everything funneled and he prayed for release, but it was not to be. He forgot about Montana, about Ricco, even about The General. All that mattered was the unrelenting pain. His stomach rolled and he thought he might vomit on top of everything else, and then the man released him. His arm hung twisted and limp across his chest, a bloody deformed thing that could not belong to him.

He closed his eyes and tried to stop the whimpering he knew came from somewhere deep inside of him. Through the buzz inside his head, he heard the General speak once more.

"Did you hear, Mr. Thomas? Did you hear the pain your brother is in? If you refuse to give me back my man, this is the life you have subjected him to. You will not find him unless I wish it. His life is mine to do with as I please. Think about that. Look at the pictures I've sent you, and I'm certain you'll do the right thing. You have forty-eight hours to think about what I'm doing to your brother. It has been a while since I've had a new subject, and I intend to take advantage of the opportunity. I will contact you with the exchange information. Until that time, use your imagination to fill in the gaps."

The General flipped the phone closed and threw it on the table, sending surgical instruments clattering to the floor. He stepped next to Dakota, grabbed his face with one hand, and turned it toward him. "Do you understand now, Doctor? Can you possibly comprehend the importance of what we do here?"

Dakota blinked, but the words made no sense to him as shock fuzzed his brain.

The General released him and turned to the man who had just broken Dakota's arm. "Take him to Ricco's cell. Keep him alive, but give him nothing for pain."

The soldier unbuckled the remaining restraints. Dakota felt the leather straps slide away as he closed his eyes. He didn't hear any reply the man might have offered, but he did hear heels clicking across the concrete floor to gradually fade into silence. He wanted to fade away with the noise, but was not allowed even that small reprieve.

The man next to him jostled his injuries as he slipped an arm under his shoulders and another under his knees. As he lifted him,

Dakota's arm screamed in protest. The last thing he remembered, besides the pain that threatened to eat him alive, was the sight of the man who had just brutally shattered his arm, looking down on him with kind, almost sympathetic eyes. He saw the man's mouth move, but no sound made it through the agony. Finally, the blackness surrounded him, giving him the temporary peace and numbness of unconsciousness.

CHAPTER 11

Montana Lee Thomas was not a patient man, nor a tolerant one. Women found him attractive, but he had been told, unreachable. Men found him intimidating; some found him dangerous. He had taken lives in the past, but killing was not an easy thing for him. It had been done out of duty and at times out of self-preservation. Never had he willfully, wantonly, taken a human life. There had never been the need or the desire–until now.

Montana always felt at odds with the darkness that simmered just beneath the surface. It was a part of him that threatened to devour the heart of who he was. He had learned, not quite to make peace with it, but perhaps to have some measure of control over it. That control was slipping.

He stared at the picture the General had sent him on his camera phone and felt the darkness grow within him. For the first time in his life, he welcomed the presence. He looked at his brother's face contorted in pain, and Montana knew only one thing—he wanted to kill. He needed to kill.

Montana gripped the phone tight and fought to keep the emotions to himself. He slipped the illusion of control back in place and handed Ito the phone. "They have Dakota." He knew his friend saw the quick play of emotions that crossed his face before he had a chance to cover them, but Ricco wouldn't know the turmoil Montana hid.

Ricco looked up quickly, his eyes betraying the uncertainty that lay just beneath the surface.

Ito examined the picture on the phone. "What do they want?"

"A trade." Montana looked at Ricco.

Ricco shook his head. "I won't go back there," he said, his face a picture of terror, the freckles standing out in contrast against skin gone pale. He looked young and scared.

Montana leaned forward and brought his face level with the boy's. "I told you once that was not going to happen. I meant it at the time. I mean it now. You will never go back there."

Ricco's voice shook a little with fear. "What about Dakota?"

"We'll find another way."

"You don't know the General."

"I think you've got that backward, boy," Ito said. "The General does not know what he has brought to life." Ito glanced at his friend. Montana looked out the window at the empty place where his Jeep had been.

"How did Dakota know the police were looking for us?" Montana asked. He had found out late last night as everyone slept. His good connections and friends in high places thought Montana might be interested in the manhunt on for him and Dakota. Montana had shared the information with Ito, and planned on telling Dakota this morning.

"Someone must have told him."

Montana nodded, still looking out the window. "Someone did, and he left thinking he could protect me." He laughed and turned around to face Ito. "He is the only person I know who can find trouble trying to stay out of it." The smile faded, replaced with anger. "Damn it, he should have stayed put. He should have talked to me." Control slipped, and Montana was dangerously close to coming undone.

Ito saved him and gave him a moment to get it together. "But he didn't. Dakota was just being Dakota. Somehow they found him. They took him, and now we will go and get him back."

Montana took the offered moment and reined the anger back in. Now was not the time. He needed a clear head, and he needed to think rationally. Later, he would drop the leash and set the monster free.

"I want him back, Ito." He looked at his friend. "I want him back alive."

Ito flipped Montana's phone closed and gently laid it on the table. "Consider it done, sir."

Montana gave a single nod to Ito and walked outside into the desert heat. He had nowhere to go; he just stood there silent and still.

Ricco took the clothes Ito had given him, walked to the window, and watched Montana. He felt stronger this morning than he had just a few hours ago. The General always told him he was a quick healer.

"What's he doing?" Ricco asked Ito as he pulled the short-sleeve t-shirt over his head. His shoulder was still stiff, but he could move it again.

"Thinking," Ito told him. "He's thinking, Private Ricco."

Ricco turned away from the window. "He scares me."

Ito laughed, but his face looked a little sad. "You have nothing to worry about. You're not the one he wants to hurt."

Ricco nodded and flexed his shoulder, working out a little of the stiffness. "I know, but that's not what I meant."

"Let it alone, boy. Montana will work it out. He always does." Ito pulled out his own cellphone and walked away.

Ricco heard him make a call, but couldn't understand the words. Turning toward the window, he stared at Montana's back. The man hadn't moved. Ricco had seen men like him before, men who cared too much. The General had made short work of them. That was what scared Ricco about Montana. He had no doubts this former Ranger could handle himself in a firefight or hand-to-hand, but the General had taken something from him that was irreplaceable. It would tear at Montana until he made a mistake. That was what the General did best, emotional warfare.

Ricco remembered, in the beginning, they had controlled him with threats of harm to his family. They told him they would do horrible things to his mother and sister if he didn't cooperate. The first time he tried to escape, they told him they had killed Emma, his Emma. He believed them, and it was the last time he fought them.

Even when he realized his family must certainly be dead, he forgot how to hope. He gave up and prayed to a God he no longer believed in, and asked for death. When that never happened, he decided to take matters into his own hands. That was when he found out he was a very hard man to kill.

When the power went out that last time, something took over and he just ran, hoping against all hope they would shoot. Ricco's hand went to his injured shoulder. They did shoot him, and he still managed to survive. But the man responsible for saving his life had somehow ended up in the exact place he had run from. Ricco knew he couldn't stand by and let someone else pay the price for this. His daddy had taught him better.

He had to make this right, but he didn't know how. Fear still held a firm grip over him. He had accomplished the impossible and made it out of that bunker alive. The thought of going back made him want to throw up.

Ricco walked to the door and opened it. The morning heat surprised him. He had spent most of his life underground in a climate-controlled environment, and the feel of the wind and sun on his face was something he needed to get used to. He shielded his eyes from the fierce rays of light, walked down the rickety porch steps, and stood a few feet behind Montana. The man didn't acknowledge his presence, but Ricco was certain Montana heard his approach.

"He won't kill him, sir."

Montana gave no indication he had heard.

"He'll use him to get to me."

"I know."

"But once he has me, he won't give Dakota back."

Montana turned to face him. "I know that, too."

The dark glasses Montana favored were in place, and Ricco realized he used them to hide his emotions from the rest of the world. "He'll kill you if he has to, but he would rather take you instead. I know this man. He has no good in him."

Montana watched Ricco for a long moment. All Ricco could see was his own reflection looking back at him. "Neither do I, Private." As he started to turn away, Ricco grabbed his arm and pulled Montana around to face him. Montana looked at the hand on his arm and back to Ricco's face.

"Yes, you do, Montana." It was the first time Ricco had addressed him as anything but sir. "That's what scares me. The General will know that, and he'll use it to get to you. It's what he does best, twisting and bending what you care about until it is not even recognizable. He'll take your soul if you let him, and then he'll own you. I can't let that happen." Ricco dropped the hand on Montana's arm.

"Is that what happened to you, Michael? Did he take your soul?

Does he own you?"

Ricco fought against the tears, and for the moment, won. He met the hidden eyes he knew were staring at him, and nodded. "Yes," he said in answer to all the questions.

"In that case I suggest we go and get it back. I will not trade your soul for another life, not even my brother's."

Ricco believed him. "I want to help."

They both turned as Ito stepped onto the porch. He caught Montana's eye and gave him a nod. Montana turned to Ricco and smiled. "Good, because we're going to need all the help we can get." He turned back to Ito. "How long?"

"Bobby and Ray should be here in a few hours. Patrick's flying in from the East coast, maybe tonight."

Ricco's gaze went from one man to the other. "What are you talking about? Who are these people?"

Montana and Ito exchanged glances, until Ito broke out in quiet laughter. "They're the best of the best, boy, and an unexpected complication for your friend, the General."

Montana put an arm around Ricco's shoulders. "Let's get back inside before you fry. We have a lot of work to do before the team shows up."

Ito touched Ricco's face as he walked by, and Ricco flinched. "Already sunburnt." Ito chuckled. "You know, you are quite possibly the whitest white boy I have ever seen."

Ricco rubbed the tingling area Ito just pinched and smiled, truly smiled. "You stay out of the sun for over ninety years and see what it does for your complexion—*boy*."

For the first time in as long as he could remember, Michael Ricco felt something stir deep inside him. He wasn't sure he recognized it, but he thought it might be hope.

CHAPTER 12

Dakota woke to shaking chills, the smells of dampness, mold, and bitter sweat. Above all else, there was the pain; he could not get away from it. The pain owned him completely. His mangled arm shifted with his slight movement and slipped from where it rested on his stomach. He screamed in agony as his vision grayed, and prayed he would pass out again, but fate was not in a giving mood. He was dead and this was hell. He was certain of it.

With his right hand, he tried to contain the pain by keeping his broken arm still and tight against his body. Somehow, that only managed to make the pain worse. As he pulled his left wrist near his side, the exposed bones twisted and scraped against one another. He bit the inside of his cheek until he tasted blood and waited for the wave to pass. Rocking and moaning, the pain subsided to a tolerable level, leaving in its wake a greasy nausea. He risked opening his eyes and took stock of his situation.

The room they had placed him in appeared to be little more than a cell, complete with a barred and presumably locked entrance. Dim lighting revealed an ancient, stained mattress thrown on the floor, his blood adding to the numerous discolorations of the material. He smelled various body fluids left behind by other occupants of the squalid, lumpy thing. He recognized urine, vomit, and feces, and decided he didn't want to know what else may have added to the aroma.

Someone had thrown him there without any thoughts to comfort. His body twisted with his legs sprawled sideways to rest on the cold concrete. Cramped muscles made him want to move, but the thought of the agony that would cause, kept him still. Finally, the cramps in his back outweighed the pain in his arm, and as gently as he could, he tried to straighten his body. His arm immediately reminded him of its presence.

Dakota tried not to scream as the pain swept through him. He succeeded, but as the nausea took hold, he rolled onto his side and vomited over the only corner of the mattress that had been reasonably clean. The room spun around him as he spit the remainder of the bile from his mouth and wiped his face with the back of his hand. The nausea was gone for the moment, but he couldn't stop the tremors that racked his body. Each shudder brought a new and exquisite wave of pain that threatened to sweep his consciousness back into the darkness.

The clinical side of him that still functioned recognized he was in shock, most likely running a high fever, and he was thirsty. Dehydration would kill him quicker than the shock and infection combined. His head rested back on the mattress as he tried to gather his strength. He lay in his own filth and didn't care.

A slight noise at the cell door caught his attention, and he was surprised to see a guard there. The man sat at a desk calmly doing paperwork while Dakota writhed in agony. His eyes widened as he recognized the man behind the desk as the one who had so efficiently broken his arm. The guy was huge, and none of it was fat. Despite Dakota's delirium, the name Big Bubba came to mind. He couldn't say why, but the man just looked like a Bubba to him. It was odd, but Dakota took a small measure of comfort in Bubba's presence. Being alone and suffering seemed so much worse than having a witness to his plight.

He tried to swallow, but he had no spit left. The taste of bile was strong, and he desperately wished for something to drink. He tried to catch his guard's eye by weakly moving his good arm. When that didn't work, he risked further bodily harm and spoke. "Hey." The word came out as a croak, but it got the desired effect.

Bubba looked up from his paperwork and stared at him. The cold glare made Dakota wish he had remained silent. "You say something?"

"Thirsty," Dakota said, and closed his eyes. He didn't expect the man to do anything about his request, but to his amazement, the sound of metal on metal had him opening his eyes once more.

The guard unlocked the door, squatted down next to him, and held out a bottle of water. Dakota reached for it, but his hand was shaking so badly he couldn't grasp it. Bubba took pity on him and helped. He put a hand under his head and lifted the bottle of water to Dakota's lips.

Dakota ignored the protests of pain coming from his arm and gulped the tepid liquid greedily. The offering was suddenly removed, much to Dakota's disappointment. His thirst demanded attention. "More, please."

"Later. If you drink too much now, you'll just puke again." He sighed and shook his head as he looked down at Dakota. "You're a mess, Doc. What you really need is an IV."

For the first time, Dakota braved a look at his arm. He felt he was looking at some foreign thing, not a piece of his own body. The break was at his mid-forearm, with the ends of both his ulna and radius protruding about an inch from the ragged, bloody flesh. Nausea threatened once more, and he looked away. "Nice job."

Bubba ignored the sarcasm and offered him the water again. Dakota sucked on the bottle, trying to get as much as he could before the man took it away again. He knew Bubba was right, and he should just sip it, but his thirst overpowered his good sense. On the third gulp, Bubba started to pull the bottle away, but Dakota clamped down with his teeth. He only succeeded in sucking the liquid into his lungs. He coughed and sputtered the water back out, then defeated the purpose entirely by throwing it all up.

Bubba helped him to his side and stayed with him until he was through retching. "Hang on a second, Doc." Dakota was beyond caring what happened to him, and was surprised when a few moments later Bubba placed a cool, damp cloth on his face. "I told you little sips." He shook his head at Dakota and sighed.

Dakota looked at him, too wiped to ask the question in his head.

"Medic," the man explained.

"Ahh," Dakota said, and winced as another spasm shook him. He felt like a dried up corn husk, the ones that rattle in winter winds, clinging stubbornly to the stalks that once gave them life.

"Tell me something," Dakota managed when the pain became more tolerable. "How can you do this?"

Bubba shook his head.

"Take care of me, after doing this to me?" He indicated his broken arm with his eyes, careful not to move as he did so.

The man simply shrugged. "Orders," he said, but it was clear he was frustrated.

Dakota closed his eyes at the insanity of the answer. He was at this man's mercy. There was no point in pissing him off with a debate he didn't have the energy to start. He heard the clank of his cell door once more and assumed Bubba had gone back to his post, but he felt hands on him and he panicked at the contact. Pushing away from the touch only caused agony to flare once more.

"Take it easy, Doc."

Dakota let the man pull him onto his back and watched through blurry eyes, as Bubba tied a tourniquet around his good arm.

The look on Dakota's face must have questioned the man's

intentions, because he explained, "It's for the pain."

Dakota watched with detached interest as Bubba purged air from a syringe and a drop of clear liquid oozed at the needle's tip. "What is it?"

"Hydromorphone. Not nearly enough, but you're a little shocky. Give you too much, I could bottom out your pressure, might even kill you."

Bubba found a vein, and Dakota felt a sharp bite as the needle pierced his flesh. Not too long after, sweet relief flooded his system. He couldn't say the pain went away, but he certainly didn't care about it as much. Before the narcotic could take him completely under, he turned to Bubba. "Hey…What's your name?"

Bubba released the tourniquet and covered Dakota with a blanket. "Carlson. Sergeant William Robert Carlson."

Dakota closed his eyes and waited to be swept away into narcotic bliss. *Still looks like a Bubba to me*, he thought.

CHAPTER 13

Montana stood in the immaculate living room of the safe house and waited for his team. He waited in silence, the external deceivingly calm, while the internal screamed for urgency. He needed to move, he needed his team.

They say once activated, Army Rangers can be anywhere in the world in eighteen hours. They had twelve, and none of the Rangers Ito contacted had been listed as active in a long time. But Rangers are Rangers for life; it's in the blood. One of their own was in trouble, and one phone call had the three remaining members of Montana's team converge on the state of Nevada. From all over the country they came. Leaving jobs and family because Montana needed them. It was as simple as that.

By ten that evening a family reunion of sorts was taking place, but it was short-lived. They had work to do. Montana introduced Private Ricco, and then briefed his team on recent events. Ito was family; no introductions were needed.

"Our mission is fairly simple." Montana passed his phone with the image of Dakota from man to man. "We need to retrieve an injured man from a secure location. I have no idea how many men are at the site or how heavily armed they might be. Ricco is our only source of information, and he was a prisoner." Montana looked at the men to whom he had entrusted his life on countless occasions. He was placing his brother's life in their hands now.

"Sweet." Ray smiled. "What are we waiting for?"

Montana returned the grin, and for the first time since Dakota had gone missing, felt like he could breathe again. He had missed this. These men were as much his family as his brother. He had no doubts that each of them would give their lives for him, if it came to that, as he would for them. Theirs was an unspoken bond few civilians could hope to understand. To them, family was more than blood. It was trust. It was loyalty. It was the training that gave them the courage and confidence to accomplish this task.

"The bastard gave me forty-eight hours until he calls with the exchange instructions."

"So, we go in now." Ray never changed. He was the equivalent of an eight-year-old with ADD on amphetamines, but the guy was good. Ray was a genius when it came to explosives and munitions. He didn't know what it meant to be afraid, and he had more adrenaline than blood flowing through his veins. Montana had seen him grow eerily calm in the face of overwhelming odds, even when grievously wounded. Ray thrived at the prospect of dismal odds and certain death. Montana would not want him as an adversary.

"Do we know where your brother is being held, Major?" Bobby was the youngest, smallest, and perhaps the smartest of them all. He stood five-four and tipped the scales at one-thirty, but Bobby had a sixth sense that kept him alive. He knew where the rounds were being fired from, and he had a knack for staying out of harm's way. Montana hoped he still had the gift. Of all of them, he felt incredible guilt at Bobby's presence. His wife of two years was just days away from the birth of their first child, but like the rest of them, Bobby had come of his own free will.

"That's another problem," Montana admitted. "I have no idea where they might be keeping him."

"I can help with that." All faces turned toward Ricco. He looked up from the picture of Dakota he'd been studying, obviously not comfortable with the attention his comment caused. "I—I mean, I think I can help."

Montana smiled at the boy's eager but unsure manner. "It's okay, Ricco. Tell us what you think."

Ricco's gaze moved from one man to the next, and then back to the small blurry picture he held. "Well, see here on the wall behind Dakota? There's an insignia. I'm pretty sure I recognize it."

Montana took the phone from Ricco and stared. He'd been so focused on Dakota's image that he had missed the details. He handed the phone to Ito. "Can you clean this up?"

Ito squinted at the image for a moment, and then sat down at the computer. "I think so. Give me a minute." He plugged the phone into the hard drive, tapped a few keys, and pulled the image up on the monitor. The picture immediately distorted as the image was enlarged. Ito played with the pixels and hit a button. "There, that's about the best I can do."

Ricco squinted at the enlarged picture. "Wow," he said in obvious amazement. "Can you make that part bigger?" He pointed to the upper corner of the screen, where numbers and letters appeared on the wall behind Dakota.

Ito zoomed in on the part Ricco had specified. Even distorted, the image was now readable. "How's that?"

Ricco leaned in closer and nodded. "Good, that's perfect," he said, still looking at the computer screen. "I know where they're keeping him." He turned to Montana with an elated smile. "I know where Dakota is."

Montana felt hope surge, but he kept a straight face. "Were you planning on keeping it a secret, Private, or are you going to share with the rest of us?"

"No, sir… I mean, yes, sir." Ricco flushed as he pointed to the black insignia painted on the wall in the picture. "There, you see that? BD-three."

Bobby stepped closer and stared at the monitor. "What's it mean?"

"It stands for Beaver Dam, location number three. I've been there before. I can't tell you exactly where it is or how to get there from here, but I know they have several bunkers in this area, and that's one of the older ones. They haven't had me there in years. I thought they abandoned it."

"Beaver Dam? But that's where we found Tommy Lawson and the others. They did abandon that location," Montana said.

Ricco shook his head. "No, sir. That was BD-one. I've been there for years. I can't really remember how long because they haven't moved me in quite a while, but I know BD-three isn't that far away."

"How far away? Beaver Dam's not a back yard—it's over two thousand acres of untouched desert." Montana let out a frustrated breath. He drug a hand through his hair and stood with his back to his team.

"I don't know," Ricco admitted. "They had me sedated whenever they moved me. Sometimes more than others. I can't say exactly."

Patrick, the remaining member of the team, spoke for the first time. "You know, that's the great thing about deserts." Every eye in the room turned to stare at him.

Patrick stood tall and lanky, his long blond hair pulled into a tail that hung down his back, dark brown eyes alert and taking in everything. It was an amazing thing to hear Patrick speak more than two words at a time. He listened, but the man was eerily quiet. In the many years Montana had known him, he could count the times Patrick had spoken on the fingers of both hands. He didn't think anyone really knew Patrick, but the man was the best sharp-shooter Montana had ever seen. He was scary-good. Tell Patrick to take out a target, and it was taken out; the circumstances didn't matter.

Montana voiced what everyone was thinking as he addressed Patrick. "What's so great about the desert?"

Patrick smiled. "It's not very good at keeping secrets."

Montana understood what Patrick was getting at. "The trail."

Patrick nodded. "They had to move him. We have a search perimeter. We track them."

"In time?" Montana asked. He knew Patrick was good, but two thousand acres was a lot of ground to cover, and Dakota's life was in the balance.

Patrick shrugged and leaned back in his chair. "Give me an hour."

"But it's dark out," Ricco said.

Patrick looked out the window at the star-filled sky and a moon-drenched landscape that appeared to stretch into infinity. He conceded the point with a shrug, and then smiled at Ricco. "Okay, ninety minutes."

As Montana stood in front of his reassembled team, pride welled up in his chest. Pride for who these men were, and for what they were willing to sacrifice simply at his asking. He had never requested anything like this from them, yet he knew there would be no hesitation. They were Rangers.

During training, they had a saying: with the tab or on a slab. It was a variation of the Spartan's mother's directive to their soldier sons: with your shield or upon it. In reality, the tab was only a small rectangular piece of cloth sewn over the right breast pocket of their uniform that read, Ranger. But it meant far more. It meant they had survived the intensive training required to be called an Army Ranger. It was a symbol of respect, and it was earned with not a small amount of blood, pain, and soul-searching.

It was this all-or-nothing attitude that got them through their missions. Active duty or not, one of their own was in trouble. Dakota might not be a Ranger, but he was the brother of their team leader, and that made him family. This one was personal. No one threaten their family and lived to talk about it.

Montana addressed his men. "I know I don't have to say this, but this General is not an honorable man. What he did to Private Ricco is unforgivable." Montana looked at Ricco as he spoke. "He goes under the guise of the military, but I don't believe he is. We go in with one objective in mind—failure is not an option."

"What would you have us do?" Bobby had pieced together a semi-automatic assault rifle and was lining up the sight as he spoke.

Without answering him, Montana took the assembled weapon, inspected it, and then chambered a round. The weapon was a thing of beauty. Montana let it distract him for a moment before tearing his gaze away from the sleek, black barrel and locking his eyes on Bobby. "I want you to bring my brother home."

Patrick stood and gave Montana an almost imperceptible nod. "Consider it done, sir."

For the next hour, five former Army Rangers, and one very rusty Marine private discussed maneuvers. Ray and Bobby showed Ricco the advancements in firepower that had occurred over the last hundred years, and reacquainted him with the feel of a weapon in his hand. But for all of them, one thought was ever-present in their minds. They had but one goal: to bring Dakota Thomas home.

CHAPTER 14

Time lost all meaning for Dakota. He drifted in and out of consciousness, and the pain followed him, even in his dreams. His fever bordered on dangerously high. His blood pressure had dipped below shock levels, and a new, disturbing congestion had developed in his chest. His arm was badly swollen, and the neglected injury was, beyond a doubt, infected. Bubba did what he could, but it wasn't much.

Dakota felt abandoned. He wondered if his brother was looking for him. He knew in his heart Montana would come for him eventually, but the more time that passed, the more his despair took hold. He was beginning to believe he had become like Michael Ricco—one of the forgotten ones—one of the fallen.

The overhead lights flared to life, and Dakota squeezed his eyes shut in protest. He had quickly learned that any change in his environment only brought more pain. He heard heels clicking on concrete and braced himself for the worst. Even now, he recognized the sound of those dress heels. The door to his cell opened, and the footsteps came to stop near his head.

"My, my, Doctor… You really don't look well."

Dakota ignored the voice he knew belonged to the General. A hand touched the side of his face, and he flinched involuntarily.

"What are his vitals?"

"Heart rate one-fifty, blood pressure eighty over forty, and his temperature is a hundred and two."

Dakota heard Bubba rattle off the numbers and realized, in a strange detached way, they were talking about him. He was in worse shape than he thought. The logical part of his brain still functioning, voiced concern. *I shouldn't be this bad this quickly*. The illogical part just wanted them to turn off the lights and leave him the hell alone. With his mind in a feverish daze, he followed the conversation without opening his eyes.

He heard Bubba plead his case to the General. "Sir, he needs fluids at the very least."

There was a pause, and then the sound of papers shuffling before the General finally answered. "I had hoped he would prove a little hardier, but I agree, Sergeant, he's no use to me dead. Do what you have to, just keep him alive."

There was a brief period of silence, and believing the General had left, Dakota opened his eyes. He found the lights still glaring down on him, and the General standing over him, watching, just watching him. That scared him, that silent observation.

"Doctor…" The General inclined his head toward Dakota, then took a step closer and squatted down next to his mattress. "It's fascinating, isn't it, the amount of pain a human being can survive?"

Under the General's clinical gaze, Dakota felt like a bug studied through a microscope. He found both humor and comfort in that odd image as memories from his childhood invaded his brain. The pictures that played inside his head felt safe, and Dakota retreated deep within himself trying to find a place where no one could hurt him, a place as far removed from reality as he could manage. He closed his eyes and tried to play dead, but the General was having none of it.

"Did you know Ricco survived over thirty-six hours of electric shock? The pain he endured must have been beyond comprehension. Yet, it took him less than a day to recover. That was an amazing thing to watch. He has had every bone in his body broken, some more than once, and I would bet that none of those injuries is apparent on radiographs. He is, in a word, miraculous. Don't you think?"

When Dakota remained still and quiet, the General slapped his face. It wasn't hard, but it had the desired effect. Dakota's eyes snapped open, and he brought his right hand up in a defensive posture.

"Are you with me, Doctor Thomas?"

Dakota slowly lowered his hand and came out of his shell. "What do you want?" He glared at the man, seeing no reason to hide the anger and hate he felt.

The General smiled and shook his head. "You really should do something about managing your temper. Considering your present circumstances, it's not healthy."

Dakota's gaze shifted to Bubba as he entered the cell. His hands were full of equipment Dakota immediately recognized, and he stiffened with fear at the thought of what the man might do with the paraphernalia.

"Relax, Doc. I'm just going to get some fluids into you."

For some bizarre reason, Bubba's presence calmed him. The man had broken his arm without mercy, but he had also been the only source of compassion in this hell. Bubba took away his pain. Bubba cooled his face. Bubba cared whether he lived or died.

Dakota felt the familiar tourniquet around his arm, only this time, he didn't even acknowledge the needle that slipped effortlessly into his vein. He watched as the IV was established and hung above his head on a small hook protruding from the wall. He ignored the General and tried to smile, but only succeeded in wincing as pain rippled through him. He knew he couldn't ask Bubba for anything, not with the General in the room. Their secret would be blown, and Dakota would lose his only salvation.

"I do hope you will learn to behave yourself, Doctor. You will find that positive behavior is rewarded…perhaps something for the pain or maybe I will allow the sergeant to set your arm. It looks extremely painful."

Dakota actually managed to grin. "I won't be here long enough for that. You made a huge mistake."

The General thought about that for a moment, and then his face took on a look of exaggerated comprehension. "Ah, I assume you are referring to your brother, the Ranger?"

The short conversation was almost too much for Dakota, and the room began to spin again. The General's face came in and out of focus, making him nauseous. He swallowed and blinked several times before finding the strength to glare up at the man.

"You have no idea the trouble you're in for." Dakota had no more strength for further conversation and turned his head away from the General, intending to find that place deep inside himself once more.

The General sighed, and more gently than Dakota would have expected, took his face and turned it back toward him. He would have jerked away from the contact, but it required more energy than he could summon.

"Yes, well, I'm afraid I have some distressing news for you, Doctor. I did contact your brother to arrange for your release, but unfortunately, he decided not to play by my rules. My men killed your brother a few hours ago, along with Private Ricco." He paused before continuing. "It is a pity. He would have made an interesting subject. I don't believe we've ever studied brothers before." The General shrugged. "His death wasn't necessary. Private Ricco put that bullet in his brain just as surely as if he had been the one to pull the trigger. We have disposed of their bodies, and they will not be found. So you see, any hopes you may have harbored of a rescue attempt, died along with them."

The General appeared sympathetic as he delivered the news. "I am sorry, but there will be no eleventh-hour pardon, no rescue, and no trade. No one knows you're here, Doctor Thomas. You are mine, just like Ricco was mine, to do with as I please."

Dakota laughed. He couldn't believe Montana had been bested by this man. "No way, you're lying." He didn't want to believe it, but his eyes filled with the possibility that the man spoke the truth.

"I understand completely. This is difficult for you." The General softly stroked Dakota's cheek as if he were a newly acquired pet. "It will take a while to get used to the fact, but this is your home now. The sooner you accept that, the easier things will be for you." Then the monster returned. He dug his fingers deep into Dakota's face and drove home his point. "Your brother is dead, and you belong to me."

Your brother is dead. Those words echoed through Dakota like the slow tolling of a funeral bell. Your brother is dead...your brother is dead. As the words faded inside his head, silence filled the room. Lying flat on his back in a dried puddle of his own vomit, with his face in the General's vise-like grip, time seemed to slow and come to a staggering halt.

Through a blurred veil of tears the General's face morphed into visions of his childhood: he and Montana raising hell and causing trouble at every opportunity; Montana, laughing and giving high fives for successful schemes and devious plots; their hearts racing as they ran from a bellowing Cal; sharing secrets in little boy whispers with only the dark of night as a witness; hiding from their mother, hiding from the world, taking the blame for each other's sins, and then turning around and setting each other up for the fall. Escaping into the desert for a taste of freedom, vowing to make his serious older brother smile more and taking pride that he was the only person able to do so. Feeling the unbreakable bond between confidants, conspirators, friends, brothers…his brother.

Your brother is dead.

The past dissolved, leaving him only with the present. As the General's face came into focus a mere six inches from his own, something primal snapped inside of Dakota. He felt no fear, no pain, no grief or self-pity, only an empty, hollow numbness. He burned with more than just the fever raging inside him, he burned with a savage hatred. He tore his face from the General's grip and struggled to his knees.

The General cocked his head and coolly evaluated him. "Now, see Doctor, that's the spirit. I was right, you would make—"

A sweeping backhand fist caught the General square on the jaw. With a stunned look of disbelief on his face, he pinwheeled his arms once, twice, three times, and then landed hard on his back on the cold cement floor.

"Jesus! Doc, what the hell do you think you're doing?" Bubba came to his side, supporting him.

Dakota had no clear idea of what his intentions were after that, and never got a chance to find out. He heard Bubba's voice through the buzzing in his head, and his vision grayed, but Dakota wasn't done yet.

The General was on his feet by then, rubbing his jaw and looking down at Dakota swaying unsteadily on his knees. "Perhaps I have not given you enough credit, Doctor. I think you will make a fine replacement for Private Ricco."

Dakota lurched out of Bubba's grasp and made it to his feet. "Fuck you! I'm not...you're not... Oh, God." The room folded in around him as he collapsed.

Bubba caught him and carefully laid him down on the mattress. As he assessed the damage Dakota's unexpected outburst had caused, the General looked on with a perverted sense of admiration. "He is stronger than he looks."

"Maybe, but he's at the end of his endurance. Sir, he needs the serum soon if he's going to survive."

"What, exactly, was he infected with again, Sergeant?"

"A version of avian influenza, sir. It was administered with the sedative when he was acquired. He'll die in the next few hours if we don't do something soon." It was as close to begging as Carlson would ever get.

"Why, Sergeant, don't tell me you've developed an attachment to the good doctor?"

Carlson looked insulted by the insinuation. "No, sir. I did what you instructed me to. He trusts me. He would believe anything I told him at this point…sir."

The General noted Carlson's indignant tone with twisted satisfaction. "Good. You have been giving him pain medication?"

"Yes, sir. He thinks you don't know about it."

"Very good." The General was impressed with the man's ingenuity. He had obviously underestimated Sergeant Carlson. "When do you think you can begin transfusion of the serum?"

Carlson reestablished the IV Dakota had dislodged, and thought for a moment. "I'd like to get a couple liters of fluid into him first. At least get his blood pressure up, to give him a fighting chance. Maybe an hour."

"Whatever you need to do, Sergeant, you have the go-ahead. You take care of the doctor…" The General turned to leave and said, more to himself than to the sergeant, "And I'll take care of his brother."

CHAPTER 15

It took Carlson longer than he thought it would to get Dakota
ready for the infusion. He hooked him up to a portable monitor, so he
could keep a closer eye on his vitals, but the sergeant had a problem:
the bunker was operating with a bare minimum of staff. All medical
personnel had been moved to decrease the risk of discovery, and the
remaining help were either spec-ops or tactical. Only Carlson had been
kept on board because he knew Ricco, inside and out. The doctor
wasn't supposed to be there. They were not set up for this, but he had
learned a long time ago to expect anything with the General.

Carlson was in way over his head. He knew how to patch them up
and keep them alive, but his training only went so far. He had a critical
patient infected with a level-3 biohazard, and he had an experimental
serum. The General wanted Dakota kept alive, and the sergeant always
did what he was told, but he wasn't used to making the decisions on his
own. He had already given Dakota two liters of normal saline wide
open. His blood pressure had responded, but it didn't stay up for long.
To make matters worse, his lungs sounded terrible. All Carlson heard

were wet respirations, and the fluid his patient desperately needed only compounded that fact.

He didn't know what to do. If he infused the serum now, Dakota was as good as dead. That would not please the General, and the General was a scary person when he was not pleased. The only thing the sergeant knew for certain, was that what the doctor needed...was a doctor.

Carlson managed to procure an actual bed and had it brought down to the holding area, mostly because his back was killing him from getting up and down off the floor. He sat on the edge of the mattress and lightly slapped Dakota's face until he opened his eyes. "Hey, Doc, you with me?"

Dakota's eyes were glazed with fever and unfocused, but he managed a smile. "Hey, Bubba. How you doing, man?"

Bubba. Carlson couldn't help but grin at the name. He was developing a strong admiration for Doctor Thomas. He had seen men twice as tough give up at this point, but as hurt and sick as Dakota was, he'd still taken a swing at the General. The doctor had balls; Carlson had to give him that. He also thought Dakota looked a little more with it than the last time he was awake, but he knew that was only temporary. The stuff inside of him was lethal, and he was as good as dead without Ricco's serum.

"I'm fine. The question is, how you doing?"

Dakota coughed, a wet, congested cough that screwed his face up in pain. He struggled for breath until his airway cleared. "Oh, hell...I'm just peachy, Bubba."

Carlson nodded. "Yeah, I know." Dakota closed his eyes, but Carlson tapped his face again and got his attention. "Listen to me, Doc. I have a serious problem here, and I think you might be able to help me with it."

Dakota blinked. Carlson could see it was difficult for the man to even try to focus. "Do tell," he said.

"You see, I have this patient—high fever, septic, hypotensive..."

"Ahh, I see. Well, Bubba..." He took a breath, trying to get air into his fluid-filled lungs. "In my professional opinion, your patient needs fluids—lots of fluids. Slam them in until his pressure is stable." Dakota struggled to keep his eyes open. The short conversation had clearly drained him.

"That's my problem, Doc. I gave him two liters wide open, but as soon as it's in, his pressure bottoms out again."

Dakota turned his head, straining to read the numbers on the monitor at the side of his bed. The slight movement seemed exhausting and his eyes drifted shut as he spoke. "Hell, Bubba...your patient looks like crap."

Carlson laughed softly. "Yes, sir, he does."

Dakota opened his eyes and blinked a few times. Carlson could see him trying to figure out the puzzle. "What you got in your pharmacopoeia? Your patient needs some major antibiotics. Fluids can only compensate for so much."

Carlson shook his head. "No antibiotics, Doc. We haven't been at this facility in years, and the shelves are empty."

Dakota sighed. "Then your patient's up a shit creek in a barb-wire canoe with a tennis racket for a paddle."

"Sir?" Carlson asked.

"He's screwed, Bubba...royally screwed." Dakota turned away from Carlson and closed his eyes again.

Carlson started to say something, then hesitated, unsure of how Dakota would react. However, time was running out, and the sergeant knew he didn't have a choice. It had to be done. He took a deep breath. "Doc?" He waited for Dakota to open his eyes again. "There's something you should know."

"What's that, Bubba?"

Carlson licked his lips; now came the hard part. "Do you know how old Ricco is?"

"Yeah, he told me."

"Did you believe him?"

Dakota shrugged, and his face contorted in pain. Carlson waited for the spasm to pass and for the doc to continue. When he did, his voice was noticeably weaker. "Yeah, I suppose. So what?"

"We were always trying to figure out how he got that way, you know? Something to do with finding the gene that controls aging. I won't pretend to know anything about that, but anyway, we would take his blood from time to time. One of the doctors here developed a serum out of it."

That got Dakota's attention. His eyes, bright with fever, but alert and questioning, turned in Bubba's direction. "A serum? They made a serum from Ricco's blood?"

"Yes, sir." Bubba held Dakota's gaze for a moment, and then lowered his head in shame.

"Bubba?" When he didn't get a response, Dakota narrowed his eyes and peered closely at the man. "Bubba, talk to me, man. What aren't you telling me?"

Sergeant Carlson slowly raised his head and looked Dakota directly in the eye. "I'm sorry, Doctor Thomas, but…you were infected with a BH-three at the time of acquisition."

"Excuse me?"

"A biological hazard, level three."

Dakota stared past Carlson. The reality of what he was just told evident on his face. "Jesus." He let his head sink down into the mattress. "Do you know which one?"

"Avian influenza."

"Fuck, Bubba." Dakota lifted his right hand and placed it over his eyes.

Although only a medic, Carlson knew enough about biological hazards to know that level fours, like the Ebola virus, had no cure.

Level threes were fatal without treatment. Even with treatment, the survival rate was only about thirty percent. He understood the Doc's reaction.

"You see my problem, Doc?"

"Your problem?" Dakota grabbed a handful of Bubba's shirt; his anger giving him momentary strength. "Fuck you nine ways to Friday!"

His outburst started another coughing fit. Dakota's face turned crimson as he fought for air, and Bubba placed a hand on his chest, hoping to ease the spasms. "Relax, Doc. You're only making it worse." He watched the monitor as he waited for the coughing to let up. "You can't keep getting yourself all worked up like that."

Dakota tried to voice a reply, but he started coughing instead. Carlson wished he knew what to do, as his patient struggled just to breathe. Dakota shook his head and let go of Bubba's shirt as his breathing became more regular. His eyes watered and tears streamed down his face. He laid his head back and sucked in short, shallow breaths. Carlson knew the doc was burning up with fever, but he shivered as if he were freezing.

"Tell me...the serum...what about Ricco's serum?" Dakota's voice was weak and barely audible.

"It's never been used successfully, but Ricco has this amazing ability to heal himself. In theory, the serum should be able to do the same thing. The problem is, you're not stable enough for me to give it to you. It's got some really nasty side-effects."

Dakota turned his head and looked at the vital signs flitting across the monitor. "I won't get any more stable than this, pal. I'm going to die."

Carlson sadly nodded his agreement. "Yes, sir."

Dakota released a raspy sigh and seemed to resigned himself to whatever fate God, and the serum, had in store. He turned back to Carlson. "Okay. Slam the fluids in, your patient can take the extra volume. Get his pressure up, and then give him the serum. Any side effects, just treat as they appear."

"You sure about this, Doc?"

"Well, I sure as hell don't want to die!" Dakota closed his eyes, and Carlson thought the doc might have released the tentative hold he had on consciousness, but to his surprise, Dakota made one final request. "You got me into this, Bubba...now get me out."

Carlson hooked up another bag of saline and gave a half-smile to his semi-conscious patient. "I'll do my best, Doc." Some days, he really hated his job.

In an expression of concern that caught him by surprise, he reached down and gently pushed a lock of sweat-soaked hair out of the doctor's eyes. Dakota lay still and gave no indication of noticing.

Serum or not, Carlson wondered if it was too late to save Dakota Thomas, but in his heart, he knew he would be damned if he didn't try. As the saline ran into the doctor's arm, he left the room and retrieved a small, five-hundred milliliter bag of yellow fluid from a refrigerated unit outside the holding area. Without a doubt, what he held in his hand was priceless...if it worked. He spiked the bag, and prepared to find out.

CHAPTER 16

Montana's associates had stocked the house with food and everything to make life in the middle of the desert bearable; Montana had stocked the armory. Accessible only through a trap door in the floor of one of the bedrooms, there existed a mercenaries' wet dream.

Montana descended the ladder and turned on the overhead light. His team followed, and one-by-one, gazed about the room in awe. Assault and sniper rifles lined the walls—M-16s, AK-47s, a couple of new XM8s, M-40s, a pair of Dragunov SVDs, and others. The shelves were stocked with a variety of handguns—Uzis, Desert Eagles, Glocks, Berettas; and beneath those, the bad boys—M8 rocket launchers, M-60 machine guns, and stacks of C-4, along with their detonators. Boxes of concussion and fragmentation grenades sat on the floor under the shelves, as well as boxes and belts of ammunition.

Patrick grinned as he lovingly pulled his weapon of choice off the wall, a Barrett XM107, .50 caliber, long-range sniper rifle with IFR and night vision scope. He caressed the long, sleek barrel like a lover.

Wrapping the strap around his arm, he hoisted the weapon to his shoulder and sighted it.

Montana stepped up beside him. "Like it?"

Never taking his eyes off the gun, Patrick gave a distracted nod. "It'll do."

"Leave it."

Patrick's head snapped around, and he looked at Montana like a little boy asked to give up his last piece of candy. "But, sir…"

Montana turned away. He had helped many people in his career, and his armory existed because some had the means to show their gratitude more than others. He had also learned many things along the way, but more than anything, he learned the value of being prepared. "Listen up, people. We're going underground. The bunker is concrete, with long, narrow hallways and very little room for cover. Choose your weapons accordingly. Concussion and flash-bang grenades only. We don't know how many other prisoners might be down there, and we don't want to make soup out of any innocents." He looked at Ray and pointed to a case of C4. "Ray, you load up. If we get the chance, I want this bunker returned to the earth from which it came. The rest of you, take what you need, but be quick. We leave in thirty minutes."

Montana turned back to Patrick, who still held the XM107, pouting. "Here, give me that." He took the weapon and hung it back on the wall. "Let me show you something I picked up a couple of months ago." He led Patrick to the back of the room, where a black plastic rifle case leaned against the wall. "I haven't even tried it yet…been too busy." He laid the case on the floor, unsnapped the latches, and smiled at Patrick. "Can't think of anyone I'd rather have break it in for me." He lifted the lid, and Patrick looked as surprised as he was capable.

"Holy shit." He dropped to his knees in front of the case. "An Alpine TPG-1… I don't believe it." His fingertips danced over the different features of the exotic weapon. "Custom molded, through-the-stock grip…full, integrally silenced barrel…ATN 16x65Z scope… I never thought I'd see one of these up close. Major, where did you get this beauty?"

Montana just shrugged, stood and slapped Patrick on the back. "Try not to drool on it, okay?"

As the rest of the team gathered their weapons and ammo, Ricco wandered around the room, looking for something familiar he could relate to. He felt like he had just entered a time warp, and with a jolt, realized he had. An odd-looking, mask-like contraption caught his eye. Tiny switches and dials lined the top of it, and two black cylinders protruded from where the eyes should be. He picked it up and turned it over, trying to make some sense of the strange device.

Bobby came up beside him. "Night vision goggles." When Ricco still didn't comprehend, Bobby took the goggles and fitted them over the Marine's head. "Watch this. Hey, Ito…hit the lights." The room became immersed in complete darkness, and Bobby reached up and turned a dial on the goggles.

Ricco's hands flew to his face and he took a step back as the room was enveloped in an eerie green glow. "Wow! I can see. I can see everything!" He held his hands out in front of him and wiggled his fingers, then turned in a circle, fascinated by the green world surrounding him. "You guys really can't see anything? You can't see me?"

Bobby and the others laughed. "Not a thing, man."

Ricco waved a hand inches away from Bobby's face and received no reaction. "Wow!"

Bobby fumbled and found the dials on top of the goggles, then flipped a switch, which left Ricco in darkness once more. The light came on, and Ricco took the goggles off, staring at them in amazement as Bobby smiled at him.

"Are we done playing around? We have work to do." Montana handed Ricco a small handgun, then gestured to Bobby. "Make sure he knows how to use it."

The weapon felt like a toy in Ricco's hand. He expected the comforting weight of the thick-bodied guns he had trained with, but he thought this would break if he gripped it too tight. It felt completely foreign to him but damn, if it didn't feel good just to be armed again.

Bobby gave him a ten-round magazine, and showed him how to fit it into the grip. "Make sure the magazine is secure, pull back on the slide, release it, and you've got a live one in the chamber. Got it?" Ricco nodded, a little uncertain. Bobby demonstrated the safety. "Make sure you're aiming at what you want to hit. If you don't want to fire or you're not sure of your target, keep your finger outside the trigger guard."

Ricco released the magazine and pushed it back into place. He thought he could get use to how the weapon felt in his hand—it felt dangerous. He liked that. He smiled at Bobby. "Sweet."

Ito laughed as he shouldered a weapon. "You've been talking to Ray."

Montana finished inspecting his own weapon and gave Ricco his attention. "No time for practice. Looks like you get to learn on live targets, Private." After loading a few more magazines into the ammo belt around his waist, Montana addressed his team. "We move out, now." They didn't need to be told twice, the fully armed men followed Montana out of the room and into the cool of the desert night.

As the team loaded their weapons and ammo in the trunk of one of the rental cars, Montana pulled a sleek Harley 833 Sportser from the shed behind the house. It was a black, low-slung, sweet ride, and Montana's favorite toy. Besides his Jeep, the Harley was one of the few possessions he hated to be parted from.

He parked the bike in front of the car, while his team stood in the dark of a desert night and waited for his final word. As Montana faced his men, he felt something completely alien to him. It was just a small seed stirring in the pit of his belly, but it was there—doubt. He didn't like it.

Ito seemed to understand his hesitation. He walked up behind his friend and placed a hand on his shoulder. "We will bring him home, Montana." Montana. Not sir or Major—Montana.

Montana swallowed the hundred excuses he had for bringing these men here. "If any of you leave, I wouldn't think less of you. This is my fight, and this is my brother. You have lives, people, and families of your own to think of." He paused, and his eyes settled on Bobby. "I should have handled this by myself."

The team stood in silence for all of two seconds, until Ray broke the tension. "Yeah? Well, screw that." He glanced at the rest of the team. "He invites us to a party, hands out the favors, and then he wants to start without us." He turned back to Montana with a grin. "Ain't gonna happen, sir."

Ito's rumbling laugh filled the night. A broad smile spread across his face, and with his white teeth and eyes gleaming in the dark, he resembled a giant, black, Cheshire cat.

Bobby spoke up. "We're not here because we have to be, sir. We're here because you need us. If you think you can do this alone, then…well, with all due respect, Major, you're cracked."

"We're not leaving," Patrick added. "Deal with it."

Montana smiled and pointed at the weapon that Patrick cradled affectionately. "You're just saying that, because if you leave, you won't get to play with your new toy."

Patrick slung the rifle over his shoulder and put a protective hand on the strap. "Yes, sir," he said with a completely straight face. Not even Montana was certain if he was serious.

Without being asked, his team gathered around him. Ricco looked small and very alone standing by the car. Montana pointed in the boy's direction, and Ray made a hole, dragging him into the circle.

Ito quoted the Ranger's motto. "Rangers lead the way."

"Yeah, and we kick ass, too." Ray laughed.

Nothing more needed to be said. Montana straddled the Harley and kicked the engine to life. He took one last look at his men. "We all good?"

He got nods as answers.

Montana trusted these men, and that was a good feeling. He had missed that feeling more than he wanted to admit. "Then, let's go get my brother." The throttle ripped back, and he tore into the quiet of the desert night.

CHAPTER 17

Twenty minutes into the first serum infusion, Dakota went into convulsions. His body arched on the bed as his muscles contracted in violent spasmodic jerks. His eyes rolled back until only the whites were visible, and saliva foamed from his mouth.

Sergeant Carlson expected that. He had seen it happen before, and had established a secondary IV for just such an occurrence. While the serum continued to drip into one arm, he straddled Dakota's writhing body and struggled to inject Valium into the other line. By the time he accomplished the relatively simple task, he was drenched in sweat.

Countering the seizures was a fine line, and Carlson prayed he hadn't crossed it. Too much of the drug, and respirations would be suppressed to the point of stopping. Too little, and the seizures that gripped Dakota's nervous system would deplete his oxygen reserve, causing irreversible brain damage. He watched and waited.

Two minutes—one hundred and twenty seconds—that's all the convulsions lasted. Carlson figured he guessed right. The doctor's body relaxed, and his heart rate and respirations returned to base line. When he checked Dakota's pupils, they were equal and responsive to the flashes of light shone in his eyes. Sergeant Carlson breathed a sigh of relief. "Good news, Doc. No sign of brain damage."

The rest of the infusion went without any problems. Carlson hung the second and final bag of Ricco's serum, as Dakota slept off his Valium chaser. He adjusted the flow of the yellow liquid dripping into the doctor's veins and wondered exactly what the stuff was doing to him. He considered Ricco to be a freak of nature. The man was over a hundred years old, but he didn't look a day over nineteen. It just wasn't natural. But he never felt guilt over what he had helped do to Ricco. That was different, that was his job.

He watched the monitor and the vital signs that moved across the screen, and then his eyes settled on the doctor's face. In the quiet of the cell, with the steady rhythm of the man's breathing lulling him to another place, another time, Carlson found his thoughts drawn to when he had first met the General. He had no wife or kids, only the military, but after everything he had sacrificed for his country, he couldn't even find a job to support him in civilian life. That's when the General found him, on the streets, strung out, and slowly dying. The General took him in and cleaned him up. He owed the man more than his life; he owed him his honor. It was a debt he felt obligated to repay.

The story was the same for everyone in the Program. The forgotten, the damned, the neglected, the rejected, the General had found them all. The man gave them back more than their lives. He gave them back something they thought lost forever; their honor and their respect. He gave them the chance to look in the mirror again.

Carlson never questioned anything the General asked of him. He followed orders. It was what he'd been trained to do. The Program had become his life, but as he looked down at Dakota, Carlson felt for the first time that what he was doing might not be right. This man spent his life helping others. He was a doctor. He had helped Ricco, and look what it had gotten him.

Carlson shook his head, ridding himself of the thoughts. He glanced at the monitors and was pleased to see the doctor's vital signs had stabilized. It gave him the leisure to do something he had wanted to do since the man puked all over him. He didn't think the General would mind. In fact, the exact words he remembered were, 'Do whatever you think you have to.' Carlson left the room just long enough to get what he needed. When he returned, he proceeded to bathe Dakota and do what he could for his injured arm.

Trying to be as gentle as he could, Carlson cut away Dakota's soiled and foul-smelling clothes. With a tenderness that belied his gruff exterior, he washed the sweat and filth from Dakota's body. Now that the task was completed, and his patient remained stable, the sergeant took hold of the doctor's shattered arm. "It's a good thing you're out of it, Doc. I'm thinking this is going to hurt." He pulled and twisted until the bones realigned themselves, then coaxed them back down into the channel of flesh and muscle they had been forced from.

Dakota made a face, but never woke, and his heart rate remained steady. Carlson knew it was only a temporary fix, fragmented pieces of bone still lay scattered in the infected wound. But with the arm stabilized, at least it wouldn't cause Dakota agony every time he moved. He finished by taping a rigid splint to the underside of Dakota's arm, and wrapping it tight with surgical gauze. After dressing Dakota in a set of scrubs, he positioned the arm across the doctor's chest and secured it with a sling to minimize movement.

Sergeant Carlson sat back, feeling pleased with himself. Although it had only been a couple of hours since the infusion began, Dakota looked better. The color had returned to his face, and he no longer sweated with fever. He looked at peace.

Carlson listened to the doctor's respirations with his stethoscope, and smiled. "Clear as a bell, Doc." He placed a tympanic thermometer in Dakota's ear and waited for the beep that indicated a reading was ready. "A hundred and one, damn near normal."

A wave of relief surged through him, and unable to contain his feelings, Sergeant Carlson leapt to his feet, punched a fist into the air, and proudly declared to the world at large, "Ladies and gentlemen, it appears as though Doctor Dakota Thomas just might live after all…yes!"

* * * *

Montana killed the single headlight and the engine, then coasted the bike to a stop on the side of the road. The rental car pulled up behind him and went dark. For just a moment before his team joined him, Montana gazed out into the quiet darkness of the desert and willed it to part with her secrets. Their relationship was a complicated one. In all the years Montana had spent asking the desert the questions of his life, he had learned more in her silence than he had through any teachings offered to him. Dakota understood that. Dakota understood that Montana spoke volumes through his silence. *Where the hell are you, Dakota?*

Montana heard the car doors open and the sound of feet on gravel as his team started to unload their gear. He forced his attention back to what needed to be done.

He shook wind-blown hair out of his eyes and stood in front of his men. "We're about a mile from where Dakota and I found Tommy's car. It's only been twenty-four hours since this all went down, so I'm thinking the place is probably still pretty hot, if not with cops, then maybe with this General's eyes. Either way, we need to assume we will not be alone out there. We go in fast, and we go in quiet. Our only advantage is that we're not expected."

Ray grinned. "Well yeah, that and superior firepower, not to mention they don't have me."

Bobby rolled his eyes. Montana just shook his head, retrieved a box of headsets from the trunk, and handed them out to his team. He fitted a wireless earpiece around his left ear. A small, blue flashing light indicated it was working. The rest of the team, save for Ricco, did the same.

"Patrick, take point. The bunker will be in a ravine about a mile due east of here. Give us a sit-rep when you find it. Approach with caution and give anyone there a wide berth. Maintain radio silence until notified otherwise," Montana said.

Patrick gave him a single nod in answer.

"Okay, com-check, channel one." Everyone checked to make certain they had the correct channel set and could hear one another. When Montana was satisfied, he gave Patrick a nod. Patrick headed off at an easy, ground-eating lope, and Montana watched as the darkness swallowed him.

Montana checked his ammo and turned back to the men behind him. "We'll give Patrick a few hundred yards, and then we move."

He noticed Ricco standing away from the rest of his team as though he knew he had no place among them. He looked lost. Montana moved to the back of the car on the pretense of looking for more ammo. His men had walked away from the car, and Ricco would be the only one to hear him. "You okay?"

Ricco jumped at the quiet words. "Yes, sir."

"You don't look okay. I need you with us, Private, not locked up inside your head. Do you understand? I don't have time to look after your ass." Montana motioned to his team. "Neither do they."

Ricco fumbled with his weapon, struggling to load the magazine properly. "Yes, sir." He didn't make eye contact. When the magazine failed to slide in smoothly, he ejected it and tried again.

Montana moved next to him, took the Glock and the magazine from his hands, loaded it correctly, and handed it back to Ricco. "All right…spill it, Ricco. Tell me what's bothering you or stay here."

Ricco stepped closer to the car. "I don't know. This is all a little weird, I guess. Being back here…well, being anywhere really. I have no idea what you expect of me. What's a sit-rep? And what's a com-check? Major, I don't want to mess this up, but I don't know what to do." The words came out in a rush, laced with uncertainty and fear.

Montana smiled as he checked an ammo mag and added it to his bag. "Is your shoulder okay?"

The unexpected question caught Ricco off guard. His hand absently rubbed his injury, and his answer mirrored his confusion. "Yeah, it's fine…I guess."

Montana nodded. "Good. Just stay with me, Ricco. That's all you need to do. I promise I won't let anything happen to you. Understand?"

Ricco didn't look confident, but he nodded his head in silent agreement. As Montana headed back to his men, Ricco abruptly stopped him. "Sir?"

Montana turned and waited for him to continue.

"There is one more thing." Ricco lowered his eyes and hesitated. His voice became a whisper. "Do you remember what I asked you, back at the hospital, about if it looked like they were going to take me again?" He raised his head and looked Montana in the eyes. "Remember the promise you made me?" He sounded like he was about to choke. "Sir, I need to know you'll keep that promise."

Montana stayed where he was. His voice was quiet and

controlled. "I don't forget my promises, Private, and I never go back on my word, but if that doesn't convince you, let me make it perfectly clear. That isn't going to happen." He stepped closer. "Now, I'll ask you one more time…do you understand?"

Ricco gave him a tentative nod. Montana walked back to the team, but decided to keep an extra close eye out for the kid. It wasn't fair bringing him back here and expecting him to keep it together, but Montana, and he supposed Ricco as well, had learned long ago that life was anything but fair.

"Come on, sir. Are we moving or what?" Ray paced in front of the car as if he was about ready to crack from nervous excitement.

Montana tried to suppress a grin. "Let's go find Ray something to destroy. Move out."

Ray waggled his eyebrows as he trotted past Ricco. "About God damn time!"

Montana followed behind his team and made sure Ricco was at his side. He shook his head at Ray. The guy acted like he was on his way to a kegger rather than to face unknown danger out there in the dark, but then, that's why Ray was Ray. Montana wouldn't have it any other way.

* * * *

They made good time, but after fifteen minutes at a steady jog, Ricco lagged behind the group. He tried to keep up, even though the pace was killing him. Physical exercise had not been a part of the

Program's routine, and his thighs quivered as underused muscles objected to the abuse. His lungs burned with every breath. Sweat dripped from his face.

Ricco stumbled once, got right back up and ran a few more steps, and then everything shut down. He tried to will himself forward, but his body refused to follow the commands his head gave it. The desert swirled around him as he fell to his knees. Lowering his head, he sucked the cool night air into his lungs in great gulps, trying to catch his breath. He wanted to call out to Montana, but afraid to make any more noise than he already was, he could only pray they didn't leave him too far behind.

He didn't need to worry. Ricco heard soft footfalls and saw Montana jogging back through the dark for him. Still gulping air, he shook his head. "I'm sorry…Major." He wiped sweat from his face with the sleeve of his shirt. "I can't…I can't keep up." Ashamed by the admission, he lowered his head again, his face sweaty with the effort and his humiliation.

"I'm surprised you made it this far." Montana knelt on one knee at his side, Ricco noticed the man wasn't even breathing hard. "You almost bled to death a couple of days ago. I'm not sure I could have done better."

Ricco's breath came easier now, but his legs still felt boneless. "You're just saying that…to let me rest, sir." He attempted a smile as Montana offered him a hand up. Ricco took it, standing on unsteady legs.

"Does it matter?"

"No, sir, I guess it doesn't."

"Then keep moving, Private. If you stop now, your muscles will stiffen up." Before Ricco had a chance to reply, Montana's hand went to his earpiece.

Montana motioned for Ricco to be quiet as he listened to Patrick.

"Major, I'm three hundred yards south of the bunker. Have eyes on two players. Please advise. Over."

"Give me a visual on our players. Over," Montana said.

"Two males. Big guys. Berets, boots, desert camo, and packing mini-fourteens. Over."

Montana nodded as he digested the information. "Stand by. Over." He turned his attention to Ricco. "Patrick has two men in his sights. They're dressed like military, berets and camouflage outfits, and they're carrying mini-fourteens. Sound familiar?"

"Mini-fourteens? Are they those black, short-nosed rifles?"

Montana nodded.

"Those are the General's men. They all carry those things."

Montana noticed Ricco tense. The one thing more unpredictable than an armed man unsure of his target, was a nervous man afraid for his life. "Relax, Private, or you'll be all worn out when the action starts." He hooked an arm around Ricco's waist. "Come on. Put your arm around my shoulder, and let's go."

Ricco half-limped, half-ran with Montana to rejoin the rest of the team. Montana filled them in, and then asked Patrick for an update.

"They're just standing there posing for me. It's an easy shot. What are we doing?" Patrick asked. "Over."

"Come on, Major. Have Patrick cap these guys and let's get on with it." Ray sounded jealous of Patrick.

Montana gave Ray a scathing look as he answered Patrick. "Negative on the shot. I repeat—hold your fire. Fall back and stand by. We are five minutes from your position. Do you copy? Over."

"Roger that. Falling back and standing by. Out."

Montana caught Ray's irritated stare. "We don't know their check-in schedule or when they're due to be relieved. If we take them out, and they're discovered before we find the bunker where Dakota's being kept, we're screwed."

Ray mumbled something under his breath.

"Stop complaining, Ray, and get moving. We have a long night ahead of us yet. Plenty of time for you to create havoc." Montana, with Ricco beside him, clapped Ray on the back as they ran past.

"Yeah, well, I'm holding you to that," Ray said as he fell in a few feet behind them.

Patrick waited for them, squatted down next to a boulder. He watched the two guards through laser ranging, night-vision spotter binoculars. "Six-hundred-twenty yards. They haven't moved, Major."

Montana bent down on one knee near him and borrowed the

binoculars. "They don't look too happy about being here, either." Montana glanced over his shoulder at Ricco. "I get the feeling a whole lot of people are pissed off at you, Private."

"Yes, sir." Ricco gave Montana half a grin and looked down at his feet.

Montana handed Patrick the binoculars, grabbed Ricco's sleeve and pulled him down next to him. "Do you have any idea where BD-three is from here?"

Ricco's face creased in concentration.

"A good guess will do, Private. With these guards here, we can't use this bunker as a starting point. If we have to sweep a wide perimeter around this place, searching for the trail, we'll never find it in time."

"I'm sorry, sir." Ricco shrugged his shoulders and shook his head. "I spent all my time underground. I couldn't tell you where we are right now, even if it was daylight out."

Montana slumped back against the boulder, the doubt he felt earlier, becoming a tight knot in his stomach. But failure and Montana never did mix, and it didn't take him long to decide what to do. "Patrick, drop our players. Do it now. We'll take our chances with the rest of it."

"Roger that." Patrick unfolded the tripod on the TPG-1, laid the weapon gently on the ground, stretched out prone in the sand, and snuggled the butt of the unique sniper rifle into his shoulder. He unsnapped the front scope cover and set the drop compensator for the .308 ammunition. With a deadly mechanical sound, Patrick chambered a round. Whispering to himself, he went through the final procedures of lining up the shot. "Six-two-zero yards...two clicks up. Windage...two miles right...one click. Target in sight...man needs a shave. Safety off." He relaxed, let out his breath, and slowly squeezed the trigger.

"Wait! Don't shoot—I remember something." Ricco's sudden outburst shattered the silence.

Patrick eased off on the trigger and turned to Ricco with a frown. Ray groaned while Ito chuckled, and Montana voiced what Bobby was undoubtedly thinking. "This better be good, Private."

"Major, the last time they moved me, from BD-three to here, it was early in the morning, and I was pretty drugged, but I could feel the sun on the left side of my face the whole way."

"You sure?" Patrick sounded skeptical.

"Yes, sir. When you don't get to feel the sun on your face for years at a time, believe me, you remember when you do with perfect clarity."

"Okay, that's good. That's very good." Montana peered over the boulder in the direction of the bunker, and then turned to Patrick. "That means they were traveling south." The knot in his stomach unraveled as he pulled a compass from his pants pocket, flipped the cover up, and placed it on the ground in front of Patrick. The fluorescent needle settled on north, and Montana breathed a deep sigh. "Patrick, I would greatly appreciate it if you would find this bunker where they're keeping my brother."

Patrick gave a quick nod, gathered up his rifle, and moved out.

Montana smiled at Ricco as he put the compass back in his pocket. "Well done, Michael." Then he stood and wagged his finger at Ray. "I don't want to hear it."

"What?" Ray feigned his innocence to Bobby. "Wha'd I say, huh?"

"We have two hours until sun up, people. Let's make this happen."

* * * *

It took longer than ninety minutes to find the trail, but no one said a word to Patrick about the miscalculation. Ito followed just behind Patrick and looked at the nearly concealed trail with admiration. "Whoever these guys are, they're good."

Montana grunted in response. He kept a close eye on Ricco. Being here again was clearly starting to unnerve the boy, but he kept it together. Montana gave him credit for that. The kid was a lot tougher than he looked. He came up close behind Ricco and spoke so only the boy would hear him. "You okay?"

Ricco's eyes appeared black in the light of the moon. The pupils had dilated, leaving only a thin rim of iris surrounding them. "Yeah, yeah, I'm good."

Montana wasn't sure that was the truth, but he put a hand on the boy's back and gave him a reassuring pat as he walked by. He followed just behind Patrick and nearly stumbled into him as the man stopped. Patrick, head down, like a dog on a scent, retraced his last few steps. He paused, went down to one knee, touching the ground and then looking intently all around him.

Montana held his breath for a moment, the only sign of the nerves that jangled and screamed for urgency. If Patrick couldn't pick up the trail, no one could. He trusted the man and held tight to that trust, he had to. It was all he had. Montana tried to put thoughts of Dakota out of his mind, and silently berated himself when he couldn't.

Patrick stood and gave a slight nod, almost as if he were reassuring what he found.

"Here," was all he said, and then his movements became more sure as he followed along an invisible path only he seemed to see.

They entered a blind canyon as the first rays of light pierced the sky above them, but night still prevailed where they walked, and they took advantage of the concealment the dark provided. The team followed Patrick in silence. He finally came to an abrupt stop and turned to face Montana. He looked confused and frustrated. Standing in front of a slight indentation in the canyon wall, he turned in small circle, looking at the ground. "What the hell? It just ends. How can it just disappear?" He kept retracing his steps, coming back to the point where the tracks ended.

"Patrick?" Montana stepped up beside the taller, thinner man, the single word asking more than he was willing to verbalize.

Ricco made his way through the men from his position at the end of the ranks, his eyes bright with fear or excitement; it was hard to tell which. "I know this place." His voice, not much more than a whisper, commanded the attention of every man there. "They didn't disappear...look." He reached out a hand and began scraping at the dirt of the wall.

Montana was the first to see what he was doing, but the rest of the team caught on fast. Together, they cleared away the edges of a door that had been camouflaged to look like part of the canyon wall. The disguise was nearly perfect. It had to have been for Patrick to miss it.

"Well, God damn." Ray let out a low whistle at the sight before him.

Ricco's eyes widened as he surveyed the area. "I've been here before. It's been a long time, but I remember." He nodded as though trying to convince himself that he was right. "This is BD-three. I'm sure of it."

CHAPTER 18

Dakota opened his eyes. Just narrow slits against the light. He blinked his vision clear, and the first thought that broke through the confusion was, *Christ, I have to take a piss*. His second thought had him realizing he was too weak to do anything about it. Then suddenly, Bubba was there by his side.

"Hang on, Doc." Bubba handed him a bottle, and helped him use it.

With that fundamental task taken care of, Dakota found Bubba smiling at him and looking very un-Bubba like. The sergeant removed the stethoscope from around his neck and placed it on Dakota's chest.

"Jesus, Bubba, that's cold."

"Shut up."

Dakota complied, but only because he didn't have the energy to argue. "Don't you ever sleep?"

Bubba pulled the stethoscope from his ears and smiled. "Sleep is highly overrated."

Dakota noticed his bandaged and splinted arm. "Bubba, you do love me."

"You have no idea, Doc." Bubba stood and headed for the door. "Lie still and I'll bring you some water. You're a little dehydrated."

As Dakota listened to Bubba's footsteps echo down the hall, the fragmented memories of his close encounter with death began to come together. At first, he thought it was all some sort of weird dream, but from the numbers on the monitor beside him, he knew without a doubt it was real. He took inventory, and realized for the first time that, despite the weakness, he felt better. With the cotton stuffing pulled from his head, he could think again. More than that, he could breathe again.

Bubba returned with a bottle of water and a smile on his face.

"What happened to me, Bubba?"

"I'll tell you what happened, Doc. You're a freaking miracle, that's what." Bubba laughed and slapped the doctor's leg.

Dakota winced at the contact and groaned as he clutched his aching arm. The biohazard infection might have been eliminated, but his arm was far from better. He asked his question through gritted teeth. "The serum worked?"

"Hell yes, it worked. Never saw anything like it before. I mean, you were as good as gone and still breathing, you know? But it brought you back, right back from the brink. God damn! You're a freaking miracle." Bubba laughed again.

Dakota smiled and tried to ease the pain in his arm. "Happy to oblige." He didn't feel like a miracle. He felt like a six-year-old girl could take him down. He closed his eyes, took a deep breath, and was happy to have the opportunity to do so.

* * * *

Dawn brought muted shades of gold and rose to the desert sky. It has always been Montana's favorite time. The quiet that existed between the ending of the night and the beginning of the day gave him a peace that renewed itself once every twenty-four hours. A peace that for the first time in his life, eluded him. Montana stood on a ridge a little outside the circle his team had formed around Ricco, and listened while he briefed his men.

"These bunkers are all the same. The entranceway is one long, narrow hallway with living quarters on one side, and a mess hall, rec room, toilets and stuff on the other. It goes down for about a hundred meters, and then splits. The hallway to the right heads to the med facility, offices, that sort of thing. The one to the left leads to the holding cells. That's probably where they're keeping Dakota."

Montana nodded, as the description matched his recollection of the other bunker. "What about guards?"

"That's hard to say, sir. They probably don't have a full staff with the quick move, but I'd expect to find one on the door, and one, at least, on Dakota at all times. I have no idea how many might be in the med lab or with the General." Michael shrugged.

"So, you're pretty much guessing," Ito said.

Ricco released a deep sigh. "Sorry, but yeah, pretty much. Nothing like this has ever happened before." He turned to Montana. "There is one thing I don't have to guess about, sir. You need to be very careful. The General, he is unpredictable and full of surprises."

"Cool," Ray said. "I love surprises."

"No." Montana shook his head. "No surprises. There has to be a back door, a ventilation shaft, something. There was a hidden door at the first bunker, one in the ground." Montana looked at Ricco and then all around him on the ground.

"Another door?" Patrick asked.

Ricco nodded. "It's how I got out."

"We need to go in quiet. If Ray blows the door, we're screwed." Montana described the door he and Dakota had found at the first bunker. "Split up. It'll be well hidden and probably overgrown with vegetation."

Ray shook his head and mumbled, "Waste of time."

As the rest of the team went to search the ground near the canyon wall, Montana walked up next to Ray, who sat on a boulder with a lump of C-4 in his hand. "Got a problem, Ray?"

"No, sir." But he didn't look happy. He scowled at the bunker door, as his hand bunched and squeezed the innocent looking lump of explosive.

"If there's something on your mind, say it."

Ray jumped off the boulder and looked at the explosive in his hand, then back at the door they had recently uncovered. "We're wasting time, sir. Give me thirty seconds and I'll get you in there. Down and dirty. We blow the door, and they'll never know what hit them. Bobby and I will cover you, you grab your brother, and we get our asses out of here."

Montana leaned against the boulder Ray had vacated. His stillness was in contrast to the immediacy he felt churning inside him. As he looked at the door and thought of Dakota somewhere down there waiting for him, it was difficult not to agree with Ray. "I know, but it's my brother's life in the balance. It's a risk I'm not willing to take. The minute we blow the door, we lose everything."

Ray sighed and looked longingly at the door once more. "Yes, sir."

"I'll try to give you something to destroy when we leave, okay?"

Ray gave a half-hearted grin just as Ito's voice came across on their headsets. "Found it, one hundred yards north of the canyon wall."

Ray perked up at the news. "I get to blow the fucker on the way out?"

"You help me get my brother out of here, and you have carte blanche, my friend."

By the time Montana and Ray had rejoined the rest of the group, the previously concealed door had been revealed. Montana looked to Ricco. "Any idea where this opens up?"

Ricco glanced over his shoulder to the canyon behind him, and back to the door before him. He wiped beads of sweat from his face with a forearm, and nodded. "Yes, sir. Right before the split. There's a secured room there. I've never been inside, but I've seen security go in and out all the time."

Montana thought for a moment. "It's probably the control room for the power, ventilation, that sort of thing. How's it secured?"

"There's a box next to the door. They use their ID badges to get in."

Montana nodded. "I saw them in the first bunker."

Bobby spoke up. "It's possible they aren't working, Major. Ricco said this bunker has been out of service for years. We're talking about sensitive equipment. Without environmental control and proper upkeep, they're probably out of commission, the connections eroded."

"Probably," Montana agreed. "But I'd rather not guess. We do this by the book." He made a point to look at Ray. "No cowboy maneuvers. No mistakes."

Ray rolled his eyes, but wisely kept any comments he might have to himself. Montana turned his attention to Ito and motioned for him to open the door. "We do this quiet. Do not fire unless you have to, understood? Two teams. Bobby, Ray, you're on the main entrance, if there's a guard deal with it, you go on my signal. Ito and Ricco, you're with me. We'll take out the control room. Patrick, stay topside and find a good spot to cover both exits. The lights go out and we move fast and silent. If our cover is blown, then Ray gets to makes some noise." Montana reached up to his earpiece and adjusted the setting. "Stick to channel one, but switch to channel two if necessary. We don't know what they're monitoring. Gentlemen, we insert in one minute. Questions?"

The only sound was of weapons checks. There was no more time for talk. Montana gave a nod to Bobby and Ray. "Move out." As the two men hustled away in the dusky light of dawn, he peered down into the bunker below. "All right…Ito, you're up. You know what to look for. Ricco, stay in my shadow. Once we're down there, do not step in front of me for any reason."

Montana waited for Ito to climb down the ladder. He was always amazed a man of Ito's size could move with the silence and liquid grace of a big cat. When Ito reached the concrete floor beneath them, Montana signaled for Ricco to follow, and started down the ladder himself.

"Good luck, Major." Patrick gave Montana a salute before he disappeared in the shadows.

At the bottom of the ladder, Montana motioned Ito forward, caught Ricco's attention and put a finger to his lips. The kid looked like he was about to puke, but he didn't hesitate or slow them down. As they crept silently down the corridor, they heard muffled voices and occasional laughter coming from the right wing of the complex. So far, so good. Their insertion had gone unnoticed, but Montana knew that was about to change.

The security door was exactly where Ricco told them it would be. Montana signaled for Ito to move ahead to the split, and pulled a metal card from his vest pocket. A small battery and a pair of wires emerged from another pocket, and working quickly, he connected the leads to the card, swiped it down the slot in the card reader, and, de-magnetized the controls. A soft metallic click indicated the lock had been neutralized. Montana looked to Ito, who gave the all clear sign, and pulled on the door. It swung open on quiet hinges.

"How'd you do that?" Ricco whispered in amazement.

Montana smiled, despite the circumstances, and blew on his fingers. "Magic."

It took Montana less than thirty seconds to find the right control panel. He slipped his night vision goggles down over his eyes, waited until Ito and Ricco had done the same, and then called Ray on the radio. "Ray—lights out in five seconds. You ready? Over."

"Ready, willing, and God damn eager, sir. Over."

"Okay, let's dance." Montana pulled the breaker, and they were wrapped in darkness until their night vision illuminated a green-tinted world.

As they left the room, they heard shouting, someone barking orders, and the crash and clatter of metal objects hitting the floor, followed by angry curses. Montana knew they didn't have long before the emergency generators kicked in, and he spurred his team quickly and quietly down the hall until they came to the split. He glanced down the corridor to the right, and saw several men groping their way along the wall toward their position. He turned, looked back down the hallway, and saw the dim outline of Bobby and Ray running their way.

Montana signaled for them to cover the split, and without waiting for a response, he took off down the left hand hallway toward, where he prayed, Dakota was being held. Before he ran five steps, he heard two short bursts of gunfire from Bobby and Ray's position and swore under his breath. They had just run out of time. The emergency generator kicked to life a moment later, and all three men ripped the night vision goggles from their eyes, as even the dim lighting blinded them. The red haze of the emergency lights now replaced the green glow.

"Move!" Montana told the two men behind him. A sudden explosion shook the bunker and almost brought Montana to his knees. He ducked his head as bits of concrete and dirt showered down on him. "God damn it, Ray! I said on the way out!" All thoughts of a quiet extraction dashed, Montana picked up speed, hoping Bobby and Ray could contain whatever went wrong in the tunnel.

* * * *

The lights in the bunker flickered. Both Dakota and Bubba looked at the fluorescents above them. They came back on once, for a second, and then an inky darkness wrapped around them.

"What's going on, Bubba?"

"Nothing to worry about, Doc. This place hasn't been used in years, and the wiring's shot to hell. Lights should be back on in a minute."

Dakota jumped as the unmistakable roar of gunfire echoed through the bunker. It sounded loud in the complete darkness. "Hope that wasn't your maintenance crew."

"Shut up, Doc." Dakota heard Bubba searching for something in the dark. "This ain't right. Something's wrong."

"Gee, you think?" The emergency lights flared to life, and the sudden red glare blinded Dakota. He blinked his eyes until they adjusted to the light and saw Bubba get up to leave the cell.

"Stay put. I'll check it out."

"Yeah, well, I was going to order some Chinese takeout, but okay, I'll stay here."

Before Bubba made it outside the cell door, an explosion reverberated through the entire complex. Bubba ran back and dove to cover Dakota as pieces of concrete rained down on them from the ceiling.

Dakota ducked and covered his head with his good arm beneath Bubba's bulk. "Jesus!"

"What the hell?" Bubba brushed the debris off his patient, and then looked up at the ceiling. His face distorted with fear and apprehension, but it was Dakota's turn to smile.

Bubba saw the smile, and it only added confusion to his fear. "What's so funny?"

Relief flooded through Dakota's soul as another shock wave

shook the cell. "Bubba, if I were you…I would start looking for a safe place to hide."

"What the hell are you talking about, Doc?"

"Trust me on this, Bubba. That's the sound of my brother knocking on the General's door, and you don't want to be anywhere near here when Montana comes for me."

Bubba left Dakota and ran out of the cell. He wasn't gone long before he returned with a sidearm in his hand.

"What are you doing, Bubba?" Dakota shook his head as Bubba locked the cell door and flicked the safety off on the gun. "Don't do it. He'll kill you."

"Shut up, Doc." Bubba strode to the bed and began unhooking the monitor probes on Dakota's chest.

Dakota could smell the fear, the uncertainty coming from the man. "He won't hurt you if he doesn't have to. Don't give him a reason."

Bubba's answer was to slide a round into the chamber and place the muzzle of the gun on Dakota's temple.

"Hell, Bubba." Dakota winced as Bubba pulled him to a sitting position and situated himself behind him on the bed. Not for one minute did Dakota think Bubba would pull the trigger, but Montana wouldn't know that.

* * * *

A rapid exchange of gunfire erupted from the main hallway. From the sound of it, Montana knew Bobby and Ray were engaged in a serious firefight, but they were doing their job. No one followed them down the left split.

He came to the first of a long line of cells and held up his hand, halting the two men behind him. Ito motioned for Ricco to stay put, and cautiously moved to the far side of the hallway, his weapon tight to his shoulder and never taking his eyes off the cell door. Montana stood with his back hugging the wall, waiting for Ito's signal. Ito nodded, and Montana snuck a quick peek into the cell. It appeared empty, but he took no chances. With his weapon at the ready, he nodded to Ito, spun around and swept the cell with the gun. "Clear."

Montana and Ito moved to the next cell, where they repeated their procedure with a quick, cautious efficiency. Ricco followed the two men, his heart pounding in his chest and the gun shaking in his hands as he covered the hallway behind them. He glanced into the empty cells and remembered when they had been his life. He peered through the hellish glow of the red lights, listening in fear to the roar of gunfire being punctuated by the sound of screams. Men were dying back there. Ricco prayed it wasn't Bobby or Ray. In his heart, he didn't count on those prayers being answered. All those years spent screaming in the dark, and not one of his prayers was ever answered. He trusted in Montana far more than he did in God.

When Montana came to the tenth and final cell without any sign of his brother, he was sure of one of two things: either they had Dakota in the medical facility or he was in that last cell. He glanced across the hall at Ito, who gave him a grim nod, and then he took a deep breath and stole a quick look. What he saw brought both relief and physical pain.

His brother sat slumped on a cot in the middle of the room, held upright from behind by an Army Sergeant who had a gun pressed to his temple. He appeared to be dressed in hospital scrubs, barefoot, and his left arm was wrapped and bloody.

Montana fought back his rage and struggled for control as he motioned for Ito to hold his position. With his back to the wall, he called out to the cell. "Dakota?"

"Montana. What the hell took you so long, man?"

"Couldn't find the address. You okay?"

"Been better. My arm's shattered, and there's a big guy holding a gun to my head. Care to rephrase the question?"

Montana sighed. Dakota's voice sounded weak and shaky, but at least his sense of humor was intact. "Can you walk?"

"Doubtful."

"Not a problem." Montana then addressed the man with the gun. "How about it, Sergeant? Drop your weapon now, and let my brother go, and we'll forget this ever happened."

"Can't do that, sir. Doctor Thomas is not going to leave this facility."

That was the wrong answer. Montana whirled around, the sergeant in his sights, and his finger on the trigger. "Oh, he's leaving here, all right. The question is…are you?"

Montana spared a brief glance at Dakota, trying to determine his condition, then turned his attention back to the sergeant. "Drop the gun or I will shoot you."

"No, sir! The General gave me strict—"

"The General's not worth dying for, Sergeant! Drop the God damn gun!"

Ito joined Montana at the door, his weapon trained on the sergeant. Dakota, looking down the barrels of both guns, blinked his eyes and started to say something. "Wait, Montana. He saved my—"

"Shut up, Doc!" Bubba tightened his grip on Dakota and dragged him to the back of the cell.

Montana assessed the possibility of hitting the man without him pulling the trigger first. He hesitated, knowing even if he killed him, the sergeant could still pull the trigger in a spasm and hit Dakota. He needed a distraction, and suddenly was rewarded with one.

Ricco yelled, "Ito!" and began firing down the hallway.

Ito pivoted behind Montana and opened up with his machine gun. As the spent casings bounced off Montana's back, he saw the sergeant's eyes follow the action, and the gun waver in his hand.

Negotiations were over.

Montana took the shot. The bullet hit the sergeant in the chest just right of dead center. His eyes widened with the realization that he was shot, and in that split second, he fired his own weapon, and went down fast, dragging Dakota beneath his bulk.

"Major, it's getting hot in here!" Bullets kicked off the walls all around them as Ito ejected an empty magazine and fed another into his weapon. Ricco was on his knees, screaming at the top of his lungs and blindly pulling the trigger as fast as he could.

"Just cover me!" Montana shot the lock on the cell door and kicked it open. He ran into the cell, dropped his weapon and pushed the sergeant off his brother, then scooped Dakota up and over his shoulders. He knew Dakota was still alive by the groan he heard as he lifted him, but the blood running down Montana's arms didn't bring him any comfort; it wasn't his.

Ito ran into the cell. "I think we stopped them, but we need to get the hell out of here, now!" Ito picked up Montana's discarded weapon, slung it over his shoulder, and followed Montana out the door. He grabbed Ricco by the collar, hauling him to his feet, and the four of them started back up the long, dark hallway.

They didn't get far.

Two khaki-clad soldiers met them at a dead run coming down the hallway. They opened fire, but Ito was quicker. The first one went down with two shots to the head. Ito didn't chance they were wearing body armor. The second one saw his buddy fall and hesitated just a moment before pulling the trigger. The shot grazed Ricco across his side, but it was enough to make him drop his gun and fall to one knee.

"Drop your weapons! Drop your weapons!" The young soldier

was sweating and nervous, but his rifle was aimed directly at Ricco's head.

Ito looked from Ricco to Montana.

"Don't do it." Ricco held his side and grimaced in pain. "Kill him."

"Doesn't work that way, boy." Ito slowly lowered his weapon.

The young soldier swung his weapon on Ito. "Drop it! Fucking drop it, now!"

Before Ito could comply, a single shot broke the tension. The guard's head snapped back and he fell to the floor, a small puddle of blood widening around his head. They all looked behind them to Dakota's cell. Dakota's guard lay on his belly in the cell doorway, his smoking weapon drawn in front of him. Blood trickled from his mouth as he looked up at Montana and struggled to speak.

"Get...the doc out...before...the Gen..." The gun fell from his hands and clattered to the floor. He collapsed in a pool of blood, his eyes already glazing over in death.

Montana thought he heard Dakota whisper something. It sounded a lot like, *Bubba.*

Ito took hold of Ricco's arm and helped him to his feet. "You okay, little brother?"

Ricco clutched his side, still grimacing in pain, "I'll live." He bent down and reclaimed his Glock, but seeing the dead guard's mini-fourteen lying on the floor, he stuffed the Glock into the back of his pants and picked up the weapon.

"Let's go. The sergeant gave us a chance...let's not blow it."
Montana repositioned Dakota on his shoulder and heard a low moan of
pain. "Hang in there, man." He wasn't sure if Dakota heard him or not.

The three men skirted the dead bodies and started down the hall.
No more firing could be heard anywhere in the complex, and the eerie
silence was disturbing. Most of the lights had either been shot out or
had failed with the explosions. They carefully picked their way down a
dark hall filled with smoke and the acrid smell of gunpowder, their feet
crunching on broken glass and chunks of concrete.

They nearly made it back to the first cell, only to be stopped short
by the sight of three armed guards waiting for them. They had them
cold, their weapons at the ready and trained on Montana and Dakota.
Ito wanted to take the shot, Montana could feel it, but he also saw his
dilemma. If Ito fired, he might take the guards out, but not before
Montana was hit.

They stood facing each other like statues frozen in time, neither
side moving, and nobody saying a word. Then a voice spoke from the
shadows. "It seems we are at a bit of an impasse."

Montana recognized the voice from their short phone
conversation. He didn't need to look at Ricco's face to know he was
right.

The General stepped out of the darkness and into the small puddle
of light behind his men, an arrogant smile on his face, so sure of

himself and his victory that he wasn't even armed. He approached them with a slow, casual air, eying each man as though judging their worth before addressing them.

His gaze settled first on Montana. "You must be the Ranger, Montana Thomas."

Montana had never felt intimidated by any man alive, and this man was no exception. He knew a pompous puppet when he saw one. "That's *Major* Thomas to you...General."

The General's haughty laugh reverberated off the walls as he turned his back on Montana. "Of course...Major Thomas." He cupped his hands behind his back and spoke in a condescending tone as he stepped behind his men once again. "My apologies. You have done well to get this far, Major." He turned around and smiled. "But now your little show is over. Put down the good doctor, if you please, and have your men stand down." He held Montana's stare for a moment, daring him to respond, then looked past Ito. "Private Ricco. So nice of you to save me the trouble of looking for you. Welcome home, my boy."

With those few words, Montana saw Ricco's courage dissolve. He knew what the kid was thinking and wanted to tell him to hang in there, they weren't done yet. But before he could say a word, Ricco did the unthinkable. Apparently not trusting Montana to keep his word, he took matters into his own hand.

"No..." He shook his head and swung the mini-14 up and thrust the muzzle under his own chin. "No more."

"Ricco, stand down!" As Montana reached for the gun, a metallic click sounded. Ricco had pulled the trigger on an empty chamber.

The General looked almost disappointed as he shook his head at Ricco. "You see, Private? Fate stands with me this morning. There is nothing you can possibly do to change that fact. What did you think you were accomplishing by running? All you have done is to cost these people their freedom and quite possibly their lives. You can't win, you belong to me."

Ricco shivered uncontrollably as Montana grabbed the barrel of the gun and pulled it away from his chin. The weapon clattered to the floor, and Montana placed his hand on Ricco's shoulder. "This isn't over yet," he told him.

"Oh, but it is, Major. I have been more than patient, but I do have my limits. Now, put your brother down and step aside or I will order my men to kill your African friend." He eyed Ito with admiration. "Which would truly be a shame, for he is a fine specimen of his race."

Ito held his ground and narrowed his eyes at the man.

Montana carefully placed Dakota on the floor next to the wall. He tried to determine how badly Dakota was hurt, but all he could see in the short time he was allowed was a bloody furrow in his hairline—the Sarge's stray shot.

Dakota's eyelids fluttered open, his eyes glassy and unfocused. Montana placed a hand on his brother's cheek. "Take it easy, bro."

"Turn around, Major."

Montana complied. As he turned, he saw the Glock in Ricco's pants—still cocked. He faced the General. "It's your lucky day. I've decided to make you a deal."

The General raised his brows and laughed, his expression one of supreme amusement. "A deal? Really?"

Montana shrugged. "Yeah, what the hell."

"Excuse me, but what part of being surrounded by my armed men, makes you think you are in any position to offer me a deal?"

"The part where you have your men stand down, and I have my man, standing behind you, not blow your brains out."

The three guards surrounding the General adjusted their grips on their weapons and looked at one another in doubt. The one to Montana's right lifted a hand to wipe sweat from his upper lip. It was then Montana knew he could bluff these men. He had been trained better, trained to ignore things like dripping sweat, discomfort, hunger, cold, heat. He had trained his team to be better. These men had no discipline, they were weak. It was something he intended to exploit.

The General spoke to his men in an irritated tone. "Hold your ground. The Major is a desperate man." He spread his hands and smiled. "And I am not nearly as gullible as he would hope. Surely you know that, Major. This game of yours is over."

Montana returned the smile and nodded. "I was counting on it." He focused just behind the nervous man on his right. "Take their asses down!"

The guard to the General's right swiveled around and opened fire into an empty wall. The gunfire prompted the other two guards to turn toward the imagined threat. The second guard looked for something to aim at, and seeing only shadows, panicked.

Montana took advantage of the distraction. He pulled the gun from Ricco's pants. With familiar ease, he threw back the slide. The guard to his left was dead before he emptied his load. The one to his right realized the ploy and swung his weapon back to engage Montana. A bullet cut through his temple, killing him instantly. He dropped to the ground in a puddle of his own blood.

The General ducked and huddled next to the bodies as the third guard hoped to find mercy as he turned to Montana. He held his weapon by the muzzle, his hand off the trigger. Montana brought his sites up and found the center of the shaking boy's head. His finger caressed the trigger. He wanted to squeeze it, but he couldn't bring himself to kill an unarmed man. He lowered the muzzle and in the last moment took a quick step toward the guard. Flipping the weapon around, he brandished the stock and hit the guard on the side of his head. He went down fast following the momentum of Montana's strike.

The General uncovered his head and looked at the blood splattered across his previously pristine uniform. He shook his head while assessing his dead and unconscious men. "No!" He turned his attention back to Montana. "No, you can't do this."

"Yeah? Guess you should have taken my deal." Montana pushed the General hard with his foot to the man's chest until he was sitting on the blood-covered floor.

"Now you see..." Ito turned the barrel of the gun on the General. "That is what you call an end game."

Montana handed the weapon back to Ricco and clapped him on the shoulder. "Always secure your weapon, Private, before stowing it." Ricco took the Glock and just stared at him in a daze. Montana bent down and picked Dakota up.

Ricco seemed to realize he was armed again—and the General wasn't. It was almost as if he didn't know what to do with the advantage. He brought the gun level with the man's face and took a step forward.

Montana positioned Dakota on his shoulders. "There's no time for this, Private." He turned to Ito.

"I'll take care of it."

Montana gave his friend a quick nod and headed slowly up the tunnel, fully aware he was unarmed and headed into the unknown. He kept his pace slow, waiting for Ito to 'take care of it'.

The General spread his arms and gave Ricco a fatherly smile. "Really, Private Ricco, just what do you think you're going to do with that?"

Ricco's face screwed up in confusion at the question. Even now with a loaded weapon pointed at the man who had taken everything away from him, it was clear the amount of control the General still had over him.

Working up the courage through anger, Ricco took another step toward the man and pulled the slide back on the Glock. The weapon shook in his hand. "I was thinking about killing you."

The General clapped and laughed at the announcement. "You don't have it in you, son."

"I'm not your son, you bastard."

The General smiled and stood, his confidence returning. He had spent a lifetime learning how to manipulate the man in front of him.

"I've know you as long as your father. In a way, I know you far better than he ever did. You don't have murder in you, Private. We both raised you better than that."

Ito stepped in front of Ricco. "Maybe he doesn't, but I do. I have no moral dilemmas to get in my way. By the way, I've never been to Africa, asshole."

Before the smile faded from the General's face, Ito squeezed off two quick rounds. The General stumbled back, his hands clutching his chest, his face ashen. He tripped over the body of one of his men and fell with his back to them.

"No!" Ricco took a step toward the downed General, then brought the Glock up and pointed it at Ito. "He was mine! You had no right!"

Ito raised his brow at the weapon cocked and aimed at his chest. "Well, either shoot me or follow me, Private. Whatever one it is, do it quick because there is no time for this. We aren't out of this yet."

Ito started back up the hallway after the unarmed Montana.

"You had no right." Ricco took one last hateful look at the still body of the General and decided he didn't want to die there with him. He removed his finger from the trigger, but kept it ready to fire and took off at a run after Ito.

They caught up with Montana, who had just reached the split. As they rounded the corner, they found Bobby sitting with his back against the far wall. His right arm hung limp and useless at his side, and blood soaked his shirt, but he was conscious.

He looked up at Montana with shocky eyes. "They came at us hard, Major. We got most of them, but there were too many." He shook his head. "Too many." He motioned to Ray, who lay with what was left of his head in Bobby's lap. "I think Ray got hit…but I don't think it's too bad."

Ito heard someone barking sharp orders in the med lab. "Sounds like they're regrouping, Major. We need to get out of here, now."

Montana nodded. "Let's move."

Ito slung his gun over his shoulder, then picked Ray's body off Bobby and cradled him in his arms. "I've got you, Ray." Without being told, Ricco went to Bobby and helped him to his feet.

Weighed down with the wounded and the dead, none of them had the ability to return fire. Adrenaline fueled their flight, as their only hope lay in getting out before the remaining troops rounded the corner. Ito carrying Ray, and Ricco nearly dragging Bobby, made it past the doorway just as the gunfire erupted behind them. Montana had nearly made it over the threshold, when he felt the heat in his back. The impact knocked the breath out of him and sent him flying forward. He cleared the doorway, but lost his grip on Dakota, who tumbled ahead of him. He made it back to his knees in time to see Ito lob a grenade past him through the rubble that was once a door.

"Down! Get down!"

Montana heard the grenade bouncing down the hallway as he dove forward to cover his brother's body with his own. It exploded a few seconds later and the air around him seemed to take on a life all its own. He waited for the concussion blast to pass, and then dragged Dakota away from the open door.

The explosion silenced the gunners inside the bunker, but the silence didn't last long. Once again, the doorway came alive in a hail of bullets as the remaining troops rushed the entrance. With no way to return fire, all Montana could do was cover Dakota and wait for a pause to make a run for it. Suddenly, he heard gunfire coming from in front of him. It had a different sound, higher pitched, and with a steady, single-shot rhythm.

"Yes, Patrick!" Montana took advantage of the cover Patrick provided and moved quickly. Ignoring the pain that shot down his side and leg, he picked his brother up, cradled him in his arms, and stumbled away from the entrance, trying not to think about the fact that Dakota had not moved or made a sound since they made their run down the hall.

Fire continued to come from the bunker, and bullets ricocheted all around him as Montana made it to the outcropping of rock that Ito and Ricco were using for cover. He lay Dakota down, but didn't have time to see to him just yet. Fragmented pieces of pulverized rock stung his face as rounds hit too close to their mark.

Ito pushed another magazine home. "You okay?"

"Not sure."

Both men ducked as another barrage of gunfire exploded around them. Patrick returned fire, but he was badly outnumbered.

"Got any ideas?" Montana asked.

"I'll let you know if I think of any." Ito pushed his weapon over the top of the rocks and blindly emptied another magazine in the direction of the bunker.

"That beautiful son-of-a-bitch!" Bobby's sudden laughter had all three men turning in his direction. He held out a remote detonator. "I found it in Ray's hands."

"What's that?" Ricco asked. It was clear from the expression on his face he couldn't understand why Bobby was so excited. "What are you talking about?"

Bobby's face was streaked with tears and blood, both Ray's and his own. "Ray was running back from the med lab when he got hit. I never got the chance to ask him what he was doing. I just pulled him in and returned fire." He looked at Ray's body next to him. "He set the charges...he had to."

Montana and Ito exchanged knowing glances, and Montana

pointed to the small box in Bobby's hand. "Do it, Bobby. Do it for Ray."

"Do what?" Ricco looked at the box, still confused.

Bobby only smiled. "Prepare to be amazed," he said, and pushed the button.

For half a second nothing happened. When the concussion blast hit, the entire canyon became engulfed in fury. The less wounded dove over the more seriously injured, and they all ducked for cover as what was left of the bunker was thrown into the heavens. Then, as if the celestial judges saw what filth had entered their domain, it was cast away and fell back down out of the sky, finding its way to hell.

No one moved for almost a full minute afterward. All that could be heard was the settling of rocks as they rolled and fell to their final resting place. Montana looked around him and took a head count. Ito and Bobby were still with him. Ricco, already on his feet, shook the dust and debris off his body, and climbed atop the outcrop of rock.

The look on his face was one of awe as he eyed the smoking crater that once had been the med lab. Montana followed his line of sight and saw the charred depressions in the ground where collapsed tunnels led off in two directions.

"Wow...Ray did all that?" Ricco asked.

Montana gave him a nod, and for the first time had a chance to determine if his brother was even alive. Dakota lay beneath him on his side. He slid a finger along his neck, and then lowered his head in relief as he felt a strong pulse. Dakota was alive; for that, he was grateful. His bound arm was soaked in blood, and so was his back. Montana examined him closer, and realized the round that hit him through his Kevlar vest, had first passed through Dakota. His brother was in bad shape, but he wasn't the only one.

Ray was dead. Bobby was wounded and in shock. Ricco's injury didn't seem to bother him, but of those who had gone into the bunker, Ito was the only one who had come out unscathed.

"We need to get Dakota and Bobby out of here." Montana tried to stand, and the world tilted.

Ito helped ease him down. "I'm thinking we're not walking out. Stay here, and I'll get the car and bring it as far as I can."

"Ray's dead." Montana's voice sounded detached and emotionless.

"Yeah, I know. Let's try to keep the body count to one, okay?" Montana only blinked. "Stay put, Major. I'll be back as soon as I can. Patrick will cover you." He gave Montana his gun and put a hand on his shoulder. "You good?"

"Go," Montana said.

Ito nodded and disappeared into the early morning light, a black ghost silently swallowed by the void.

CHAPTER 19

By the time Ito made it back to the car, the sun was on the horizon and the desert day had started coming to life. The sedan was a rental, a Ford Taurus, and as he leaned on the hood and tried to catch his breath, he realized there was no way that car would make the drive through the desert back to the bunker. His body reeled from the heat and the exhaustion of his long run, while images of his injured teammates swirled through his mind. He knew their survival depended on him, but he needed help.

Ito wiped the sweat from his forehead with the palm of one hand, then made a decision. He opened the car door and reached for the cellphone. Montana might be pissed, but he didn't give a damn. He had just killed over a dozen men, and Ray's blood and brains covered him. No one else was going to die if he could help it.

* * * *

Montana thought the hallucinations had finally taken over his mind. He rubbed his eyes with the heels of his hands, and looked twice before he realized the sight was real.

Patrick had come down from the bluff and stood guard over them all. He watched in silence along with Montana as the cavalcade approached. A dozen police and FBI vehicles closed in on their position. Two medi-vac helicopters swooped down and hovered above them. Out of reflex Montana tried to chamber a round, only to find the slide stuck open. He was out of ammo.

Patrick lowered the barrel. "Relax, Major. They're the good guys." He handed him a pair of binoculars. "Lead vehicle, passenger side."

Montana suppressed a groan as he straightened up. He focused the binoculars and there, in the lead car, was Ito. "He was supposed to bring the car, not an army."

Patrick shrugged. He leaned back against a boulder and silently appraised Montana. "How you doing?"

Montana struggled to his feet. "Still breathing." He stood on shaky legs, one hand bracing himself against the boulder, and the other holding his side. He inclined his head toward Dakota and Bobby. "How are they?"

"Still breathing," Patrick said, echoing Montana's words. "Ray's not so lucky."

Montana had nothing to say to that. He bent down next to Dakota as sirens cut through the air. "Help's coming," he told his still unconscious brother. "Hang in there."

The rotor wash had them covering the wounded as the helicopters found places to land. The FBI unit reached them first. Three men exited the vehicles with their weapons drawn and ran toward them, heads ducked against the sand kicked up by the helicopters.

"Drop your weapon, now!" the lead agent yelled at Patrick as he approached.

"Well, hell…" Montana said under his breath. "I thought they were the good guys." Patrick shrugged again, and gently laid his weapon on the ground, then stood and raised his hands, lacing them behind his head.

Montana didn't care when they pushed him to the ground. He didn't care when they wrenched his arms behind his back and cuffed him. He heard Ito yelling from behind the mass of men, "They're wounded! Take it easy!" But his eyes never left Dakota. He breathed a sigh of relief as the medics found his brother and loaded him into the first helicopter.

One of the Feebs pulled him to his feet and started screaming questions at him, but Montana felt his weight give out from under him. The agent caught him on the way down, then pulled back his hand and saw blood on it. "What the hell? Hey, buddy, you hit?" He turned and yelled to the medics. "We have more wounded over here!"

Montana heard the man's voice as if it came from the end of a long tunnel. He pitched forward and fell face down in the sand, wanting the desert to wrap its arms around him and bring him peace. Someone rolled him onto his back, and he opened his eyes to see Ito's face hovering above him. "Get these freaking cuffs off him! I got you," Ito told him, as the world grayed out around him. "I got you."

* * * *

Montana woke up in the Carson City trauma bay. The bullet that passed through his body armor had cracked a rib and exited out the other side without hitting anything life threatening. He agreed to a quick clean and patch-up, but nothing more, even though the doctors insisted on admitting him. Montana's only response was to ask about his brother.

One of the doctors applied another piece of tape to the dressing. "He's still in surgery." He checked Montana's pulse, and gave him a stern look. "And you belong flat on your back in a hospital bed for the next two days."

Montana ignored him.

Ito found him a short time later and helped him into a wheelchair. It didn't occur to Montana to object as Ito pushed him to the waiting room. Montana settled into one of the chairs very much aware that Ito watched his every move with concern. He suppressed a groan as he adjusted his position. "Fill me in."

Ito sat down in the chair next to him and made himself comfortable. "Well, they dropped the charges against you and Dakota. Your good sheriff made that happen."

Montana nodded. The pain meds they had given him were starting to take hold. His head felt fuzzy, and the pain backed down a bit.

"And Bobby?"

"He lost a lot of blood, but he's stable now. They think he's going to be okay."

Montana lifted his head and met Ito's eyes. The last question was the hardest to ask. "What about Dakota?"

Ito shook his head. "They don't know. He's been in surgery for hours. Montana, he didn't look good."

Montana leaned his head back on the chair and closed his eyes. Dakota had to be okay. Ray could not have died for nothing. That one thought kept repeating in his head. Dakota could not die. It simply was not an option.

A doctor in wrinkled surgical scrubs entered the waiting room. He looked almost as tired as Montana felt. His eyes went from one man to the next as if he were unsure who to address. "Montana Thomas?"

Montana tried to stand, but didn't get far.

The doctor motioned for him to stay seated, pulled off his surgical cap, and scratched his head.

"I'm Doctor Santos." He offered Montana his hand. "I'm the staff surgeon on your brother's case."

"How is he?" Montana winced as he shook the hand.

The doctor frowned at Montana's show of pain and sat down in the chair next to him. "The short version is we have him stabilized. He's in recovery right now, and they should be moving him up to ICU shortly."

"How about the long version."

Doctor Santos sighed. "The bullet passed through a lung. He has a chest tube, and his breathing is stable, but his arm is another story altogether. He's going to need multiple surgeries later on, but at the moment, we're mostly concerned with the infection. All in all, I'm surprised he's doing as well as he is."

"He's going to live?" Montana got right to the question that weighed most heavily on him.

"Nothing's definite, but if I were a betting man, yeah, I'd lay odds on him coming out of this."

It was all Montana needed to hear. He felt his eyes fill. Blinking back tears, he nodded to the doctor. "I want to see him."

"You sure you're up to it? You looked a little wiped yourself."

"I want to see him." Montana hung his head and covered his face with his hands. He took several deep breaths, attempting to control his emotions and keep from sobbing outright. Exhaustion almost had him loosing it, but even if he didn't fool anyone, he managed to keep it together.

Doctor Santos laid a hand on Montana's shoulder and gave him a moment to compose himself. "Yeah, okay. I'll make sure they tell you when he gets to ICU." He turned to Ito. "Make sure he doesn't over do it or they might end up as roommates."

"I'll do my best," Ito promised. "But he's not an easy man to keep down."

"I can see that." Doctor Santos gave Montana a gentle pat on the back and left to see to his patient.

* * * *

Intensive care units and their staff are not big on visitors. There are no chairs in patient's rooms or any amenities to welcome long stays. Regardless of that fact, Montana stayed by Dakota's bedside. After a few hours, one of the nurses took pity on him and brought him a chair. He moved out of the way when they needed to care for his brother, but he refused to leave, and no one had the courage to ask him. Ito brought him clean clothes and news of what the Feds were doing, but Montana never left Dakota for long.

As the hours passed, memories of their childhood drifted in and out of Montana's mind. For as long as he could remember, it had been his job to look after Dakota, but more often than not it had been Dakota taking care of him. They were only thirteen months apart; two wild boys raising hell and causing trouble through the quiet streets of Caliente. Lilly Thomas had never married and worked long hours to support her boys, which left Montana and Dakota alone far too long, and far too often. Trouble was a close and constant companion.

Montana had been ten the first time he tried to run away. He didn't get far, and nine-year-old Dakota followed him. Montana threatened him, pushed him, and finally bloodied his lip, but Dakota wouldn't back down. He stood, tearful and bloody, and told Montana that he had to come home. That time Montana relented, but he got sneakier as the years went by.

At every turning point, every crisis in his life, Dakota had been there for him. His brother was the one constant in his turbulent, unpredictable existence. An unspoken bond held them together, a union of shared trusts and secrets of the soul. They were confidants and conspirators, but above all, they were friends, and to Montana that was an amazing thing.

A sad smile tugged at his lips as he stared at Dakota's pale face. Dark lashes stood out against almost translucent skin. Montana had never seen his brother so still before. It scared him, and the only person who could understand that was Dakota. Tears welled and spilled down Montana's face. Too tired to care, he let them slide unheeded and unconcerned as to who might see them. He sat in the calming quiet of the ICU and held his brother's hand. Laying his head on the mattress next to Dakota's arm, Montana closed his eyes and waited for him to wake.

Michael Ricco had once again become property of the United States Government. Neither Montana nor Ito had been allowed to see or talk to him since they had been seized in the desert.

On the second day, Cal Tremont came—to ask questions, and out of genuine concern for Dakota. He told Montana the Feds had excavated what was left of the Bunker, and what they found there, only gave them more questions to ask.

Cal shook his head as he looked at Dakota. "I never should have called him, never gotten him involved. I should have just gone looking for Tommy myself."

"You aren't to blame for this, Cal."

"Maybe not, but that doesn't make Tommy and the others any less dead, now, does it?"

Cal stood at the foot of Dakota's bed and shifted his considerable weight from one foot to the other. It was clear to Montana the man had something to say, but he let him get to it in his own way.

"You know…" Cal began. "The Feds had been all over what's left of that bunker. They found forty-two bodies. Most have been identified as ex-military. Some were AWOL, others had been dishonorably discharged."

Montana kept his eyes on Dakota, but his attention was with Cal. "They already briefed me, Sheriff."

"Yeah, I know what they told you. I also know what they didn't tell you."

That brought Montana's eyes to Cal's broad face. "What didn't they tell me?"

Cal hesitated, started to say something, and then turned away from Montana and looked down at Dakota. "I've known you and Dakota all of your lives." A fond smile formed on his lips, followed by a husky chuckle. "Little monsters, the both of ya. I'd be lying if I said otherwise." The smile broadened as he shook his head. "I can't begin to remember how many times your momma sent me chasing after you when you ran away. Always into one thing or another… I'm surprised I have any hair left at all after dealing with the two of you." The smile faded, and Cal sighed. He pointed a meaty finger at Dakota. "He gonna be okay?"

"They think so, eventually, yeah. Cal, what didn't they tell me?"

The sheriff ignored the question and just nodded. "Good. He's a good boy, always was. I gave him a lotta' grief growing up, but only 'cause I knew he could make something of himself. He didn't disappoint me."

Impatience clawed at Montana. "Cal?"

With another sigh, Cal finally told Montana,. "They pulled everyone out of that bunker, boy, and your General wasn't one of 'em."

Montana blinked several times. "That's not possible. Ito said he hit him twice in the chest, and Ito doesn't miss."

"I'm not saying he did. I'm only telling you what I know as fact. Forty-two bodies—all non-coms. Not one of 'em matches your description of this General. Is your man sure he was dead? The guy could'a had a vest. You did…saved your life."

Montana looked away and shook his head. "There wasn't time. I don't know." His mind raced through the events of that morning: where they were, where the General was, the only two exits they knew about, and Patrick was covering those. He would have seen him if he climbed out. Montana was having a hard time believing the General could have escaped, and an even harder time with what that meant if it were true. "You're telling me he got away? That the man who did this to my brother is still out there?"

"I'm just telling you we don't have a body."

Montana took Dakota's hand and stared at the wall ahead of him. He had no expression on his face, but his mind was churning.

Cal turned to leave, and then stopped at the door. "Montana, you did good. You got your brother back, and you shut down that hellhole. Don't go spoiling it by doing something stupid, boy. Let it go. Let the Feds do their job, and just let it go."

Montana continued to stare at the wall. "One of my men is dead, and they haven't even released the body to his family yet. Another is badly wounded and might lose the use of his right arm. Ricco, and who knows how many others, spent most of his life at that man's mercy." He squeezed Dakota's hand. "And the son-of-a-bitch tortured my brother. Now, you tell me he is out there somewhere, still breathing?" Montana's voice was measured control. "Don't worry, Cal. I don't do stupid. I never did."

Cal sighed and scrubbed one meaty hand over his face. "Damn, don't make me come after you again, boy. I'm gettin' too old for this shit."

Montana simply stared at him, and then turned away again.

Cal, having said what he came to say, left Montana alone with his thoughts and his brother. He wasn't worried. Montana Thomas was the one person he never worried about. If anyone should be worried, Cal thought it should be the General. If the man knew Montana only half as well as he did, he would start running and never look back.

CHAPTER 20

The first thing Dakota saw upon opening his eyes was Montana's face.

"You done having all the fun yet?" Montana asked him.

He smiled and wanted to say something witty, but fell asleep instead.

The next time he opened his eyes, it was Ricco's face staring back at him. "Where's Montana?" he asked. His voice didn't sound like it belonged to him. It was thick and gritty, and it hurt his throat to speak.

"Not far," Ricco told him. "In the waiting room, sleeping. He's hardly left this room for three days."

Dakota looked around the clean, bright room. His last clear memory was of Bubba holding a gun to his head in a dark, filthy cell. Everything after that was a mirage of images and half-remembered dreams. "How we doing?"

Michael shrugged and stuffed his hands into his pant's pockets. It was clear being here made him uncomfortable. "One of Montana's team members, Ray, he died at the bunker. Another one, Bobby, he got shot pretty bad, but you took the worse of it."

Dakota tried to process that information and put faces to the unfamiliar names, but he couldn't. As more memories came to the surface, one stood out crystal clear—his life and death struggle with the avian influenza. "Did you know about the serum?"

Ricco looked puzzled. "The serum? Yeah, I knew about it. They took my blood all the time, and talked a lot about a super-serum that would cure anything, but they were afraid to use it. Everybody they gave it to...died." He peered closely at Dakota. "They gave it to you?"

Dakota nodded. "You saved my life, I think."

A bright smile broke out on Ricco's face. "You saved mine, I'm happy to return the favor."

Seeing his boyish smile, after having had a brief taste of what Ricco went through for over eighty years, left Dakota in awe of Ricco's strength. "Jesus, Michael." Dakota didn't know what else to say. He couldn't believe the hell that had been this man's life. "What about you? What happens to you now?"

Ricco sighed and ran a hand through his hair. "Everybody seems to want a piece of me."

Dakota noticed his hair had grown a little longer, and the boy looked like he had gained some weight. "Everybody? Do you mean the government?"

Ricco nodded and pursed his lips in frustration. "The government, people from the military, the FBI, medical research people from who knows where. It seems I am a person of great interest." He tried to smile again, but the attempt was pitiful.

"Is that what you want?"

Ricco shrugged his shoulders. "Don't know that I have a whole lot of choice."

"Yes, you do. Everyone has a choice."

"It's okay. If they can figure out how to do some good, you know, with what they did to me, I can't say no to that."

Dakota raised his eyebrows. "You're a better man than I am, Michael J. Ricco. I sure as hell don't want them to know I'm carrying the serum. If they do, they'll never leave me alone."

Ricco gave him another half-hearted smile and a shrug. "They don't need to know—they have me." A worried look replaced the smile, and Ricco took a deep breath. He turned around, stepped to the window, and stood staring into the distance.

Dakota could tell there was something more on his mind. "What is it?"

He didn't answer right away, and shifted his weight nervously, as though trying to decide whether to speak at all. "Doctor Thomas, you need to know something. They told me not to tell you, but I think you have a right to hear it."

Dakota wrinkled his brow. "What?"

Ricco turned to face him. "He's still out there…the General. He got away."

Dakota fell quiet, as what Ricco told him sunk in. When he spoke again, his voice was barely audible. "It's not over, is it?"

Ricco shook his head. "No, sir, I'm afraid it's not."

"He's not going to stop looking for us, is he?"

Ricco confirmed Dakota's fears with a matter-of-fact statement born from a lifetime of experience. "He'll either take us or he'll kill us. He thinks he owns you now. You know that."

Dakota did know, but hearing it put that way sent a cold fear creeping down his spine. He didn't answer Ricco, there was no need. Dakota turned away, and noticed the armed guard outside his door for the first time. The man was obviously military. "Who's he here for, you or me?"

Ricco glanced over his shoulder. "He belongs to me. Guess they're afraid I'll take off."

Dakota suddenly felt exhausted. "I'm sorry, Michael."

"It's okay, sir. I'm not sure how I would handle complete freedom anyway. It's been too long."

A nurse came up behind Ricco and cycled Dakota's blood pressure cuff. Apparently, she didn't like the numbers she saw. She looked at Ricco. "I think he's had enough for today." Her voice was quiet, but it was clear she wouldn't tolerate an argument.

"Yes, ma'am." Ricco smiled at Dakota. "I'll see you later, Doctor Thomas." He started to turn away, but Dakota stopped him.

"Ricco, I need to talk to Montana."

Ricco nodded "Yeah, he needs to talk to you, too." He glanced over at the nurse. "They'll only let one of us in at a time. It was supposed to be Montana, but Ito wouldn't wake him."

"That's good. Let him sleep. I'm not going anywhere for a while." He smiled at the nurse. "I have a feeling they will be amazed at my recuperative abilities."

It was Ricco's turn to smile. "I have no doubt about that, sir." His guard fell in step behind him like a shadow, as Ricco walked back to the waiting room and let Dakota sleep and heal.

* * * *

By the end of that week, the government had finally relented and released Ray's body to his family. He was from Virginia, ironically, not far from where Ricco had grown up. Montana and Ito were going to the funeral, Patrick would meet them there, but Bobby, much to his dismay, was not well enough to go.

Dakota, as predicted, had amazed his doctors with his remarkable recovery. He still needed the additional surgeries on his arm, but the chest tube was out, and he was moving on his own again. Granted, he hurt all over, got dizzy when he stood, and felt weak and useless, but he was alive. The same could not be said of Ray.

"I'm going," he told Montana.

"They won't release you."

Dakota made a face and waved off Montana's comment. "I'm a

doctor, remember?"

"No, you're a patient, remember? Dakota, you almost died seven days ago. You aren't ready for this. It's a five hour plane ride just to get there, and that's not including the service or the burial. Besides, you never even met Ray."

"He died saving my life. I'm going."

They stared at each other in silence, until Montana finally blinked. "I'm not going to talk you out of this, am I?"

"Not a chance."

"Then you have to promise me, you will listen to Ito."

"If I have to."

Montana sighed and stood up. "I don't think it's a good idea, but I'll make the arrangements."

Dakota smiled as he watched his brother walk out of the room. For the first time in a long time, he felt as though he had just won an argument with Montana.

* * * *

He was tired, and all he wanted to do was sleep, but they wouldn't let him. Every time he drifted off, he would find Bubba next to him, jabbing him with needles, hooking him up to one monitor or the other, observing him, always observing him, a specimen in a glass cage.

The General was impressed that he had healed so quickly, and wanted to see what more he could do. What limits could he push and still keep him alive? Dakota was certain he didn't want to find out, but there were no more choices left to him. No one was coming to rescue him this time. All the good guys were dead, and no one knew where he was. Desolation, hopelessness, and isolation owned him as much as the General did.

Bubba jostled his still healing arm. "Sorry, Doc." He grabbed Dakota's wrist and elbow.

Dakota knew what came next, and he tried to brace himself for the pain.

"Orders," Bubba explained. He applied pressure to the mending bones, and the snaps could be heard over Dakota's screams.

Dakota came out of the nightmare with a sudden start. His left arm, encased in a fiberglass cast and resting in a sling, had slipped beneath his weight as he slept. The plane seat reclined as far as it went, but he still slumped to one side, with the injured arm wedged between his body and the window. The dull, steady pain the position caused was what woke him in the guise of a nightmare.

Sweat ran down his face and back as he tried to orient himself. The hand gently touching his arm caused him to jump. He turned to find Montana sitting next to him.

"You okay?"

Dakota tried to slow his breathing. He could feel his heart beating in his ears. He tried to shake off the effects of the dream, but could tell from the look on his brother's face that he had failed miserably.

"Where are we?" he asked, instead of lying to him and telling him he was fine. Montana was right about one thing, he was not ready for this, either emotionally or physically. The nightmares plagued him whenever he closed his eyes. The drugs they gave him helped for a while, but then the dreams started sneaking through, and with the sedatives in his system, he couldn't just wake up. He had to endure whatever the General and Bubba did to him until the drugs wore off. He was jumpy and sleep-deprived, and despite Ricco's magic serum, he had a long way to go before he recovered completely. Simply put, he was a wreck.

"We just entered Virginia. Should be landing in about ten minutes or so." Montana's eyes silently appraised him.

Dakota knew Montana didn't like what he saw, and there wasn't squat he could do about it.

"Do you need Ito? Something for pain?"

Dakota wiped a hand over his eyes. "Just stop, already! I don't need Ito, and I sure as hell don't need something for pain. What I need is for you to stop bugging me. Think you can do that...big brother?"

Montana stared at him as though he spoke a foreign language.

Dakota saw the look and immediately regretted his tone, even though he didn't have much control over it. "Shit, Montana. It's as good as it's going to get, okay? Just let it alone."

Montana slowly shook his head, his expression difficult to read. His words were not. "Understand something. You have no choices here. You were discharged against medical advice and against my better judgment. You gave up any right to express your opinion when you signed those release papers. You'll do what I say, when I say it, or I swear I'll have you flown, under military escort and heavily drugged, back to the hospital. Are we clear…little brother?"

The plane dipped in altitude as it made its descent and preparation for landing.

"Can I go take a piss without your permission?" Dakota asked.

Montana stood up and helped him to his feet, making sure he was steady as he guided him to the coffin-size bathroom at the end of the aisle.

Dakota turned to him before closing the door. "Gee, want me to leave the door open so you can make sure I don't drown in the toilet or something?"

Montana ignored the sarcasm. "I'll wait outside."

Dakota shook his head and closed the door. Only when he was alone did he let go. He leaned against the door and started shaking. He couldn't stop. Then the tears came. Sliding quietly down to the floor, Dakota dropped his head to his chest, and muffled the sound against his arm. The sobs tore through his body until his chest hurt. The shaking didn't stop, but settled to the point where he could hide it. He sat with his knees pulled up tight, his eyes squeezed shut, and his head buried in the crook of his arm.

He stayed like that until he thought he could stand again. He saw the reason for Montana's concern when he looked at his image in the polished metal that passed for a mirror. Dark circles shadowed his eyes, now puffy and red from the tears. He had lost weight, and his face was gaunt and pale. Green eyes looked back at him with a haunted expression.

"Get a grip," he told his reflection. He turned the faucet on, splashed cold water on his face, and then gathered what dignity and courage he had left to him, and prepared to meet his brother's concern once more. The constant, silent appraisal was almost more than he could take. As close as he and Montana were, this was the one thing they could never share.

The only other person who might understand what he was going through, would be Michael Ricco. He wondered how Ricco dealt with the nightmares, if he feared sleep or if they had managed, after all that time, to kill the part of him that dreamed. In his conversations with Ricco, he felt an emptiness about the man, as if that part of his soul where hope lies had been taken from him. Michael Ricco did not know how to hope. Dakota started to shake once more as he realized why.

CHAPTER 21

Several Humvees met them at the airport, complete with an armed military escort, who obviously were not there to pay their respects to Ray or his family. Not one dress uniform in sight. These troops were all business, and their weapons were not for show. They came loaded and ready for battle, with full body armor, helmets, and ammo belts bulging with additional rounds.

Dakota stepped to the cabin door and blinked against the bright Virginia sunlight. After the dim interior of the plane, it blinded him. Not having much choice in the matter, he allowed Montana to take him by his good arm and ease him down the steps of the plane. He eyed the impressive escort with a mixture of concern and awe. "I didn't know you were that important."

"I'm not." Montana gestured toward Ricco, who was in front of them, walking steadily toward the waiting vehicles.

From behind them, Ito's voice registered his disgust at what had become of Private Ricco. "The government's just protecting its property."

Dakota watched as Ricco climbed into the Humvee without any expression on his face. "He says he's okay with all of this."

"Bullshit," Ito said under his breath, but still loud enough for Dakota to hear, which brought a smile to his lips for the first time in a very long time.

A soldier opened the door for him, and Dakota froze. A sudden, unwanted image slammed into his brain: a different car, alone on a desert road, three armed soldiers, and the feel of gravel under his back as they forced him to the ground. He took a step back, and then another, and shook his head.

"No." He couldn't tear his eyes away from the dark interior.

"Dakota?" The voice was quiet in his ear, but the light touch at the small of his back made him jump. He blinked, and the present came into focus with a dizzying rush. His knees started to buckle. His stomach leapt to his throat, and he struggled to swallow the bile back down. His every sense was suddenly running in high gear. He felt the sun scorching his back and the cold sweat running down his spine. The light hurt his eyes and he wished for his sunglasses, but remembered they were in his bag, which had just been stowed in the Humvee.

Montana stepped in front of him, demanding his attention. "You don't have to do this."

Dakota took a deep, steadying breath, stiffened his shaking knees so he wouldn't fall down, and pushed the memory of his capture out of his head. "Yes, Montana...I do."

It took more courage than he liked to admit, but he climbed into the Humvee and sat next to Michael Ricco. The soldiers gave no indication of witnessing the incident. They never said a word. Everyone split up into their respective vehicles, and forming their own small cavalcade, the band of survivors went to say goodbye to Ray.

* * * *

God help them all, Ray's family was Catholic. The service itself was over an hour-and-a-half long and attended by half the county. People crowded in the back of the church, standing when all the pews filled up.

Ray's family took up the first two rows on both sides, with Montana, Dakota, Ricco, Patrick and Ito, sitting just behind them. The temperature inside the tiny church bordered on stifling, and even the priest sweated and fanned himself as he praised Ray's virtues.

One of the parishioners sitting next to Montana, nudged him with a boney elbow and pointed to the sleek communication device Montana had curled around his ear. "That one of those new digital hearing aids? I wanted to get one of those beauties, but medical assistance won't pay for it. Go figure." The man gave Montana a knowing grin, exposing tobacco stained teeth.

Montana stared the man into silence, and then turned his attention back to the service. Ray would have hated this. Montana knew it. The man being canonized in the church, and the Ranger who had been instrumental in saving Dakota's life, were two very different people. Montana took a closer look at his brother. Dakota should not be there, but when the FBI and the federal government learned that Ricco, as well as Dakota, planned to attend Ray's funeral, a plan was put into motion. Montana had no choice in the matter. His safe house and his weapons stash had been confiscated, his private investigator's license revoked, and his standing as a retired Ranger was in question. Montana was allowed to help with the official operation on one condition: Dakota had to remain oblivious to the fact that he was human bait, a lure along with Ricco, meant to draw the General out from hiding.

Montana refused until they informed him the charges against him and Dakota, involving the murder of the man who had tried to kill Ricco at the hospital, could and would be reinstated. It was bullshit, all of it, but Montana knew that guilty or innocent, the charge alone meant Dakota would never practice medicine again. It didn't matter what they did to him, but Montana would not have Dakota's career ruined. He conceded to the conditions with one of his own: he was in charge of security. In the end, they agreed to a compromise. The government would supply the men, Montana and Ito would deploy them, but Montana reported directly to a government official. It was hardly a compromise, but Montana took it, as if he had the choice.

Dakota tried to concentrate on the words the priest spoke, but his mind kept wandering. He wondered what Ray had been like. All he had to go on were Montana's and Ito's description of the man. "Ray bordered on crazy," Ito had told him on the plane. "Part of that is why he made such a good Ranger. Fear meant nothing to Ray. He hasn't seen or talked to his family in years, and they're only here now, because the government is sending them his pension."

Sitting in the tiny church in rural Virginia, Dakota didn't care about any of that. He just wanted the service to end so he could have some air. He couldn't breathe. He didn't know if it was the priest's rambling monotone or the cloying incense combined with the heat, but he had to have some air—now.

He stood abruptly, and excused his way out of the pew in the middle of a eulogy by one of Ray's brothers. The man, who could have been Ray's clone, stopped speaking, and every eye in the churched watched as Dakota made his way down the pew. Small, old women gave him disgusted looks, and Dakota mumbled apologies for stepped on toes and the interruption. The last man in the pew took his arm lightly, and asked if he needed help. Dakota just shook his head, took his arm back, and walked as quickly as he could up the aisle.

Montana came halfway out of his seat to follow, when Ricco, of all people, stopped him with a firm hand on his arm. His whisper was lost in the murmur of the crowd. "Let him alone, Major. Where can he go?"

Montana reluctantly sat back down. He knew Dakota needed time to himself, and Ricco was right—where was he going to go? However, Dakota was not like Montana. Dakota felt everything too much. What had happened to him inside that bunker was not over for him. He relived it every time he closed his eyes. The smart-ass, wisecracking brother Montana had always counted on had disappeared, and he didn't know what to do to get him back. Dakota was dying inside, right in front of Montana's eyes, and it was killing him. Dakota was the nurturer, the one who took care of things, but now he was the one who needed help. Everything Montana tried to do only pushed Dakota further away.

Montana understood Dakota needed time alone, but the thought of what happened when he was left alone in the safe house came to mind. He heard the back doors of the church open and close. Dakota was safe. Montana had seen to that. He tried to stop worrying and focused on the service, reminding himself of Ray's sacrifice, but that lasted all of five minutes before jangling nerves got the better of him. Jumping up, he stopped the service yet again. He shook his head at Ricco and Ito, silently telling them not to follow. Making no apologies, and ignoring the glares from disgruntled parishioners, Montana strode down the aisle to the doors at the back of the church.

* * * *

Dakota pushed the church doors open and gasped for air. He was suffocating; he needed fresh air, and he needed space. Truth be told, he didn't know what he needed. If he could have, he would have started running right there and not stopped until he collapsed. But he knew no matter how far away he ran, he could never outrun himself. He couldn't outrun the pictures in his head, either. They followed him wherever he tried to hide.

With some discomfort, he sat on the stone steps of the church, hung his head, and waited for his breathing to slow. It didn't take long for the beautiful Virginia day to seep into his awareness, and canting his head upwards, he saw a cloudless, captivating blue sky. A soft breeze carried the delicate scent of honeysuckle, and the sun felt warm and soothing. His troubles momentarily forgotten, he closed his eyes and let the healing rays bathe his face.

"You okay, boy?"

Startled, Dakota's eyes snapped opened and he turned in the direction of the voice. An old woman sat on one of the benches near the church door, smoking a hand rolled cigarette. At least, he thought it was a cigarette, until the smell wafted his way.

She could have been eighty or a hundred; it was difficult to tell. Her face was lined and leathery, the face of someone who had spent their entire life outdoors. Her shoulders were stooped, and her fingers gnarled, but from the humorous glint in her eyes it was evident that hard work had bent, but not broken her.

She offered Dakota the joint. "You want a hit, kiddo? You sure as hell look like you could use one." She started out laughing, but ended up in a coughing fit that made her eyes water.

Dakota had to smile. He shook his head. "No, thanks. I'm good."

"Bullshit." She cast him a toothless grin, and offered the joint again. Dakota glanced over his shoulder at the closed church doors, and then looked back at the old woman. "Oh, grow some gonads. They'll be in there a goodly spell yet. Father Andrews ain't never seen such a crowd, and I reckon he'll make the most of it. Carries on like a shut in on visiting day, he does, why the hell you think I came out here?" She held out the joint. "Come on…it ain't killed me yet."

Dakota shrugged. "What the hell." He took the joint, inhaled a long drag, and immediately started coughing. He hadn't smoked anything, let alone pot, since his undergrad days. The old woman cackled and slapped her knees at his reaction. When his eyes stopped watering and he could speak again, he handed the joint back to her. "Lady, that's some seriously good shit."

She inclined her head in recognition of the praise. "Thanks. I grow it myself." Then her toothless grin reappeared. "Ray used to be one of my best customers, but don't you go tellin' his mama on me now, that woman never did want to hear the truth about her boys."

Dakota smiled at the grinning, silver-haired, pot-smoking outlaw of an old woman, and realized he hadn't had anything to smile about in weeks. "Thank you, ma'am. My world's been a little screwed up lately. You're a refreshing change."

"Nothing wrong with this world that can't be fixed, sonny. And if it can't be fixed, well then, this surely does help make it seem—"

Dakota watched in confusion as the woman jerked back suddenly. It was just a small movement, then a thin stream of blood trickled down the bridge of her nose from a round hole in the center of her forehead. The joint still dangled from her fingers, and for some reason that was the image he fixated on…until he heard the voice.

"You have caused me a great deal of trouble, Doctor Thomas."

Dakota froze. He couldn't turn around. If he didn't look, it couldn't be real. The sound of soft footsteps come up beside him. Looking down, he saw black dress shoes. He knew those shoes. Swallowing down the bile that wanted to come up, he slowly turned his head away from the dead woman and looked up.

The General smiled down at him.

In desperation, Dakota blurted out the first thing that came to mind. "The army has men all over the place. You'll never get out of here alive." He hoped he sounded more sure of himself than he felt.

"If you're referring to the men who escorted you from the airport, or the ones who have been carefully positioned all around this church and the cemetery, most of them are mine. The ones who weren't are now dead."

Dakota followed the sweep of the General's arm and saw that he was right. It was a small rural church with a cemetery off to one side, where an open grave sat waiting to receive Ray's body. Surrounding it were armed soldiers, the same soldiers he thought were there to protect him, but they all had their weapons trained on Dakota, not the General. Dakota glanced involuntarily toward the church, where Montana and Ito sat.

The General merely shook his head, as if reading his thoughts. "There are explosives rigged to the entire church. Unless you want more innocent people to die, I suggest you forget the heroics and come quietly with me."

Dakota felt his world shrinking, the lens of the microscope bearing down on him. "How?" It was a useless question, but all he could think to ask.

"You are wonderfully naïve, Doctor, not a jaded bone in your body. It's quite amusing. The fact is we have cells everywhere, in every branch of the government. You can't stop this anymore than you can stop the sun from rising. All you and your brother have accomplished is a momentary delay. The Program has been relocated, and it will go on, with you as its primary subject."

Dakota stalled, hoping for a miracle. "Ricco's inside. You'll kill him if you blow the church."

The General sighed. "That would be unfortunate, but as I said, we have you now, don't we? We're wasting precious time, Doctor. Come quietly and no one else has to die—not Ricco, not your brother, not any one of the men, women or children in this church, who have no idea their lives depend on the choice you make at this moment." The General pulled a large handgun from under his jacket, chambered a round, and pushed the safety off. "Now, choose."

Dakota slowly stood, his knees shaking. "I don't have a choice."

"I was so hoping you would see it that way."

Dakota glanced back at the church doors once more and the old woman sitting there. "You didn't have to kill her. She was no threat to you."

"She was nothing, just an old woman, long past being useful to anyone. I gave her a quick, clean death, probably better than she deserved. Now move, Doctor."

Dakota felt like he was trapped in a bad dream and waited to wake up. He walked in a daze down the steps, his movements ushered by the General and two armed guards who had moved in closer. One came up behind him and gave him a shove with the barrel of his rifle.

"Over there." He motioned to a white cargo van with a flower shop logo on the side, parked on a narrow stretch of blacktop that served as a road between the cemetery plots.

They had covered half the distance to the van when Dakota heard the door to the church open. He turned to see Montana standing in the doorway, his eyes on the dead woman. Montana looked up and their eyes met. For a fraction of a second, time seemed to stand still as two brothers stared at one another across an unbreachable chasm. Then the spell was broken, and hell lashed out.

"Take care of it!" The General pushed Dakota hard, while the soldier raised his rifle and fired, his silenced weapon not making a sound. Montana was on the move and reaching for his own weapon when the bullet hit. Dakota watched him fly backward as if a great hand had swatted Montana like a bug.

"Move!" The General shoved Dakota again.

He stumbled, regained his footing and looked back over his shoulder. Montana didn't move, and stayed exactly as he had fallen. All

Dakota could see was blood flowing down the side of Montana's head.

"No!" He didn't know if the word was meant as a denial that Montana was down, or in response to the General's order. All he knew was this had to end. He would not have his life taken from him as Ricco's had been.

The General urged him forward once more, and this time when Dakota went down he stayed there, feigning helplessness, until the General reached down and grabbed him by the shirt. "Up, Doctor! Get up!" As the General hauled Dakota to his feet, he looked back at the church, and in that moment of distraction, Dakota wrenched the gun out of the General's hand.

With his left side still useless, Dakota took several steps back, fumbling with the heavy, unfamiliar weapon in his one good hand. He shook so bad he almost dropped it, and in his panic, all he could think about was getting his finger on the trigger. When he did, the gun roared like a cannon and the recoil nearly pushed him back to the ground.

He missed the General completely, but the shot served another purpose—everyone in the church must have heard it. He regained his balance, and with the roar still ringing in his ears, he turned around and ran. Shots cut the air around him, one so close he could feel the heat as it passed by his ear.

"Stop!" The General yelled at his men. "Do not kill him, you idiots! Wound him, but nothing mortal. I need this man!"

Dakota hid behind one of the large granite memorials, thankful, for the moment, that his life had some value. He had to think fast or they would take him, he knew that. Montana was probably dead, but he would have to deal with that later. Ito and Ricco had to know there was trouble, but he couldn't count on their help. If there was any way out of this, he was on his own to find it.

He risked peeking around the headstone, which brought immediate gunfire, and shards of granite ripped open the flesh of one cheek. "Shit!" He dropped the gun and ducked back behind the stone, wiping the blood from his stinging cheek with the palm of his hand. "So much for non-lethal force!"

His eyes watered as he picked up the gun, and without looking or aiming, he poked the barrel around the corner of the headstone and pulled the trigger. The roar was deafening, and the recoil snapped his wrist back so hard the gun almost flew out of his hand. He stared at the smoking weapon in disbelief. "What the hell is this thing?" He didn't get a chance to find out as more gunfire caused him to flinch and tighten up his position behind the granite grave marker.

Then he realized the gunfire wasn't directed at him. He heard the General barking rapid orders and risked another glance around the stone. He felt some measure of relief to see armed men pouring out of the church, but more importantly, the General and his men no longer paid attention to him. His heart pounding in his ears, Dakota jumped up and ran.

He reached the far side of the cemetery and took shelter at the side of a large mausoleum. He was surrounded, it was daylight, and he had little cover. With his hand shaking, and using his cast for support, Dakota checked his ammo. Minus the two he had fired, he had five rounds left. That would never be enough, and he knew it.

Ricco's request to Montana came back to him, and right then he made a promise to himself—if it came down to it, he would save the final bullet to deprive the General of his prize. He wondered if he would have the courage to take his own life.

"Drop the fucking gun or I swear to God, I'll blow your fucking hand off! Let's see you try and heal that."

Dakota froze. The gun was in his hand, but pointed away from him, and away from the voice behind him.

"Drop it, asshole! I won't say it again."

Closing his eyes in defeat, he let the weapon fall with a quiet thud to the grass, and then held his hands out to his side as he blinked the blood and sweat out of his eyes.

"Stand up, you fucking little prick!"

Dakota complied the best he could. The lack of adrenaline left him numb and off balance. The soldier came up behind him, bent down, and retrieved the gun. "Now, turn the fuck around!"

Dakota started to turn, but before he got halfway around, the soldier took a quick step toward him and slammed the butt of his weapon into the soft underside of Dakota's chin. Dakota went down hard, landing flat on his back. Black specks danced in front of his eyes, and his vision blurred. Blood now flowed from his chin as well as his shredded cheek. When he could focus once more, he saw the soldier looming over him.

"That was for Carlson, you sorry sack of shit!"

"Who?" Dakota's mind reeled along with the black specks. "You mean Bubba?"

The soldier gave him a vicious kick in the side with the toe of his boot. Dakota felt a rib crack, and cried out in pain as he curled himself into a ball.

"Carlson, motherfucker! Sergeant William Robert Carlson! You got it? He was a good man, and he's dead because of you!"

"Okay, okay…" Each breath brought a stabbing pain to his side. "Carlson… Great guy… I got it."

"Fuck you!"

Dakota grimaced as the soldier jerked him to his feet and pushed him forward. Any thought of escape abandoned him, as staying on his feet required his complete attention. Gunfire continued to rip through the air from the direction of the church, and Dakota prayed that Ito was winning the fight.

The soldier herded him down a small incline and without any warning, punched Dakota in the back of the head and knocked him to the ground. "Carlson saved your fucking, worthless life!" He picked Dakota up and a sadistic grin spread across his face. "That ain't my fucking style."

Dakota saw the punch coming, but was helpless to defend

himself. A whole galaxy of stars exploded in his head as he flew backward, and once again, landed hard on his back. On the verge of passing out, he watched the soldier walk toward him with his fists clenching and unclenching and a glassy, wild look in his eyes. The more pain he caused Dakota, the more out of control he became.

"Just give me a fucking reason, you puke—that's all I ask." He dragged Dakota to his feet and drew back a fist.

Dakota feared for his life and frantically sought a way to dampen the man's rage. "What…what about your orders…the General?" Every word was punctuated with pain, and Dakota groaned as he clutched his side.

The sadistic smile broadened when the soldier saw the source of Dakota's pain. This time, the punch hit Dakota in his broken ribs, stealing his breath and leaving mind-numbing pain behind. The soldier grabbed him by the front of his shirt and kept him from falling down, and then hauled him up until they were face-to-face. "Understand something, you piece of shit." His face twisted into an ugly mask of hate. "I'm not Carlson. I don't give a damn about orders. And I don't give a fuck about the General. All I need is an excuse, and I'll put a bullet in your fucking brain."

"But you won't, Captain, because I'm paying you an obscene amount of money to keep this man alive."

The captain dropped Dakota to the ground and stepped back. Dakota lay in a broken, bloody heap, gasping for breath, but in a turnaround he found ironically amusing, he actually felt relieved to hear the General's voice.

"Get him loaded into the van, and without further incident, Captain. Once we're moving, I will ignite the charges."

The General didn't sound as collected as he had earlier. Dakota prayed, to whatever God might be listening, that they had met with some opposition. He still heard sporadic gunfire coming from the cemetery, as the soldier he now thought of as Evil-Bubba picked him up and threw him into the back of the empty cargo van, and the doors slammed shut on any hopes he might have had of getting away.

Evil-Bubba sat on the floor opposite of him. "I ain't done with you, pal." He glanced to make sure the General wasn't watching, and then kicked Dakota in the head with the heel of his boot.

As the engine turned over and the van started to move, there was a muffled explosion. A shock wave rocked the van, and debris rained down on the metal roof as they sped away. He rolled onto his side, his thoughts choked with despair.

It's over, and the bad guys have won.

CHAPTER 22

Poor Ray's service was interrupted once again. This time by the sound of a single gunshot. Ito was on feet racing to the back of the church, followed closely by Ricco, Patrick and the dozen active duty Delta Force Rangers who had been placed undercover in the church. To avoid spooking the locals, the Rangers had been ordered to wear civilian clothing. They twitched and sweated in the uncomfortable suits, but they were ready for action. Their jackets concealed handguns, and larger weapons were hidden and ready at a moment's notice.

One of the Rangers at the door stepped in front of Ito and grabbed Ricco before he got to the door. "You stay here."

Ricco wrenched his arm away and glared at the man. "Like hell!"

Ito intervened before things got out of control. He pushed between the Ranger and Ricco, using his size to his advantage. "There's no time for this, son. Let him go, I'll watch after the private."

The ranger didn't look happy, but apparently he agreed with Ito. "If you say so, sir. But he's going to need this." He handed Ito a weapon and he, in turn, gave it to Ricco.

"Stay close, don't get hit," Ito told Ricco.

Ito made it out the doors first and immediately drew small arms fire from the cemetery. Bullets snapped into the stone walls all around him as he dove for cover behind a large iron planter and tried to assess the situation. A host of would-be Army Rangers surrounded the perimeter, Dakota was gone, Montana was down and next to him, an old woman lay dead with a gunshot wound to the head. Their security had obviously been compromised, and the church was in a vulnerable position. It sat raised and exposed, with only the front doors as an exit. Montana had argued from the beginning about the church, but Ray's family refused to budge. The church was over two-hundred years old, and Ray had been baptized there—he would be buried there.

Ito realized the team they had positioned around the cemetery were either dead or infiltrated. The only men he could trust were inside the church. Ito keyed his earpiece and gave his men orders. "Blue team leader—our perimeter has been breached. Repeat—hostiles inside the perimeter. Load up, now!"

The team leader gave directions to his men, and assault rifles were retrieved from hiding places inside the confessionals, put together and loaded with practiced ease. They split up and poured out of the church with amazing speed.

The confused congregation asked questions and tried to leave. One Ranger was left behind to ensure the unarmed parishioners' safety, but as soon as they were told to stay put, the word bomb was heard from outside.

One of the Delta team's demolition experts raced back into the church and spoke quietly but urgently to his teammate. "There are explosives rigged to a remote control all around the exterior. Get these people out of here!"

That was all anyone needed to hear. Ito pulled Montana up and threw him over his shoulder, while panicked churchgoers spilled from the building and ran as fast and as far away as they could.

It was a nightmare for the Rangers. They were taking fire from the cemetery, had unarmed civilians and wounded in harm's way, and a bomb that could go off at anytime. They returned fire to the cemetery, and then realized the numbers were in their favor. Whoever was out there had counted on surprise, not force. The Rangers advanced, and it didn't take long before the fire being aimed in their direction ceased. A few moments later, the church exploded. A red-orange fireball engulfed the small wooden structure, sending burning debris, like hell's rain, descending down on them.

Ito covered Montana with his body. The disturbed air formed a shock wave that pinned them all to the ground until it passed. Delta force wasted no time and advanced.

"They took Dakota…there." Ito pointed to the white van just over a slight rise in the cemetery. "I think I saw him there."

The Ranger nearest him gave him a slight nod and touched his earpiece, relaying the information to his team leader. He looked at

Montana. "How's the major?"

Ito hadn't had a chance to check. He didn't even know if Montana was alive. He slid slippery fingers along the side of Montana's throat, and let out of breath of sheer relief. "He's alive. I think the bullet just grazed the side of his head. There's a lot of blood, but no real damage."

As if on cue, Montana moaned and opened his eyes. At first, they were unfocused and confused. Blinking the blood out of his eyes, he looked from the Ranger to Ito and tried to sit up. Ito helped him. He looked a little shaky, but he was still with it.

"How you doing?" Ito asked.

Montana shook his head and staggered as he tried to get to his knees. Ito helped steady him.

"Take it easy," Ito said.

"What the hell happened?" Montana asked. He put a hand to his head, and it came back bright red with blood. His eyes seemed to snap into focus and he tried to stand, but Ito kept him still.

"Where's Dakota?" Montana asked.

"In trouble," Ito told him simply.

"Sir." One of the Rangers from the church ran up to Ito, his hand over his earpiece. "I just got word, the major's brother has been taken. He's in the white van and it's on the move." He pointed down the hill to the van driving away from their location and out of the cemetery.

Montana leaned heavily on Ito, but he stood. "Stop the van," he told the Ranger.

"Sir?" The Ranger turned to Ito, a question on his face.

"Stop the Goddamn van!" Montana yelled. He squinted his eyes and held his head.

Ito put a hand on Montana's shoulder and addressed the Ranger. "I would stop the van if I were you," he advised.

The Ranger gave Ito a brief nod before he dropped to the ground to lay flat on his belly. The van was two hundred yards away and picking up speed. Ito knew it would be a difficult shot and hoped the guy was as good as he thought he was. The Ranger sighted the rifle and gently squeezed the trigger, taking the recoil in his shoulder. At the same time the shot registered, the van's left rear tire exploded. When the vehicle kept moving, he squeezed off another shot, which hit the left front tire.

"Yes!" The Ranger grinned, but his elation was short-lived. The van careened from one side of the road to the other, jumped the curb, tilted precariously on two wheels, then followed gravity and started a slow roll down the hill. It flipped four times before coming to rest with a metallic crunch against an ancient oak tree next to a towering War World I memorial. The tree creaked and groaned in protest to the insult, but it held strong.

"Shit," the Ranger whispered.

Ito bent down to speak quietly in the Ranger's ear. "Not quite what I had in mind," he said.

"Dakota is in there?" Montana struggled to stay on his feet. It was obvious he was dizzy and not in the best of shape. He looked to the Ranger who had just taken out the van. "I need a weapon."

"No, sir." The man shook his head.

Montana looked at Ito, who smiled and handed him the Glock he kept concealed under his shoulder harness. "Live one in the chamber, nine in the mag. Try not to kill any of the good guys, okay?"

Montana said nothing. He checked the weapon, pushed the safety off with his thumb, and started running, unsteadily, toward the overturned van.

"Sir, do you think that's a good idea?" the Ranger asked Ito. "He has a head injury."

Ito smiled and clapped him on the back. "Son, you just rolled the vehicle with his brother inside, I would think arming the major would be the least of your concerns." He checked his own weapon and followed Montana down the hill.

* * * *

The van lurched forward, and Dakota was thrown against the side, reminding him of recently injured ribs.

Evil-Bubba smiled at his obvious pain. "I can't wait to get your ass back to base. We have all sorts of fun planned for you and Ricco."

A thought occurred to Dakota. "Why wait?" If he couldn't get free, and if Montana was dead, maybe Dakota could piss this guy off enough to kill him, despite the General's orders or promised payment. He looked as if he hated Dakota enough to do him that small favor.

"Don't tempt me," the guard growled. "There is nothing I would like better than to put a bullet in your brain, but I can't."

"Ahh, yeah, that's right, orders." Dakota straightened himself up against the side of the rocking van. "You know, I often wondered if Bubba ever made one decision of his own. I doubt it. He probably needed permission to take a dump."

The guard narrowed his eyes at Dakota, and without warning, slammed the rifle into the fiberglass cast on his broken arm. That was exactly the reaction Dakota had been hoping for, but the pain caught him by surprise. Everything grayed out for a second, and then a steady, sharp pain brought him back to the moment.

Sweat rolled down his face, and he felt half sick, but he continued his taunts. "You sure you didn't need an order to do that?" Dakota saw the man's nostrils flare in anger and gave one final push to send him over the edge. "You and Bubba, you're just the General's puppets. He pulls the strings, and you pull the trigger. The bastard walks away with clean hands, while you wind up with blood on yours. Bubba ended up dead."

Something inside Evil-Bubba snapped. He dropped the rifle on the floor of the van and pulled a wicked looking knife from a sheath at his hip. "No amount of money is worth this." He threw Dakota down on his back and straddled him. "You don't deserve a clean death."

Dakota didn't fight the man, he closed his eyes and waited for the blade. He tried to think of Montana and his mother. The pain wasn't important, as long as the man killed him in the end, as long as the

General never got the chance to turn him into another Ricco.

A sudden explosion jarred Dakota's eyes open. The vehicle lurched to one side as the driver fought to keep the van under control. Another explosion, another sideways lurch, and the van flipped on its side and then rolled onto its top. Dakota and Evil-Bubba were thrown violently inside the rolling tin can. The gun became a lethal weapon without ever being fired as it smashed into doors, windows, and the ceiling. They both lunged for it, but neither had a chance as their bodies flopped around the inside of the cargo hold like rag dolls. Everything seemed to happen in slow motion as the van made its fourth and final flip.

Dakota fought for breath and realized the guard's weight had settled directly onto his chest. Thankful, at least, that the man was unconscious, he struggled to push the body off him with his one good arm. He finally emerged in one piece, dizzy from the abuse and covered in blood, but Evil-Bubba wasn't so lucky. During one of the flips, he fell on top of his own knife and embedded it up to the hilt in his chest. The man had achieved exactly the same death he had planned for Dakota.

Dakota scooted away from the body and found himself pressed against the roof. The motor of the van raced out of control, accompanied by the screeching sound of metal grinding against metal. Steam and the smell of burning rubber filled the interior. He heard voices coming from outside the van, but his still reeling mind couldn't decipher them. Expecting the worst, he searched through the steamy haze and found the rifle. With a shaking hand, he pulled the weapon to him and held onto it like a lifeline, determined to kill anyone who came through the doors. He was aware enough to make sure the safety was disengaged and a live round chambered, but he had trouble holding it steady. Then he realized that in the confines of the mangled vehicle, it was unlikely he would miss anything in front of him.

* * * *

By the time Ito and Montana made it down the hill, the Rangers had set up a perimeter around the van. They had killed twelve armed men in the fields surrounding the cemetery grounds, and were convinced that any remaining enemy troops were either inside the van or already dead.

They prepared to open the cargo doors, when Ricco stopped them. "Where's the General?" Ricco had seen his own bit of action on the short trip down the hill. His face was speckled with blood that Ito knew was not his own. The blue-green eyes were dilated nearly black, and he was breathing heavily.

The look on Ricco's face reminded Ito of how he had seen him in the bunker. Fear and pure hatred stirred in that boy's soul, and Ito was certain Ricco was right on the edge. He came up behind Ricco, put a hand on his shoulder, and could feel the adrenaline in the quivering muscles beneath his touch. "Most likely, the man is inside the van, Private."

Ricco thought about that, and shook his head. "Not in the back. He wouldn't be in the back." He brought his rifle up and checked the load, then climbed up the side of the downed van and moved to the driver's door, which now faced the sky.

The team leader, entrusted with Ricco's safety, was about to stop him, but Ito halted the man with one look. "Let him do this," Ito said. "He needs to do this."

The team leader looked uncomfortable, but he understood. He motioned for two of his team to clear the driver's section of the van before Ricco could open the door.

A Ranger entered the cab weapon first. "We have one dead driver, one injured passenger." He pulled out the driver and the passenger, letting the injured man fall to the ground. Another small team began to pry open the impossibly smashed rear doors of the van to get to Dakota.

Ricco jumped from the wreckage and watched as the General stood in front of him. The man was bloodied and unsteady on his feet, but he was alive. Ricco approached him slowly, with the rifle aimed at his head. "I should have done this when I had the chance." He stepped forward until the barrel of the weapon touched the General's temple, pushed it into the wound that already existed there, and smiled when he saw the man flinch. "Does that hurt, General? Maybe we should record it and study how you react when I blow your fucking head off!"

The General closed his eyes, and his body began to tremble. "Ricco...don't."

"Not good enough! Beg me not to kill you. Beg like all the men you tortured begged!"

"Please…" The General's lips quivered, and then he burst out with a wailing sob and fell to his knees. "Please don't kill me. I'm sorry. I don't want to die. Please!"

Ricco closed his eyes for just a moment. When he opened them again, Ito could see the years of pain and indifference that triggered the hatred he felt coming from the boy. Ito couldn't imagine the hell that had been Ricco's life.

The Ranger next to Ito got his attention. The man looked uncomfortable at the exchange in front of him. "Sir, how long are we going to let this go on?" he asked. "We have wounded inside the van as well as out here." He motioned to Montana trying to open the van doors, despite the blood still trickling down his face. The mangled rear doors were proving to be a challenge.

"He's waited a lifetime for this, Corporal. Give him a minute," Ito told him, keeping his eyes on Ricco. Ito wasn't sure how much the team with them knew about Ricco. From the expression on the man's face next to him, whatever they knew, it wasn't enough.

Ricco's eyes were bright with tears of rage. He pushed the muzzle of the rifle against the General's head. "Not nearly good enough," he said, and pulled the trigger.

The General screamed, a surprisingly high-pitched sound, as the rifle clicked on an empty chamber.

Ricco grinned at the large, wet, dark patch that spread across the crotch of the General's pants. The man had pissed himself out of fear. Ricco threw the weapon to the ground and pulled the General to his feet. "Way too quick and clean for you."

"Michael…" The General tried to smile. "Think about what you're doing. What would your father think of what you're doing? He would be disappointed in you, don't you think?"

With the mention of his father, Ricco froze. Ito watched with concern, his hand on his weapon, ready to come to Ricco's aid if needed. He gave the boy a moment and saw the anger flare once more in his eyes.

"Don't you dare mention my daddy to me, you son-of-a-bitch! He was a better man than you could ever hope to be." Ricco circled the General, Ito could almost feel the anger radiate from him. Anger built up over nearly a century of torture and inhuman conditions.

"He gave me life, he taught me how to be a man, all you ever did was cause me pain."

"For the greater good, Private. You never understood that." The General seemed to reclaim some of his dignity.

"I understand." Ricco stopped his circling and stood within feet of the General. "I understand that you did everything to me but kill me, even when I begged for it! It's you who never understood. It's time to change that." With that, Ricco threw himself at the man in front of him. Ito and twelve armed Army Rangers watched while Michael Ricco beat his tormentor without mercy.

When Ricco could no longer lift his arms, he fell to the ground exhausted. The General's blood covered his face and hands. The General lay unmoving on the ground. No one bothered to check if he was even alive.

Montana had watched patiently while Ricco executed some long deserved payback, and the remaining Rangers struggled to open the van doors. "If we're done having fun, can we open the God damn doors and see about Dakota now?"

* * * *

Dakota must have passed out at some point, as the sound of someone pounding on the back doors of the van brought him back to consciousness. It took him a few seconds to realize where he was, and then a bright light seared his eyes as the bent and twisted doors flew open on groaning hinges. They rebounded closed once before several pairs of hands held them open.

He knew it had to be the General, but he had the gun this time, and there was no way he would let the bastard live, not after what he had done to Montana. God, Montana is dead. The reality of that slammed into him, and he almost dropped the gun.

As a figure stepped into the narrow doorway, silhouetted against the sunlight behind him, Dakota raised the rifle and steadied it on his knees.

"Dakota Rain, drop the gun."

He paused with his finger on the trigger. There were only two people in the world who knew his middle name, and he believed both of them were dead.

"It's me, man. Drop the gun."

Dakota felt certain it was a cruel trick of his imagination. The figure leaned inside the van, blocking the sunlight, and Dakota saw the face for the first time. He lowered the rifle and shook his head in confusion. "I watched you die. You're dead."

Montana knelt in front of him, covered in blood, his dark hair matted and stuck to the side of his face. "I might look like hell, but I assure you, I'm still breathing." He took the weapon from Dakota, and looked at the dead guard. "Can't leave you alone for a minute, can I?"

Dakota still had trouble believing what his eyes were showing him. "Montana?"

Another figured appeared behind Montana, and Dakota reached for the gun once again only to find it gone. "Behind you!"

Without looking, Montana put a hand on Dakota's arm. "It's okay, man. They're the good guys."

Dakota shook his head. "There are no good guys." Then he recognized Ito standing behind his brother.

Ito smiled as he squeezed past Montana. "Doctor Thomas. What a mess you've gotten yourself into, yet again." He gently touched Dakota's face and slid a hand down to his wrist. He felt Dakota's pulse for a moment, and glanced at Montana. "He's shocky. Let's get him out of here so I can see what there is to see."

Out sounded good to Dakota, but his fear lingered. "The General..." He couldn't seem to get a complete sentence formed. Thoughts pinged around inside his head until nothing made sense. The one thing that made it through was that Montana wasn't dead. That was the thought he held onto, nothing else mattered.

He kept a tenuous hold onto consciousness as they took him from what he had convinced himself was his coffin. He remembered Montana's face and Ito's gentle hands, a helicopter, and a lot of pain, numbness and cold, and then nothing—sweet, peaceful nothingness.

* * * *

The FBI was not known for their handholding or their patience. A field medic had seen to Montana and patched him up, but thought it best if he saw a real doctor. Before Montana had a chance to tell him that wasn't going to happen, Ito and he were taken to a makeshift command office near the remains of the church. The trailer had only a small circulating fan to push the hot humid air around, which did little to cool anyone. Montana and Ito were brought in and told to wait.

Montana took one of the hard plastic chairs. He lifted a hand and wiped a mixture of sweat and dried blood from his face. "What's the deal?"

Ito stretched his legs out in front of him and hiked his shoulders. "As far as I can figure, we're caught in a pissing match between the FBI and the government. Neither one wants to admit to any wrong doing."

Montana nodded in understanding. "So, of course, both sides are trying to figure out how to blame us."

"I have a feeling Private Ricco might have something to say about that."

"What do you mean?"

"Think about it. The government wants Ricco almost as bad as the General. We saved his life. Do you really think he'll let us take the fall for any of this?"

Montana smiled for the first time in what felt like days. "It's good to have friends."

"That it is." Ito swiped a hand over his face, trying to clear it of sweat, but new beads immediately sprang up on his brow.

They were silent for a while, and then Ito's chest started to shake. Montana watched as the shaking turned into full-blown laughter. Montana raised his brow. "Something amusing about all of this?"

"I was just thinking." Ito's grin split his face like a sharp axe through soft wood. "The commander of the Deltas told me they got all the civilians out of the church before it blew."

"Yeah, I know. They told me…so?"

Ito's grin broadened even further. "But, they didn't have time to get Ray out."

Montana finally understood, and a smile crept onto his face. The smile evolved into a quiet chuckle, and unable to contain it any longer, both Montana and Ito laughed until tears streamed down their faces and their sides ached.

The laughter gradually quieted as their thoughts returned to their fallen brother. Ito sighed as he leaned back in his chair. "Getting blown up in a church while still in his coffin. Damn, Ray would have loved that."

Montana wiped his eyes and gave a small nod of approval. "I can't think of a more fitting tribute."

Ito nodded back. He gave Montana a sad smile and gave him his best impression of Ray. "Fucking sweet."

Montana agreed. "Fucking sweet."

They sat in the silence of their memories until the FBI came back to question them in detail.

CHAPTER 23

Michael Ricco was alone. He could not honestly remember the last time he had been truly alone. He wandered around the spacious apartment with absolutely no idea what to do with his time. He knew the feeling of freedom was an illusion. The United Sates Government had set him up in the one-bedroom accommodations, given him clothes, introduced him to plasma televisions, CD players and computers, and all they wanted in return was his cooperation.

They would keep him comfortable for the remainder of his life, however long that may prove to be. He was promised no pain, and no life threatening experimentations. They only wanted his blood from time to time, it was all he had to give them, that, and of course, his freedom.

Michael sat on the sofa in front of the blank television screen, staring out the window and watching the leaves on the trees blow backward. "There's a storm coming." He remembered his daddy telling him that. After a humid afternoon, if the leaves start blowing so you can see the underside, you know a storm is not far behind. His daddy had never been wrong about that.

He closed his eyes and heard his father's voice in his head, the quiet southern drawl that could be soft and sweet like honey or hard as steel, depending on his mood, but never loud. His daddy never needed to raise his voice to his oldest son. Michael never wanted to disappoint him.

God, how he missed his father and his family. It upset him that he had trouble recalling their faces. He tried, almost making out his brother Mattie's mischievous grin and Sarah's shy smile, but he could never get the whole picture. It had been too long. Sarah and Mattie were long dead and buried; he knew that. They had grown old and lived an entire lifetime, believing he died as a nineteen-year-old Marine. The injustice of that made him angry. He wondered what he had been doing when they married, when they died. He had been denied the simple thing that most people took for granted—a family—and now, his were all gone.

A possibility invaded his thoughts, something that had never occurred to him before. Mattie and Sarah had grown up; wouldn't they have married? Had families of their own? Maybe Michael was not as alone as he thought. Maybe he did have family out there somewhere.

He picked up the phone on the table next to the sofa. No dial tone; it was a direct line to his caretakers. No outside contact was allowed unless pre-approved. He had agreed to that as well.

"Yes, Michael?" a friendly female voice asked. "What can I get for you?"

"I need to talk to…well, I'm not sure who I need to talk to, but I have a condition of my own. Do you think you can help me with that?"

There was a brief moment of silence before the woman answered him. "I'll see what can be arranged, Michael. Perhaps within the hour. Would that suffice?"

"Yeah, I mean, yes. That would be great. Just make sure you tell them it's important."

"I will. Is there anything else? If you get hungry, there's dinner in the refrigerator. Do you remember how to use the microwave?"

"Yes, ma'am. I'm not real hungry right now, but thanks."

"Okay. I'll make arrangements for Geoffrey to come by and speak with you. Call if you need anything."

"Yes, ma'am." Michael hung up the phone and tried to remember which one was Geoffrey. It didn't matter. As long as he had the authority to do this thing for him, he didn't care. Unless they agreed to this one request, they weren't getting another drop of blood from him, unless they took it by force.

He needed this. Maybe this would give him peace at night. Maybe he could actually sleep once it was over. He didn't count on them giving him what he wanted though, he didn't think he could take the disappointment if he counted on it and they said no.

Michael stood and watched the sky grow dark and the wind pick up. Knowing a number of unseen eyes were on him at all times, he stepped out onto the bricked patio and sat at the glass table there. He could smell rain in the air and decided to wait and see which came first, the lightening or the rain. Either way, the storm would be well under way before the hour was up and Geoffrey came to hear what he had to say. His daddy had never been wrong about those things.

* * * *

The lack of control, Dakota had difficulty getting used to that one thing. The daytime usually went by smoothly; he could handle it as long as the sun was out. Nights were a different story altogether. He would put sleep off for as long as possible. On a good night, he made it to sunrise without closing his eyes once. On a bad night...well, a bad night happened when the exhaustion overwhelmed him and his body shut down. Then his mind controlled what happened next, and he had no choice over the images that played out inside his head. The best he could do was try to hide the nightmares from his therapist. The woman did not fool easily, though, and she usually picked up on Dakota's moods the moment the session started.

Life one month after the abduction attempt in the cemetery consisted of simply making it from one day to the next. His medical license had not been suspended, but he had been put on administrative leave, with the promise he could return to work after a full psychiatric evaluation and clearance. That was the main reason he tried to keep the nightmares to himself.

Between his daily therapy sessions and further surgeries to repair his arm, they told him not to expect to practice medicine again for at least a year, and then only on a supervised basis. Montana was up his ass too, playing mother hen and sincerely bugging the hell out of him. Dakota found himself on edge and being pulled in every direction. If they would just leave him alone, he could figure this all out on his own.

Sometimes they had him wait to see his therapist, Mary, but today the blond receptionist, whose name he could never remember, ushered him right in. Figured, on a day when he could have used the time to get it together.

He sat where he always sat, in the comfortable armchair opposite her desk. There was the prerequisite couch available, but he avoided even looking at the thing, as it just seemed excessively clichéd.

"Dakota." Mary smiled at him as she rose from her desk. Even her smile irritated him today.

"That's me," he replied.

Mary, Doctor Stromm, wasn't bad, really. Dakota supposed she was quite brilliant at her job. She was maybe in her fifties with prematurely gray hair worn very short, and very stylish. An unlined face gave the impression she was much younger. Dakota had learned the hard way not to treat her in accordance to his moods. She had the unnerving ability to see right through any defenses he put up.

Mary sat back down, steepled her perfectly manicured hands, and appraised him.

After a full minute of silent observation, he couldn't take it any longer. "What?"

"Bad night?"

He rolled his eyes. There was no use in denying it, so instead of confirming the truth, he simply shrugged. Exhaustion weighed heavily on him. The few hours he managed to sleep were haunted and far from restful. Dredging it all up again for the woman's amusement did not appeal to him.

"Same dream?"

"Yeah, same one. It's always the same one. Look, I'm dealing with it, okay?"

She made no comment to his obvious hostility. "Your brother tells me you're not sleeping in your bed. When you do sleep, it's in a chair, and only when exhaustion forces it on you."

Dakota made no reply. He stared anywhere but at her. His leg started bouncing as the seconds ticked by.

"Dakota, you've been coming here since your release from the hospital, twelve visits in all. In that time, you've lost weight, you don't sleep, you never leave your apartment except for these mandated sessions, and you have grown increasingly hostile, agitated and defensive. I trust you did a psyche rotation in med school, so you know the diagnosis as well as I do."

Dakota's leg stopped bouncing, and he let his gaze rest on her face at last. In his best clinical voice, he presented her with the diagnosis. "Your patient has been through an intense emotional and physical ordeal. It is clear he is suffering from post traumatic stress syndrome…Doctor."

She ignored his sarcasm. "I agree. What would you suggest as a form of treatment?"

Dakota broke eye contact with her, leaned back in the chair, and stared at the ceiling. "Haven't a clue. You're the shrink. I'm just the fucked up bastard you're supposed to fix." He stretched his legs out in front of him and feigned indifference.

Mary chuckled. "Ahh, but I don't fix anything. I merely make suggestions until my patients realize they had all the answers the entire time, and then I charge them outrageously and declare them cured."

That got a smile out of Dakota.

"Well, there's progress." She folded her arms on the desk and leaned forward. "Dakota, this isn't going to go away, you know that."

He closed his eyes, admitting the truth for once. "It's hard."

"If it were easy, you wouldn't need me."

He knew that too. "I wish I could have watched Ricco beat the crap out of him. That would have been sweet."

"Who? The General?"

"Yeah. At least Ricco got that small satisfaction. He got to kill the sick son-of-a-bitch."

"Kill him?"

Her tone, and the question, had him opening his eyes and looking over at her. "Yeah, kill him." He dared her to tell him he was wrong.

She did.

"Dakota, who told you he was dead?"

"Well, I…" His face screwed up in concentration. "No one, I guess. I just assumed. Are you telling me he's not dead?" His heartbeat doubled and cold sweat trickled down his back.

"I thought you knew." Mary leaned back in her chair, obviously concerned that she was the one to tell him. "The General is currently being held in a maximum security psychiatric facility for the criminally insane. I thought someone told you. I'm sorry you had to find out about it like this."

"Yeah, me too." He sat up straighter. "Does Montana know?"

"You'd have to ask him."

"That son-of-a-bitch! Why didn't he tell me?"

"Maybe because he knew this is how you would react. How do you feel knowing this man is alive?"

"Oh, please, don't get all shrinky on me." Dakota turned away, and his leg started bouncing again. It was bad enough when he thought the General was just a figure in his dreams, but now, to find out the man was alive and out there…somewhere. Suddenly, a thought came to him. "I want to see him."

That took her by surprise, and the flustered look on her face delighted Dakota.

"You want to see the General?"

"Is that a problem?"

She hesitated. Dakota could feel her watching him for some clue to his motive. "I'm just not sure it's a good idea. The man was responsible for grievously harming you."

"I know what he was responsible for, Doctor. I was there, remember?" His voice became more insistent as he stood up and paced in front of her desk. "I want to see him."

"Why?"

Dakota whirled on her. "Why the hell do you think?"

"I think you want to kill him, Dakota," she said and held his glare with unflinching ease. "You won't be able to, you know. You won't even be allowed to touch him, and they'll search you carefully before they let you anywhere near him."

"I just want to see him, okay? I don't know why. I just know I need this. Mary, please…" He let the request hang there between them.

She considered what he asked and sighed. "Maybe it would help bring you some closure. I'm not at all convinced this is good for you, but I'll see what I can do. No promises, is that understood?"

He nodded. "Understood."

The truth was, he didn't understand. He only knew he would never be completely whole until he confronted the man who stole his sleep, the man whose face haunted his dreams—the keeper of his sanity. If he ever hoped to live a normal life again, he needed to find a will he wasn't sure he possessed any longer. He needed to face down the demon who took his soul and claimed it for his own. He wondered if he had the strength to go through with it. He prayed he had the courage.

CHAPTER 24

Montana let himself into Dakota's apartment. He had taken the keys to Dakota's car away on Doctor Stromm's request. She also didn't think it was a good idea for him to leave Dakota alone, but Montana could only push his brother so far. He knew Dakota better than anyone, and maybe he was being naive, but he refused to believe Dakota was suicidal. He was depressed, yeah, but Dakota would not take his own life. That went against everything the man believed in. Montana placed a lot in that trust, but when it comes right down to it, trust is all one ever has.

Dakota would either prove him right or prove him wrong. He knew suicidal men before, and if they were serious, nothing could stay their hand. If Dakota was headed down that road, nothing Montana did or didn't do would make any difference. All he could do was be there for him, whether Dakota wanted him or not; but the man gave "being difficult" a completely new meaning.

Montana crinkled his nose up as the stench of ripe, unwashed maleness assaulted him. All the shades were drawn, shutting out any outside light, and leaving the apartment in perpetual darkness.

Dakota threw an arm over his eyes and turned on the sofa, away from the brief invasion of offending daylight. "Jesus! Ever hear of knocking?" Dirty dishes and debris littered the floor near where he lay.

"Ever hear of bathing?" Montana went from window to window, flinging the shades up, and letting sunlight cut through the gloom.

The sight of the cluttered, filthy room disturbed him almost as much as the sight of Dakota. The man lay in the same wrinkled clothing Montana had seen him in for the last two days. Dakota may not have a lot of style when it came to what he wore, but he had always been fastidious. Even as a kid, he didn't mind getting dirty, but he didn't like staying that way. Montana barely recognized the man in front of him.

Dakota not only neglected his personal hygiene, he hadn't cut his hair since that night when Ricco had been brought to his ER, it lay in heavy, unwashed tangles. Three weeks worth of growth on his face deserved to be called more than stubble. His clothes hung on his body, and not having been a heavyweight to begin, his recent weight loss was devastating to his six-foot-two-inch frame.

Montana knew the meeting Dakota requested had been approved, but he wondered if leaving Dakota in the dark about it was a good idea. Doctor Stromm insisted that was the way to play it. "He'll obsess over it," she told Montana, and he reluctantly agreed. The information would only make Dakota more of a mess than he already was. Her advice to

Montana was to be patient.

As he stood, surveying the trashed apartment with disgust, he thought, Well the hell with that. He had nearly killed himself being patient with Dakota, and the end result only served to push him further away. Montana put patience on the back burner and decided to do what he wanted to do from the very beginning. He considered his brother for a long, quiet moment, and then he pushed. "You look like hell."

Dakota squinted one eye against the glaring light. "Thank you, so much. You can leave now."

"Get up."

Dakota rolled over on the sofa and hid his face in the back pillows.

"Get off the damn couch, Dakota."

"Go away."

Montana moved the coffee table out of the way, then walked around to the back of the sofa and gave Dakota one last chance. "Are you getting up?"

Dakota's answer was to offer the middle finger of his right hand.

"I gave you a chance, remember that." Montana unceremoniously tipped the sofa over, spilling Dakota onto the floor.

Dakota came up fast on his feet. "What the hell!"

"You need a shower." Montana pointed down the hallway. "The bathroom's that way, if I recall."

Anger flared in Dakota's eyes. "Screw you, Montana! I didn't ask you to come here. I don't want you here, and I sure as hell don't need you here, so leave!" He stepped toward Montana, his hands clenched into fists.

Montana smiled. "Well, you sure as hell need something. Have you looked at yourself lately? You're a mess."

"Go to hell." Dakota paced in front of Montana, rubbing his left arm. A splint had replaced the cast, and his last surgery had been postponed indefinitely. His surgeons were amazed at how quickly and completely he healed.

Montana resisted the urge to ask if he was okay. "One of us there is enough. What happened to you, man?"

Dakota stopped his pacing and gave Montana an incredulous look. "What part did you miss?"

"Save the pity party. I know what that bastard did to you was bad, but come on, are you just going to let him win like this? This isn't you, Dakota." Montana shook his head, appraising the man in front of him. "You never gave up on anything or anyone in your entire life, so explain to me, why are you giving up on yourself?"

"Leave. Now." Dakota enunciated each word carefully.

"Make me." Montana imitated the taunt they used on each other as children. "Tell you what. If you manage to push me out the door, I'll leave and never come back, because to tell you the truth, I'd rather remember you fighting me, fighting something, hell, fighting anything, than remember you like this." Montana spread his arms and motioned with his hands. "Come on, tough guy. Make me leave."

Dakota was already breathing heavily. Montana could see the anger getting the better of him, and he smiled. Then he winked.

That was all it took.

Dakota threw himself at Montana. He had fought with Montana enough to know his weaknesses. The man was top-heavy, so Dakota aimed low at his knees.

Montana expected the attack and tried to dodge him, but he wasn't quite fast enough and went down hard, clipping the side of his head on the coffee table. It wasn't bad, just enough to draw blood. Both men rolled to their feet and circled each other. Montana wiped at the blood trickling down the side of his face and grinned.

Dakota returned the smile. "You'll leave me the hell alone?"

"I'm not out the door yet." Montana stepped in quickly, dodged the punch Dakota threw, and released a wicked uppercut that connected under Dakota's chin, sending him staggering backward.

Montana had started the fight holding back his punches, considering his brother's depleted physical condition, but after Dakota had drawn first blood, all bets were off. Besides, even underweight and malnourished, the little shit was stronger than he looked.

Dakota regained his balance, shook off the daze in his eyes, and with a fierce yell came at Montana once again. Montana was ready for him this time. He waited until the last possible moment, then stepped aside and gave Dakota a hard shoulder block that sent him flying into the small end table next to the overturned sofa. The lamp gave up without a fight, and the cheap plywood table crumbled under his weight.

As Dakota scrambled back to his feet, Montana egged him on. "I forgot to tell you, bro…I'm not paying for any damages."

Dakota picked up what was left of the lamp and threw it at Montana. Occupied with dodging the projectile, Montana couldn't avoid the pending assault. Dakota jumped on his back, pelting his head and shoulders with blows, most of which made solid contact.

Amid the flurry of fists, Montana managed to grab an arm. He spun around, pulling hard as he bent over at the waist, and slammed Dakota back to the floor. The blow stunned Dakota and knocked the wind out of him. Montana took advantage and grabbed both wrists in one hand, and lifted Dakota up and over his shoulders.

"Bath time, little brother." He carried a wheezing and struggling Dakota down the hallway to the bathroom. He kicked the door open, threw the fully clothed Dakota against the back wall of the shower, and turned the water on full force.

"Hell, Montana, that's cold!"

Dakota tried to get to his feet, but Montana pushed him back down, and then stepped inside the tub with him. He grabbed the pitiful sliver of soap left in the dish and began lathering Dakota's hair and any visible skin. After a minute or two of protest, Dakota gave up, and

Montana realized he was laughing. He gave his brother a playful shove.

"I guess that means I win."

Dakota scooped the dripping hair out of his eyes and raised his hands in surrender. "I give…I give" Puffing and trying to catch his breath, he plopped down in the corner, out of the direct assault of cold water. Montana sat opposite him, and with the water streaming between them, they both started laughing at the absurdity of it all.

Still laughing, Dakota shook his head. "I'm so fucked up."

"Yeah, you are that. But we'll get through it, we always do." Montana sighed. "You gotta' help me though, Dak. I can't handle it when you shut down on me like this."

Dakota was silent for a while, and then, looking directly at Montana, he made a difficult admission. "He did things to me, Montana. He changed me…here." He tapped his chest. "I'm not sure I can be the same person I used to be."

"I'm not asking you for that, man. I'm not asking you to forget or even forgive. I'm telling you to find a way to get around it, not over it. What happened might have changed you, but it doesn't have to define you. Do you understand?"

Dakota thought about that. "What if I can't live with those changes?"

"If you're asking me for permission to off yourself, you have to know that's never gonna happen."

"I've thought about it, you know?"

"Yeah, I figured as much."

"So, now what?"

Montana stood and offered Dakota his hand. "Well, for starters, you can finish taking a shower." He reached down and turned on the hot water. "And don't skimp on the soap, 'cause damn—you really reek."

Dakota pulled his waterlogged shirt over his head and threw it at Montana. "And then?"

Montana sighed and made a decision. "And then, we have a plane to catch."

"Oh yeah? Where are we going?"

"Washington, as in DC. You have a meeting with John McKinley."

The smile froze on Dakota's face, and then disappeared altogether. "The General? Mary got me in?"

Montana nodded. "Think you're up for it?"

"I asked for it…guess I'd better be. Don't let it define me, huh?"

Montana shrugged and stepped out of the tub. "You're not the only one talking to shrinks lately."

"Not a bad line. Hey, Montana?"

Montana looked at him.

"Ever think of going into psychology?" He rubbed his jaw where Montana's fist had made contact. "You have this warm, fuzzy thing going for you."

Montana threw the wet shirt back at him. "Lather, rinse, repeat."

Montana closed the door behind him, leaned against it, and closed his eyes. The thought of how close to the edge Dakota had been, had him shaking. He knew his brother was far from over the trauma, but it was a first step. Maybe seeing the General as a human being, a simple man, instead of the embodiment of all evil, would be another one. Walking back out to the Jeep to claim a bag of clothes he always kept there, he truly hoped so. If Dakota chose to walk to the edge again, Montana wasn't at all certain he could stop him.

CHAPTER 25

Doctor Stromm and an armed military escort met them at the airport. Montana had phoned and informed her they'd be late, because Dakota insisted on stopping to get a haircut and shave. She sounded surprised, but delighted by the news.

The transformation in Dakota was startling. Still painfully thin, pale, and sporting an impressive, blossoming bruise where Montana had nailed him, he was beginning to look like the Dakota Montana remembered. Even his walk had a little of the old Dakota cockiness to it. If you failed to look at his eyes, you might miss the fact that something was wrong with the man.

Mary Stromm watched Dakota board the plane, but hung back and waited for Montana. "How in the world did you get him to do that?"

Montana adjusted the Ray-Bans and cocked his head at her. "I beat him up."

She raised her brows. "Hmmm, interesting technique."

Montana gave her what could have been considered a grin and

followed his brother into the plane.

Not even first class could alter the fact that the flight was long and tedious. Montana spent most of it reclined and inert, the dark glasses making it impossible to tell if he was actually asleep or not. Dakota stared out the window at the nothing, silent, despite Mary's numerous attempts to draw him into conversation. He ate only because she threatened to cancel the visit if he didn't.

A half-hour later, he sincerely regretted relenting to her demands. He held his cramping stomach, and looked miserably at Mary. "I think I'm going to hurl."

"Nothing but crackers in your system for two days, it would serve you right. But you puke, and it's a deal-breaker. Or, if you prefer, I could have you admitted for IV nutrition...your choice."

"Oh, that's nice."

She laughed. "If that's what it takes to get you to eat, then so be it."

Dakota graced her with a smile and shook his head. "I think I'm feeling better, thank you."

"You have a nice smile, Dakota. You should do it more often."

He lowered his eyes, still grinning, and looking very much like a little boy. As he turned to the window once more, Mary was certain she detected a quiet reply. "I'm working on it," she heard him say, and for the first time, Mary Stromm held a small flame of hope in her heart for Dakota Thomas.

* * * *

They landed at a private airstrip just outside of Washington, DC. A long, sleek, white limo waited for them, and as Dakota made his way down the steps, he noticed they were the only traffic. Apparently, the airport had been shut down just for their flight. On closer inspection, he saw armed military personnel surrounding the landing strip. They stood like silent sentinels, weapons held across their chests, dark glasses and attitudes.

Dakota hesitated when he saw them. It was all a little too familiar.

"Relax." Montana came up behind him and spoke quietly in his ear. "They're on our side." He walked ahead of him and disappeared inside the limo.

"Yeah? How can you tell?" Dakota took a deep breath and reluctantly followed Montana into the limo, as it seemed safer than standing on the blacktop. "If I see 'Bubba' on one name badge, I'm out of here."

* * * *

The hospital was located an hour outside the city, on a quiet forty acres of green pastureland surrounded by several layers of electrified fencing. The peaceful setting was deceiving, as some of the most deviously brilliant, dangerous minds in existence were housed behind those fences.

The security spoke for itself. The limo was stopped three times before reaching the main compound, searched thoroughly, and their personal belongings scrutinized. The real fun came once they actually entered the building. Thankfully, the strip search was waived, but only as a courtesy to Doctor Stromm, who had been a colleague of the facility director.

Montana kept a close eye on Dakota throughout the process. As they made their way deeper into the complex, he became increasingly quiet, which was never a good sign with Dakota. They finally were brought to a narrow, windowless room and told to wait, while Mary left to discuss the meeting with the director. The only furniture in the room was a scarred plywood table and an ancient, green vinyl couch. The vinyl was cracked and worn through at the corners, and it squeaked and groaned whenever Dakota moved.

Montana elected to stand rather than squeeze onto the thing. The position also offered him a good vantage point to observe Dakota. He leaned against the far wall, his arms folded across his chest and his legs crossed at the ankles. They took his glasses at the last checkpoint, and in the silence of the small room, he stared at Dakota until his brother looked up to meet his gaze.

Montana spoke before Dakota could say anything, his voice quiet and direct. "Do you remember the coyotes?"

Dakota gave him a confused look. Montana watched as he seemed to search the confines of the room for some point of reference to the question. Understanding surfaced in his eyes. "You mean, when we were kids?"

Montana nodded once. "I was fifteen. Do you remember?"

"That would have been the eighth or ninth time you took off, right?"

"You found me before Cal that time, remember?"

Dakota grinned. "I always found you before Cal. I just never let you know about it."

Montana tried to suppress a smile.

"Is there a point to this, or are you just reminiscing at a wildly inappropriate time?"

Montana uncrossed his ankles and slid down the wall to sit on the floor, his legs stretched out in front of him. "You asked me why I kept taking off. All those times, and you never asked me why until that one time."

"You told me you were listening to the coyotes sing…that you needed to understand their song. You said if you figured it out, you might understand why Dad never came back. I never quite understood what you meant."

Montana leaned his head against the wall, the memory very clear for him. "And do you remember what you said to me?"

"I think I said that you already knew what the coyotes were telling you. That you understood their song long ago."

Montana closed his eyes. "You told me it didn't matter if I was there to hear them sing. The important thing was that I wanted to listen, because the song would be the same either way. I always remembered that." Montana opened his eyes again and searched his brother's face for understanding. "You don't have to do this, Dakota. Nothing that man has to say to you is of any consequence. You already know his song."

Dakota digested that thought, and after a long moment, he nodded. "Maybe. But maybe it's not what he has to tell me. Maybe it's what he needs to hear from me."

"Are you sure about this?"

Dakota shrugged. "As sure as I can be."

"I still don't like it."

"Montana, what if I was wrong all those years ago? What if I do need to listen to the song? All I know for sure, is that I need to do this."

"Then do it. I'll be here if you need me."

"I know." Dakota nodded. Montana knew his brother understood and was grateful for that simple fact.

Thirty minutes later, a guard came to inform them that John McKinley was in the next room, waiting.

Montana turned to his brother. "You good?"

Dakota stood and nodded.

The guard gave him a list of last-minute instructions. "No contact whatsoever. Mr. McKinley will be on one side of the table, you on the other. He'll be shackled to the floor, and two armed guards will be in the room with you at all times. You have ten minutes."

Mary came into the room and stood alongside him. "I still don't think it's a good idea for you to go in there alone, Dakota." They'd discussed the procedure earlier, and Dakota had insisted. His business with the General was personal, and it was bad enough that guards had to be present. He simply looked at her. There was nothing more to say.

The guard led him out the door, down the hall, and into the next room. This was possibly the last thing he wanted to do, the last person he ever wanted to come face-to-face with, but it was also the one thing he knew he had to do, if he ever wanted to live a semblance of a normal life. The sight of the armed soldiers did little to ease his feeling of dread as he walked over the threshold.

The room was small, and there were two doors: the one he had just entered, and one in the opposite wall. A plain wooden table occupied the center of the room, and behind it, in a simple metal chair, sat the General. He wore a light-blue jumpsuit with a prison ID number stenciled in black over the left breast pocket. His hands were cuffed to a thick leather strap around his waist, and his feet shackled to a heavy metal ring protruding from the concrete floor.

Dakota's first impression was that the General looked smaller than he remembered. In his dreams, the man loomed over him like a giant. His smartly pressed uniform, with its broad shoulders and shiny brass buttons, dominated his nightmares, demanding fear and obedience. But here, dressed in a wrinkled blue jumpsuit and confined behind the table, the General appeared shrunken and powerless.

Maybe that's what gave Dakota the courage to take the chair opposite the man and sit down. Or perhaps it was the fact that he wore slippers. The memory of those black dress shoes and the sound they made, clicking across the concrete floor of his cell, made Dakota sweat, even now.

"Doctor Thomas." The General inclined his head toward Dakota as he took his seat. "Forgive me for not standing, but…" He jangled his chains and smiled. "I am somewhat incapacitated."

A five-hour plane ride, almost two hours of security checks, and suddenly Dakota had no idea what to say. He simply stared at the man, sweating uncomfortably while the seconds ticked by.

The General examined him with his cold, clinical gaze. "You look a bit thin, Doctor. I do hope you haven't been ill." When Dakota didn't respond, the General continued. "And I'm told you are no longer practicing medicine." He leaned forward, his eyes bright with a mocking gleam. "Lost the desire to heal?"

Dakota turned away, unable to match the General's stare, but he could still feel those eyes boring into him, digging for control. As he nervously shifted his weight in the chair, he questioned whether he had the strength to break free from this man. Maybe Montana and Mary were right, Maybe all Dakota would accomplish here would be relinquishing the small piece of himself that survived back to the General.

The General took pleasure in Dakota's discomfort, smiling with sinister glee as he sliced deeper into Dakota's psyche. "Tell me, Doctor, how are you sleeping at night? Care to share your dreams, your nightmares, the things that claw around at the back of your brain and won't let you be? How about the demons that keep you chained in your room, afraid of the light?"

"You're the one in chains, not me." Dakota heard the words as though they came from a different person. They sounded weak and infantile to his ears.

The General chuckled, and then relaxed in his chair, a touch of resignation in his voice. "So I am...so I am. Somehow, I think the ones that keep you prisoner are far heavier than mine."

Another minute passed by in silence. Dakota stared at the floor and picked at nothing on his pant leg, while the General watched him carefully. Decades of practice had made him adept at the game of emotional manipulation, and it was a game he never lost.

He finally broke the silence with a sigh. "Well, let me see…as you do not appear inclined to talk about personal matters, what other topics can we discuss that you might find of interest?" He leaned his head back, and an exaggerated frown distorted his features as he scanned the ceiling for clues. Suddenly, he sat up straight. "Oh, splendid. Here is something I am certain you'll find fascinating." He lowered his voice to a near whisper, as though imparting a great secret to a close ally. "I have heard on the news about the threat of an avian influenza coming to the United States." He clucked his tongue in disgust. "The uneducated morons on the television are calling it the Bird Flu."

At the mention of the avian influenza, the memory of his ordeal in the bunker swept through Dakota like an arctic blast, causing an involuntary shiver to ripple through his body. He absently rubbed the scar along his left arm.

The General noticed and smiled knowingly, then struck the final blow. "That would truly be a shame, don't you think? All those lives needlessly lost, all the pain, the suffering." He paused as Dakota turned to face him. "Pity...since you have so much to share."

Dakota exploded out of his seat, sending the chair flying backward. "You bastard! You can't lay that on me!"

The two guards rushed to his side and each grabbed an arm. "Hey, buddy, calm down or you're outta' here."

He ignored them and spat at the General. "What the hell do you know about pity? You're the one who gets off on other people's pain and suffering! You're nothing but a sadistic monster!"

"Am I?" The General smiled again, unfazed by the accusations. "I know what haunts you, Doctor. It's quite simple, actually. If you give in, and do what your conscience tells you is right, your life will never be your own again. But, if you protect yourself, and turn your back on humanity and your oath, millions will die." The General leaned back in his chair. "And it's within your power to save them all."

Dakota couldn't breathe. The room closed in around him, suffocating him with the truth of his dilemma. He fought his fate and strained against the guards, leaning forward into the General's face. "You kidnap me, break my arm, infect me with your shit, and nearly kill me with your God damn serum, and now you expect me to follow my conscience and do what's right? You're one sick fuck!"

"That's it, pal. You're done." The guards dragged him away from the table, but the General intervened.

"Gentlemen, please. The good doctor is understandably upset, however, he is no threat to me, and I am sure he will promise to behave himself for the remainder of our time together. Isn't that right, Doctor?"

The guards hesitated and looked closely at Dakota, who gave a sharp nod while still glaring at the General.

"You see, gentlemen? All is well. Doctor, come and sit. We have much more to discuss."

"Let go of me!" Dakota twisted out of the guards' grasp. He focused on the General's smug smile, and something played at the back of his mind—a truth, a reality he had yet to face.

"This is your last warning." The guard glanced at his watch. "You have four minutes. One more outburst, and this meeting is over. You understand?"

"Yeah, yeah." Dakota turned around and retrieved his chair. The General's song had struck a chord in his consciousness that continued to reverberate, growing louder with each repeating echo. He returned to the table and sat down to face the General once again, only this time, it was without fear.

"You see, Doctor? I am still in control of those around me, and of you. I own you. For as long as you live, I will own you. I control your thoughts, your desires, even your dreams. I am the one who keeps you from sleeping at night, and that will never change."

Dakota realized that the moment of choice had come. He could let the General's words rule him, own him, or he could take control and reclaim his life. The simplicity of the decision had him laughing. "You don't own me. You're nothing. You take what was never yours to have. You hide in the dark because you have to. You destroy, because you can. There is nothing good about you. You have no power other than what you take. You're just a delusional, sick son-of-a-bitch…and you do not own me.

"Two minutes, Doctor Thomas."

Dakota nodded to the guard and returned his attention to the man in front of him. The General seemed more pitiful than frightful. "Your days of controlling and hurting and owning people are over. I'm the one who gets to walk out of here, *John*. It's finished. We shut you down."

The General laughed softly. "Did you? The Program isn't just me or the men you killed. It's not even a place. Name a major pharmaceutical company, Doctor. The Program is funded by at least three of them. What about research facilities, all those public donations to help find cures for cancer, diabetes, AIDS? The Program has made them all possible. Every time you prescribe an antibiotic for one of your patients, will you ever be sure I wasn't the one responsible for it? How many men's lives were sacrificed for that new baby's vaccine? You'll never know. Just like you'll never know how many more Riccos, how many more Dakotas are out there, right now, at this very moment, going through unimaginable hell, just to make your life a little more pleasant." The General's eye started to twitch as his face took on a manic look. "I am a hero to every cancer patient who prays a cure will be found before they die, to every twenty-year-old victim of arthritis, to every human being who might die of avian influenza." He locked eyes with Dakota. "I am a God, Dakota Thomas, minus the moral fiber."

Dakota shook his head in disgust. "You are nothing. A monster with delusions of grandeur."

The General leaned back and chuckled. "Oh, really? I gave you the gift of life, the ability to heal like no man before you, and you're too weak and selfish to do anything with it. Now, tell me, Doctor, who is the real monster here?"

Dakota felt his breath catch.

"We could have saved millions of lives together, but all that will be wasted now." The General smiled sadly. "I hope you can live with yourself. I hope you can find peace in the darkness that has become your life."

Dakota motioned to the guards. "Get him out of here."

John McKinley maintained eye contact with Dakota as the guards unlocked his chains from the floor and pulled him to his feet. They ushered him out at a slow, shuffling gait. He turned to look at Dakota over his shoulder, and laughed as the guards pulled him from the room. "Sweet dreams, Doctor."

Dakota sat at the table, perfectly still, with the General's words ringing in his ears. He had to sit because he wasn't entirely sure he could stand. The man had been right about a lot of things, most of which were beyond his control, and he could accept that, but McKinley was wrong about one thing: no one owned Dakota Rain Thomas. He was done with letting that man rule his life.

Dakota stood and was pleased to find his legs steady beneath him. He walked out the same door he had entered ten minutes earlier, feeling lighter in spirit and better able to confront the monsters that sought to shred his soul. He turned his back on John McKinley and everything the man represented, but he could not turn his back on what the man had done to him, not anymore. He knew for the first time in weeks what he needed to do, but hadn't had the strength or the courage to do until now. For that, and only that, he owed the General.

As he entered the waiting room, Mary quickly stood up from the couch, concern etched on her face and worry tightening her voice. "How'd it go?"

Montana remained seated. Dakota gave him a solemn nod, he hoped Montana understood, he was back now, it was going to be okay. Then he turned to Mary, his words came without hesitation, remorse or regret. "I was infected with a variant of avian influenza while being held by the General. They infused me with a serum made from Ricco's blood, and it halted the progression of the disease." He paused for a moment, his eyes going from Mary to his brother and back again before continuing. "I carry within me the cure for a possible pandemic."

With that single declaration, Dakota reclaimed his life, and the monsters backed down.

CHAPTER 26

Maggie Riley scanned the cameras in Michael Ricco's apartment. A necessary evil, that's how she convinced herself of the validity of her job. The things that had been done to the man created an irreplaceable freak of nature, and one who could possibly save untold thousands of lives. Nevertheless, she had a problem thinking of him as over one-hundred-years old—a real problem.

She kept telling herself he'd volunteered to be a human guinea pig, and they didn't keep him locked in a cell away from the rest of the world. He had a beautiful apartment and everything he could ever want, except his freedom. She wondered what he would do with freedom, anyway. It was only an illusion. He had to be happier here, or so she tried to convince herself. She had no problem with the job if she just kept that in mind. But then, she would look at his face, look into his eyes, and her resolve would melt. Through her monitors, he looked like a lost little boy, when he didn't look completely empty. Michael Ricco made her sad, and she hated him for that…well, she tried to hate him for that.

Thirty-two years old, and Maggie had worked for the National Security Agency the last seven of those years. Her long, dark hair framed a deceptively young face, and most people mistook her for someone ten years younger. That was a considerable advantage when she went undercover, however, she wasn't undercover now. She had guarded far more dangerous men than Michael Ricco, but none more fascinating.

She'd been assigned this job because her superiors felt a woman might make Ricco feel more comfortable in his new environment. Environment—as if he were a zoo specimen. Watching him day in and day out, she imagined that was exactly how he must feel.

Maggie downloaded the last twenty-four hours of data to the hard drive, reset the cameras, and was checking to be certain they were all up and functioning, when her desk phone rang. From the extension, she saw it was the director of the research center, Geoffrey, and picked it up.

"What is it, Geoffrey?" He bugged the hell out of her, because he thought no more of Ricco than the specimen he made the man to be.

On camera, Ricco just sat on his couch. No television, no music, he just sat and stared at the walls. Maggie wondered, not for the first time, what was going on inside his head. They had psychologists and a therapist talk with him, well, sit with him and ask questions. Michael Ricco wasn't big on talking.

"How's he doing, Maggie?" Geoffrey asked.

"The same."

"Yeah, well I have some news that might perk him up."

"You got approval?"

"Yep. Virginia, here we come. A team is headed there now to brief his family. Apparently, the Ricco clan has been quite prolific. There's about a million of them down in Corbin County. We had to narrow it down to a dozen or so, direct descendants from his siblings. I was just coming down to tell him the news."

Maggie glanced at the monitor once more. Ricco had disappeared from the camera she'd been viewing. She angled it to another location and found him on the back patio, one his favorite places. *Hell, if I hadn't felt the sun on my face in over ninety years, I'd spend all my time outside, too.*

"Hey, Geoff…I was just going to go down to check a stuck camera." She lied. "Unless you have a burning desire to make the trip down from the main building, I could break the news to him."

"Yeah? Sure, go ahead. I have to make transportation arrangements, anyway. Thanks, and tell him we leave in the morning. We have both stops arranged, everything he wants."

"Maybe that'll make him smile." She said that more to herself than to the man on the phone. She tried to remember if Ricco had smiled once since arriving here.

"I just want him cooperative, Maggs. This guy is costing us a fortune. We need to see some return on our investment, you know?"

"Yeah, I hear that. See you, Geoff." Maggie hung up the phone and turned her attention back to the monitors, and Michael Ricco.

She knew all about his story. One-hundred-and-ten years old, and he didn't look any older than her nephew in high school—unless you looked in his eyes. Without thinking, she zoomed in the shot and tightened the high quality, full-resolution image on Ricco's face. Half-turned away from her, all she could see was his blond hair fluttering in the early morning breeze. Suddenly, he turned and looked directly into the camera, as if he knew she watched him. Those blue-green eyes accused her, but she didn't know of what. Maybe of being no better than the psycho who did the things to him that made him the way he was. That look, it made him seem ancient and hidden.

Maggie quickly zoomed out to a normal shot and felt ridiculous, like a schoolgirl caught peeking into the boy's locker room. She didn't like it that Michael Ricco made her nervous. She didn't like a lot of the things he made her feel. In her line of work, feelings could become a liability.

Before walking down to Ricco's apartment to tell him about his long waited for family reunion, she paused the camera feed and fed a loop from the last sixty minutes of video. Anyone looking at the cameras would believe they were watching a live feed, when in reality, the cameras in Ricco's apartment were no longer recording. They were simply replaying the same sixty minutes of tape over and over.

* * * *

Maggie knocked lightly on the door and waited, when she

received no answer she let herself into Ricco's apartment. She didn't need a key, as there were no locks on the doors. Ricco couldn't go anywhere even if he wanted to, and he certainly couldn't keep anyone out. Privacy didn't exist for him, except for now. For the next few minutes, the only people who would know what Michael Ricco did or said, were Maggie and Michael Ricco.

She found him on the back porch, as expected, and called his name so she wouldn't startle him, which was something she hadn't been able to do yet. He always seemed to know when she came within touching distance. He looked up at her through the glass doors and smiled.

God, he looks like such a little boy when he smiles. She paused, her hand on the door. *Stop it, girl! For God's sakes, just tell him and leave.* She wanted to control her feelings, but she couldn't control the heart that beat just a bit faster at that smile.

He motioned for her to join him outside. She took a deep breath, slid open the patio door, and walked out onto the small, bricked porch.

"Hey," he said. His voice was soft with just a hint of a twang that identified him as a southerner.

Maggie returned the smile. "Hey, yourself. How you doing?" She felt stupid asking. She knew how he was doing. She had watched every aspect of his life, both live and recorded, since he came to stay there.

Ricco shrugged. "I'm good." He looked up at the cameras above them. "Something wrong?"

Following his gaze, she understood. The only time she ever came to see him in person was to introduce herself that first day, and to resolve any technical problems that occasionally arose with the equipment.

"Oh, no…everything's cool." *Cool? Jesus, I sound like a twelve-year-old.* "Umm, I just got a call from Geoffrey, and everything is set for tomorrow. Just thought you would want to know."

That got a reaction out of him. It was subtle, but Maggie had learned to read the slight nuances of his body language over the last few weeks. The news brought him to full alert. He straightened in the chair, his eyes locked on hers, and she noticed a slight increase in his respiratory rate. "He found my family?"

Maggie nodded. "You leave tomorrow for Virginia."

"Tomorrow? That soon?"

"Is that a problem? I mean, for the last week that's all you've asked anyone about. You made it clear…no visit, no tests. So, we got you your visit."

Ricco licked his lips. The self-assuredness she felt from him moments ago had evaporated. Now, only nervousness came from him. She stepped around a small table and sat down in the lounge chair across from him. "What's the matter, Michael?"

He shook his head, and she heard quiet laughter. "I'm not sure. I guess, I never really believed you would find them."

"Well, we did. You don't have to go, you know. It'll piss

Geoffrey off to the nth degree, but that's okay with me." She grinned, feeling very conspiratorial.

"No, no—I want to. I just...I don't know, this is kinda' weird. Who did you find? Who am I going to see?"

"I'm not sure. Geoff said something about the descendants of your siblings."

Ricco stood and walked to the edge of the patio. Maggie followed him, standing just behind him. They were almost the same height, with him being an inch or two taller.

"Mattie and Sarah," he said quietly.

"What, who are they?"

"My younger brother and sister. It's strange to think of them having descendants." He wiped his hands on the front of his thighs, a nervous habit she recognized.

"I'm not so sure this was a good idea." He spoke with his back to her. "I mean, how do I explain who I am or how I am?"

"Michael..." She put a hand on his shoulder. "We'll take care of it. Geoff has already sent a team out there."

He turned around, and suddenly Maggie found herself much too close to the man. Instead of stepping back, she held her ground. She left it up to him, to move or not.

He stayed where he was and looked down at her. "They won't understand."

"We did. It won't be any different for them."

He laughed at that, took a step back and looked back out the window. "I'm nothing but the next big dividend for Geoffrey. I'm still in a cage, and I get that, I accept that..." He shook his head. "But my family won't."

It surprised her he had confided as much to her, and it upset her he had no delusions as to his place in the scheme of things. "Is that how you feel about yourself? A specimen...something to be studied?"

"Tell me I'm wrong."

She couldn't, so she said nothing.

"You know, I had a life once. There was a time when I was just Michael. But Michael doesn't exist anymore, he's dead and buried just like my brother and my sister. There's only Ricco now."

Maggie shook her head, a little surprised that she was the one he chose to open up to—surprised, but grateful. "That's not true, Michael."

"Yes, it is. You don't know me, who I was, who I am. All you know is what's written in a file. Words can't ever tell the whole story."

"You're right, but I can't know the whole story unless you tell me. Let me get to know Michael, can you do that?"

Until now, he had been looking out at the little yard, but at Maggie's question, he turned and stared at her. Maggie met his gaze, never flinching once in the face of the intensity of that look.

"Why? So you can add it to my file? Why do you care?"

Maggie thought about that for a moment before answering. "I've watched you since you came here. I mean, I know everything there is to know about the man in the files, maybe even more than you do. They have files going back almost sixty years. The things they did to you, medically it's fascinating, but personally, I find it reprehensible. They took your life and compressed it to a culmination of facts. Why do I care? Because I want to make it right, or as right as anyone can. Because I want to give Michael a chance to exist again. Will you tell me about him, about Michael?"

"No reports?"

Maggie shook her head. "Just me. One person talking to another. For the record, anything you tell me is just between us." She motioned to the ever-present cameras all around them. "I turned the cameras off before I came down here. For the moment, we are all alone, just you and me."

Michael narrowed his eyes at her. "Why?"

"I don't really know. Maybe I felt guilty about my part in making you nothing more than a specimen in a glass cage. I'd like to try to change that if I could." She offered him her hand, and smiled. "Hello, Michael. My name is Maggie, and I would very much like to get to know you, if you'll let me."

He took her hand cautiously, his eyes never leaving hers. He wanted to trust her, she could see it, but trust still didn't come easily for Michael Ricco. Maggie watched him struggle with the dilemma and waited him out.

Michael released her hand, walked back inside and sat on the sofa. Staring at nothing, his eyes focused somewhere in the past, Michael Ricco started talking about someone he had almost forgotten— someone he used to be before the summer of 1917.

He began in a low voice. "My name is Michael John Ricco. I was the first of three children born to Thomas and Katherine Ricco. My earliest memories are filled with smells. The smells of my mom's cooking and the smells of a barn filled with cows, the smells of picking potatoes and apples in the fall." Michael closed his eyes and took a deep breath almost as if he could recall what he tried to remember.

Maggie sat down next to him, and listened. For almost two hours she listened as his world became real to her, as he became so much more than just words in a report. The enormity of what had been done to this man began to take shape in his story. His hopes, dreams and fears, had ruthlessly and carelessly been taken from him on a rainy day in July. Those who took him cared nothing about what he wanted or who he was. All they saw was the specimen.

"I had a girl, Emma," she heard him say. "We were supposed to get married as soon as I got home. She told me she would wait for me. As long as it took, she would wait for me." Ricco looked at Maggie for the first time since he began talking. "I don't think she counted on waiting over ninety years." A small smile played across his lips, and Maggie couldn't help but return it.

"I wouldn't think so," she agreed. "I bet she was beautiful, your Emma."

"Truthfully, I can't remember. I know I thought she was. She had blond hair and green eyes, but I can't see her face anymore. They took those, too—my memories."

She watched her hand, as though it had a life of its own, reach over and lightly touched his. "Maybe it's time to start making new ones."

He looked up at her, a little surprised by the contact, but he didn't move away from it. Instead, he turned his hand over and held hers. He was right; no one could give him back what he had lost, but maybe she could give him something to replace the memories he no longer carried with him.

Leaning over, she touched his face with the other hand and placed a whisper of a kiss on his lips, and waited for his response. She expected reprisal, rejection, even shock at her forwardness. What she did not expect was for him to return the kiss.

He brought his hand up and wove his fingers through her hair, then pulled away to look at her. "It's so soft, your hair. From the first time I saw you, I wanted to touch it and see if it was as soft as it looks." He smiled. "It is."

Maggie Riley, scientist, doctor, had no reply to that. Those incredible eyes studied her and a smile tugged at the corner of his mouth. Now, she felt like the specimen in a glass cage. "I'm sorry." Flustered and embarrassed by her actions, she pulled away. "I don't know why I did that."

"I didn't mind." He smiled that little boy smile once more. "It's been a very long time since I was kissed by a beautiful woman." His face creased with a question. "Why are you sorry?"

Maggie shook her head. "It's just not that easy. Things could get complicated."

Michael softly touched her face with the back of his hand. "Life is complicated. This is what makes it all worthwhile."

Maggie felt something curl deliciously inside her belly and wasn't sure she wanted to walk away from it. He was right; life could get complicated all by itself. It didn't need her help.

She moved closer to him and ran a finger lightly along his jaw, then let it travel down his throat, his chest, along his ribs, and finally coming to rest on the edge of his jeans. She let it linger there for a moment, until she saw the reaction she was waiting for. She appreciated the noticeable bulge and undid the top button of his jeans. "Are you trying to seduce me, Michael?" She smiled at him.

"I believe you started it." Red-faced, he returned the smile. "I think you should know, I'm not sure what you expect, but I'm a little out of practice."

Maggie laughed, and the tension melted. "I don't expect anything you don't want to give, Michael. And I can't possibly imagine how you would disappoint me."

"I never did this before," he admitted. "I mean, Emma was the first girl I ever kissed. We never... We were waiting until we were married."

Maggie winged a brow up at that. "I don't believe I ever slept with a one-hundred-and-ten-year old virgin before, but I assure you, Michael Ricco…" She smiled as her fingers found the tab to his zipper. "Some things never change."

"Glad to hear it." He reached for the buttons of her blouse. "Glad to hear it."

CHAPTER 27

Dakota watched through the tinted windows of the government limousine as the Black Hawk helicopter landed on the blacktop. He did a double take as Michael Ricco exited the side door of the chopper and jumped to the ground. The man he saw bore little resemblance to the Michael Ricco he remembered.

As difficult as the last two months had been for Dakota, the same time appeared to have been kind to Ricco. He had gained much-needed weight, and his face no longer had that haunted, vacant look. His cheeks blushed with the healthy glow of someone who had spent time in the sun. His blond hair tickled the tops of his ears and showed streaks of red through it. Michael Ricco looked like the Virginia farm boy he had once been. He wore jeans, a khaki t-shirt, a pair of white Nikes, and in his hand, he held a bouquet of wildflowers. Dakota looked closer and realized it was more than a physical transformation. The change went deeper than that. It took him a moment to figure it out, but then he saw it—Michael Ricco was smiling.

Ricco bent low and ducked his head from the rotor wash, protecting the fragile flowers with his body. He waited for "the suits" to follow him out, and hung back as a woman jumped down from the holding bay. A slow smile spread across Dakota's face as he watched Ricco put a protective arm around her as they ran for the car.

"Good for you, Michael."

As soon as they were clear, the helicopter lifted off again, leaving a swirl of dust and debris in its wake. The suits climbed into the unmarked car parked next to them, while Ricco opened the back door of the limo and ushered the woman inside. They took seats opposite Montana and Dakota, and with a bright smile, the woman nodded in their direction and introduced herself. "Special agent, Margaret Riley...Maggie."

Her smile was contagious, and Dakota grinned from ear to ear as he shook her hand. "Dakota Thomas. This is my brother, Montana."

Maggie glanced back and forth between them as she shook Montana's hand. "I've heard a lot about you two. It's good to finally meet you." She turned and slid open the screen to the driver's compartment. "We good?"

The driver, armed and dressed in military fatigues, spoke into his radio, and gave Maggie a nod.

"You ready?" She directed the question to Ricco, who had not taken his eyes off her since they landed.

"Yeah, I'm ready," he said and turned to Dakota and Montana for the first time. "Thanks a lot for doing this, for coming all this way. I really wanted you guys here with me."

"Not a problem." Montana spoke behind the veil of his Ray-Ban's, but for once, he didn't try to hide the smile.

Ricco turned his gaze to Dakota and looked him over carefully before saying anything. "You doing all right? You look a little tired."

Dakota opened his mouth to deliver his patented, 'Yeah, I'm fine,' response, but thought better of it. "I'm getting there, Michael." That was as close to the truth as he was willing to share at that moment. There would be plenty of time for them to talk. Right now, though, they were there for Michael Ricco's family reunion, and he wasn't about to spoil it.

Ricco nodded in understanding as the limo pulled out of the airport. "It gets better after a while. You'll see."

Dakota had trouble believing that, but he smiled anyway.

* * * *

The cemetery where Geoffrey had located Ricco's family plot was a twenty-minute drive from the Corbin County airport, through rolling green hills and recently mowed fields. Michael and Dakota spent most of the ride absorbed in their own thoughts, while Maggie and Montana chatted about their years in government service.

The cemetery itself was quite large, and bordered all around by a black wrought-iron fence. Their driver had obviously studied the layout, because he knew exactly which turns to take in the maze of blacktop that divided the lots, arriving at last, at a spot near the center of the cemetery. He slid open the divider and turned to Michael. "Three rows straight back, then four in…just to the left. Take all the time you need, sir."

Michael gave him a nod. "Thanks."

The suits parked behind them and exited their vehicle, split up and formed a loose perimeter around Ricco. Ignoring their presence, Ricco stepped out of the limo and held the door open for Maggie. Without waiting for Montana or Dakota, they walked through the rows of headstones toward the area the driver had indicated. Dakota watched as Maggie reached down and held his hand, their fingers intertwining. Montana saw it too, and exchanged a brief glance with his brother. A slight nod to Dakota indicated his approval. Michael Ricco had found happiness, and no one could argue that he deserved it.

Ricco's eyes searched the names etched into the cold granite, walking slowly in case he missed something. He stopped before one of the stones and stared at the name, his shoulders sagging slightly as he tightened his fingers around Maggie's hand.

Dakota came up beside him and read the name on the tombstone. "Thomas Michael Ricco. Is this your father?"

Michael seemed mesmerized by the name. "Yeah." His finger traced the individual letters etched deep into the granite. "My daddy. He was only forty the last time I saw him." Michael touched the death date and did a quick mental calculation. "He died at ninety-six. I beat him by fourteen years, so far." A sad smile crossed his face. "I wish…"

He stopped and shrugged. He let go of Maggie's hand and knelt on one knee in front of the marker. It was abundantly clear that regardless of the audience around him, for Michael Ricco, at that moment in time, all that existed were his memories.

"I hope I became the kind of man you could have been proud of, Daddy. I wasn't always strong, and I've done some things…" Michael dropped his head, and when he raised it again, his face glistened with tears. "I've done things, I haven't been proud of. Sometimes I forgot to fight back, but it was hard. I know that ain't no excuse, and I'm not trying to make it out to be one, I'm just telling you I tried until I couldn't try anymore. I hope you understand that." He reached out and placed a hand against the cold stone. "I'm so sorry." Michael stood and wiped the tears from his cheeks. "I have thought of you every day since I last saw you, and I will think of you every day until I breathe my last. I love you, Daddy."

He stood there for another minute and then turned his attention to the name etched next to his father's. Katherine Ann Ricco.

"Hi, Mom." Bending low, he gently laid the bouquet of wildflowers on the ground below her name. "I promised I would come home. I'm sorry it wasn't exactly what either one of us thought it would be, but I never broke a promise to you. I wanted you to know I kept this one." He took Maggie's hand, and turned back to the headstone. "This is Maggie. She makes me happy."

Maggie's fair skin flushed red from her neck to her hairline. She cast her eyes down, but stepped closer to Ricco, pressing her shoulder into his.

He walked to the next two markers and stood in silence. His brother Matthew and a wife Michael never knew, and his sister Sarah, buried next to her husband. "She was such a little thing the last time I saw her. I can't picture her married with a family of her own."

Michael looked at the two men and one woman who had come with him. "One more, then we can go."

Maggie checked the map the driver had given her and looked at the plots around her. It took a minute to get her bearings. She pointed toward the grave stones. "That way. It should be two rows up and one over."

The plots were overgrown, and they passed the low marker twice before Maggie found it. "Here…" She bent down and began pulling weeds from around the site. "She's here."

Michael turned back and bent down to help Maggie. When they had cleared the marker, he sat in the grass next to it and brushed his hand across the name. "Emma Faulks." He looked up at Maggie. "The last name is different."

"She married, Michael."

A fleeting look of disappointment crossed his face, and suddenly it vanished in a sigh of resignation. "She forgot about me."

Maggie laid a gentle hand on his shoulder and shook her head. "No, she didn't. She made peace with it and moved on." Her voice softened as she stroked his cheek. "You were her first love, and we never forget our first love…you didn't."

He thought about that, and nodded as he stood. He took Maggie's hand firmly in his once more, and turned to face Montana and Dakota. "Thank you for coming with me to see my family one last time." He made direct eye contact with each of them in turn. "Thank you both, for giving me my life back."

Montana stepped toward Ricco, and surprised Dakota by taking off his sunglasses. "Understand something, Michael. You could have given up long before Dakota and I ever met you, but you didn't, you chose to survive. The General never owned you. That was something he wanted you to believe, but you were the stronger one. You took your soul back, and it takes a strong person to do that. I believe your father would have been proud of the man you've become, and I'm damn proud to know you, Michael Ricco."

Montana extended his hand, but Ricco stepped in, threw his arms around both their necks, and held them in a fierce embrace. "You are men my daddy would have been proud of."

Dakota knew there was no higher compliment in Michael Ricco's world.

Ricco released them, slipped his arm around Maggie's waist, and then looked out at the rows of monuments and headstones. Dakota could see him fighting his emotions. He gave Ricco credit, Dakota wasn't certain, if their positions were reversed, that he would do as well with such long buried feelings. Dakota knew they had one more stop to make before the glass walls would once again close in on Michael

Ricco.

"I would be honored if you all would come with me to meet the family my brother and sister left for me," Ricco said.

They took a final, slow walk through time, and prepared to meet the family Ricco never knew. Dakota followed at a distance, reading the names of the dead along the way. So much history and so many secrets. He wondered who spoke for the dead, once they were locked, silent and forgotten beneath their granite tombs.

CHAPTER 28

Michael Ricco stared out the window as the Virginia countryside sped by. His head was full and his heart was heavy, and long-suppressed memories encroached despite his best efforts to prevent them. The finality of seeing his father's grave brought unwanted tears to his eyes. His hand lay in Maggie's, but he made no effort to hold it. Although he knew the reality of his age, in his mind he remained that nineteen-year-old boy who left for war so very long ago.

Dressed in overalls, sitting on the front porch and waiting for the bus to take him away, he clearly remembered the last conversation he had with his daddy. The words were forever etched in his memory, but his father's face had faded with the passage of time. He could recall the blond hair bleached nearly white by the summer heat, the tanned leathery skin, the thin gold wedding band, dented and nicked by hard work, the sparkling blue eyes and the easy smile, but the details of his face were lost.

"You scared, boy?" his daddy had asked him.

Nineteen-year-old Michael thought about lying, but he had never lied to his daddy before, and couldn't think of a good enough reason to start now. "Yes, sir. I am."

He looked down at his father's mud-caked boots. It was rich, dark Virginia dirt, the kind that got under your fingernails and wouldn't come out even with scrubbing, the kind his mother used to yell at him for when he sat down at the dinner table at night.

Yeah, he was scared—scared right down to his soul. He didn't want to leave home, didn't want to go kill people. He wanted to stay and marry Emma, help his daddy with the farm.

His father nodded at him and put an arm around his thin shoulders. "Me too," he said. "Listen to your COs, they'll keep you safe. And listen to that little voice in the back of your head, it'll keep you out of trouble."

Michael nodded, unable to meet his father's eyes. He stayed frozen in place, secretly hoping the bus would never come for him.

"I love you, Michael John."

Michael looked up then and saw something he had never seen before—tears in his father's eyes.

"Keep yourself safe and come home to your mother…you hear?"

Michael felt the tears, hot and wet on his own face as he whispered, "Yes, sir. I'll do my best."

It was a promise that took a long time in the keeping. His father had died believing his oldest son had perished, a faceless, nameless casualty of war. Michael could never change that, and he couldn't decide whether to be angry or sad over the fact.

The rolling countryside had only been background to his thoughts, until something changed. Michael sat up a straighter, his attention focused on the view. "I recognize this place. It's different, but I still recognize it. This is the back road to my house." He looked to Maggie for confirmation, but didn't need any as the limo rounded a bend in the road, and a large, white, rambling farmhouse came into view.

Michael came to life, his eyes roving over the landscape and the house before him. "I'm home." His quiet words fulfilled a lifetime of hopes and dreams.

The driver stopped the limo halfway down the long dirt road, in the shade of an ancient elm tree that left Michael's face in the shadows. He saw a man leave the comfort of the padded rocker he had been sitting in, and walk down the wide porch steps. It was clear he was unsure whether to wait or walk down the path leading to the limo.

The driver opened the slide and spoke to Maggie. "Let me go brief him." He stepped out of the car, and they all watched as he met the man halfway up the path and shook his hand.

"It's bigger than I remember." Michael's voice was soft and dream-like.

"What is?" Dakota asked him.

"The house. I don't know why, but I always thought if I ever saw it again, it would seem smaller. But it isn't—it's bigger."

"They've added additions over the years," Maggie explained.

"But they never sold it." He had secretly feared that one thing, never having a home to go back to.

"That was specified in your brother's will. The house and the land were to remain intact. It's pretty much the same as when you left."

"Trees are bigger." He gave her a sad smile. "Life went on without me."

"Sounds to me like it waited for you," Montana told him.

"Who is that?" Michael pointed to the man the driver spoke with on the road.

Maggie referred to a clipboard in her lap. "That should be your brother's grandson. His name is Matthew, too."

Michael's breath caught in his chest. "Mattie has a grandson?"

Maggie laughed. "He had several grandsons. Your family has been quite prolific, Michael. Most of Corbin County is populated by Riccos."

Michael licked his lips. "I know I asked for it, but I'm not sure I can do this." He looked over at the men who had brought him to this point in his life, and the woman who would take him beyond it. He fought the urge to laugh, as it seemed wholly inappropriate. His stomach clenched, and his legs felt like they were made of water.

Dakota came to his side. "You can do this, Michael. Just take it one step at a time. This is your family, and family is the one thing in your life you can always count on." His eyes went quickly to Montana before returning to Michael. "Trust me on that."

"Will you come with me?"

"We came with you this far, Private." Montana opened the limo door, and the scent of freshly mowed grass and tilled fields washed over them.

Michael lifted his head and closed his eyes, letting the scents fill him. If he kept his eyes closed, he could almost believe he was that nineteen-year-old kid again. He shook his head as he opened his eyes and looked up at Montana. "No, sir. Not Private, not ever again. It's Michael...just Michael."

Montana gave him a respectful nod and held out his hand "Let's go meet your family, Michael."

As he slid toward the open door and took Montana's hand, a thousand reasons not to get out of the car ran through Michael's head. That old house on the hill held the ghosts of a life that had nearly been wiped from his memory, ghosts he wasn't sure he had the strength to face. He stood behind the limo door as if it could shield him from the unknown, from his fears and his future, until only one thought remained, one compelling reason to walk up that dirt road and face the ghosts of his past. They are my family.

He stepped out from behind the door and started the long walk toward Matthew Ricco.

* * * *

It was like watching mirror images approach the glass. Dakota half expected them to stop and put a hand out to touch the reflective images in front of them. He wondered if Michael could see it; the way they walked with both hands tucked deep into the back pockets of their jeans, their blond heads lowered and eyes downcast, but occasionally peeking up through bleached lashes.

They looked like reluctant gun fighters as they slowly approached each other on the dirt lane. Matthew Ricco had a good twenty pounds or more on Michael, but it was more than obvious they shared the same DNA. They stopped five feet apart, and Michael's head raised as he appraised the man in front of him. "You look just like my daddy."

Matthew smiled. "I know. I've been told that since I was old enough to understand." Matthew did his own thorough assessment, and then nodded in approval. "So do you. Look like my grandfather, I mean. You're a carbon copy of Pappy."

Michael raised his brows and let out a low laugh. "Pappy? Mattie let you call him that?"

"Well, I got the broke-in model. I was his third grandchild."

Michael looked past his great nephew to the large house and wiped a hand over his face. Dakota recognized the gesture for what it was—nerves and overwhelming emotions threatening to break through the thin veneer of calm. He stepped forward with the intention of providing a distraction until Michael could get it together again, but it wasn't necessary, as Matthew seemed to understand. "There's a whole house full of people in there, who have come from three counties, and waited an awful long time just to meet you, Michael Ricco."

Michael lowered his head and nodded.

"I don't think it would hurt any if they waited a bit longer."

Michael's eyes met the man's in front of him, hope emanating from the look.

"Would you like to take a walk with me? Maybe we could talk. I could answer anything you like. If I were you, the questions I had, would take a week's worth of answering."

The relief in Michael was obvious. His hunched shoulders relaxed, and the tension visibly drained out of him. "Yeah, I would like that a lot."

Matthew held out his hand. "I don't think we've been properly introduced." As Michael took the hand, Matthew made it official. "My name is Matthew Thomas Ricco, and on behalf of three very excited generations of Riccos, it is my great pleasure to welcome you home, at last."

Michael swiped a hand over eyes that were shiny with unshed tears. Dakota couldn't begin to guess what he might be feeling at that moment.

Matthew led him away from the house and pointed through the woods. "Do you remember the pond?"

Michael nodded. "Daddy and I fished there all the time. There used to be a big catfish in there. We called him Walter. He was at least four feet long."

"Still is." Matthew smiled. "Only my kids named him Otis. He's probably a relative."

Dakota heard them laugh as they walked away, their gaits identical, like clones separated by a hundred years. Watching them, he believed Michael had truly reclaimed his soul after all those years of hopelessness. He felt tears on his face, and lifted a hand to wipe them away. He hadn't realized he had been crying.

Maggie gave them all their space and walked up the path to the house with the driver. Dakota had forgotten about Montana until he heard his brother's voice.

"Dak...you okay?" Montana came to stand beside him, resting a hand on his shoulder.

Dakota took a deep breath and let it out slowly. "You know, I really think I am."

The first subtle signs of twilight painted the Virginia sky with haunting shades of red and purple, and for once, the coming night didn't seem so endless. He turned to face his brother, his family, and for the first time since meeting John McKinley, he felt hope of his own.

He looked at Michael Ricco, walking alongside a nephew he was never supposed to know, and flexed his healing arm. If Michael Ricco was strong enough to reclaim his past and make it real, maybe he had a chance as well. Mary Stromm was right; it was his choice. He would find a small seed of strength and nurture it, until he too, reclaimed what had been taken from him. He thought he owed Ricco that much, at least, to try.

Dakota cast his eyes to the horizon and his thoughts to the future. A weight lifted from his soul with the realization that a new life lay before him, the blank pages of a story yet to be written. Montana's words came back to him: 'Find a way around it.' He thought Michael Ricco might have done just that. He found a way around the life he had been given, back to the one taken from him all those long years ago.

Dakota watched the sun give way with one last dazzling display of color and light and made a decision. He would not let the second chance he'd been given be for nothing. The future was not yet written, but he had a pretty good idea of how he wanted to fill the blank pages before him. Dakota Thomas would not only find a way around his past, he would find a way to survive his future.

About Ann Simko

http://www.lyricalpress.com/ann_simko

I have always believed the most powerful question is, What if? That is how Fallen was born. In my twenty-five years as a nurse, I have seen amazing advancements, injuries that would have killed a person a few years ago are now survivable. But what if those advancements came with a price? What if innocent blood and pain was the cost of your survival? Would it be worth it? Would you still want it? These are the moral and ethical dilemmas I asked myself as I wrote this book. Dakota is the one who has to make that terrible decision. I hope, in reality we never do.

Ann's website:

http://www.annsimko.com/

Reader eMail:

sheadakota5@gmail.com

ABOUT THE COYOTE MOON SERIES

Book 1: Fallen
Available in ebook from Lyrical Press

Book II: Through the Glass
Coming soon from Lyrical Press

Book III: The Coyote's Song
Coming soon from Lyrical Press

WHERE REALITY
AND
FANTASY COLLIDE

Discover the convenience of Ebooks
Just click, buy and dowload -it's that easy!

From PDF to ePub, Lyrical offers
the latest formats in digital reading.

YOUR NEW FAVORITE AUTHOR
IS ONLY A CLICK AWAY!

LYRICAL PRESS
INCORPORATED
WWW.LYRICALPRESS.COM

Shop securely at www.onceuponabookstore.com